in her dreams

BOOK ONE

JOANNA REEDER

REED IT & WEEP

Reed It & Weep

In Her Dreams
Copyright © 2018 Joanna Reeder
joannareeder.com

Cover Art by Angel Leya
angeleya.com

Edited by Katrina Beckstrand
editsbykb.com

For Mom

another one

"Nora, wake up! Please wake up!" a frantic young boy pleads. "We have to move!" His sniffles are loud, and he chokes on his words. "Nora, c'mon, c'mon, *c'mon!*" A small hand tugs at my arm again and again. "C'mon, c'mon, c'mon!"

My head throbs between my brows, past my temples, and around to a sharp pulsing at the back right side of my head. I struggle to open my eyes without success. My fingers are already woven through my thick hair, so I can feel the wet, sticky blood pooling against my scalp. The blood is warm, almost hot in the freezing temperature and trickles through my fingers at a steady drip.

Drip. Drip. Drip.

From my head to my heels, wherever my body touches the frozen ground is numb.

Drip.

Drip.

Drip.

"Nora, please!" The boy's voice is softer now, despondent. But he doesn't stop talking. "Please, Nora. C'mon, c'mon, *c'mon!*"

With great effort, my eyes open, rimmed with fine white crystals. I blink to unstick my ice-encrusted lashes. My shallow breath is barely visible against the gray winter sky streaked with branches going every which way above me. Blocking half of it is a blond, baby-faced boy: the source of the incessant babbling.

Colin, my memory provides. My brother. His face is pale and streaked with dirt, tears, and blood.

"Are you hurt?" I ask, reaching a hand to touch his face. His eyes widen, but he does not answer. "Colin." I say his name. Firm. The way Mama scolds him when she's caught him eating pastries meant for the widows. "Are. You. Hurt?" I speak slowly so that his shocked mind can comprehend.

"But how did you—?"

"Colin!" I close my eyes when my shout sends more shooting pains into orbit around my crown.

"No," he says, clutching my hand with blood-stained fingers. He is sobbing harder now. "Please, Nora." His voice cracks. He finally breaks from his daze. I wonder if his head is somehow injured too. Gently but firmly, Colin tugs at my arm to help me to my feet.

I resist again.

"Nora, the ice is breaking. We'll fall through."

As if hearing its name called, the frozen river underneath us groans and cracks. I can feel the vibrations and almost hear the rushing current beneath, despite Colin's continued noise.

"What happened?" I wonder, not fully understanding the danger. My head feels fuzzy.

"The branch. It broke." Colin points to the tree above us, then to a large tree limb only inches above my curls. I crane my neck—sending lightning-sharp pain through my head.

Everything flashes purple. Then blinding white.

And I know myself.

It's rare. I'm usually so immersed in the experience that I can't really see myself or my surroundings. I start cataloging the facts. Through Nora's eyes I see the limb, at least two feet in diameter. The far end of it has punctured the edge of the ice, sending spider-web cracks everywhere. And although I can't turn my head, somehow I can sense similar cracks shooting in all directions around us. The snow-saturated appendage still hangs sickly from the tree, attached by less than a sliver of wood.

The branch will fall.

I gasp, and the minuscule movement causes more pain. A moan escapes my—Nora's—lips. Twitching my fingers locked in my hair, I feel a jagged edge that falls into an indent. My heart lurches with panic. *How is she still conscious? How is she still alive with a giant gash in her skull?* The sound of dripping blood has ceased. A steady flow now silently pools past my fingers, creating steam on the ice.

Nora is dying.

I've died fifty-seven times, and it sucks. Every. Single. Time. I brace myself for number fifty-eight, wondering how long the branch will last. *How should I catalog this?* I think to myself as a distraction. *Head injury? Yes. If the dying happens fast. If it's not fast, maybe hypothermia. Or shock or blood loss.* Any of those could take a while. And while I am no expert, my eyes keep darting back and forth between the precariously angled branch and the cracking ice... It could be drowning.

I shudder. Drowning isn't pleasant.

Colin. My heart lurches again. If the ice breaks, he could die too. There isn't much hope for Nora, but Colin can get to safety.

"Get off the ice, Colin," I say. *Good, my voice is steady.*

Colin's sobs and mumbling abruptly stop, and his eyes widen. "Nora, you—"

"Please go!" My shout is pathetic.

"Not without you. *Please,* Nora," Colin cries and resumes incoherent speech.

"Nora! Colin!" a voice from the bank calls.

"Papa!" Colin calls back. "The ice is breaking."

"Don't make Mama and Papa lose us both," I say, my voice so

weak I am not sure Colin hears me. I can feel myself fading, but Colin hasn't left.

Quickly I search through her head. What's her last name? Is there anything I can say to get him to go?

Do not panic him. It's the only thought I get from Nora before she is silent again.

"Colin, what is today's date?" I ask, scrambling.

He looks puzzled. "February the twelfth."

"February twelfth," I repeat. "Nineteen hundred and…" I guess, hoping he will fill in the rest.

"*Eighteen* forty-nine."

Wow. Way off. I snap back to the moment. "Right, February the twelfth, *eighteen* hundred and forty-nine." I take a deep breath in an attempt to clear my head and stay conscious a moment longer. "Next year, on February the twelfth, eighteen hundred and fifty, I want you to remember how much fun we had today. *Before* this." Nora floods my thoughts with the two of them laughing and playing, skating and sliding on the frozen river— their favorite pastime. "How much fun we always had in winter together."

"But—"

"Remember that, *okay?*" I plead.

He nods, scrunching his face to hold back a yowl as tears stream down his dirty cheeks.

"And remember how you were so brave—" I choke. Taking a deep breath, I clear my throat and continue. "You were so brave because you got off the ice quickly and saved yourself." I smile weakly.

Colin nods again and is suddenly and finally quiet. "I love you, Nora Violet Harker." He squeezes my hand.

He sounds so old, so grown up, Nora thinks. "I love you too, Colin William Harker."

His smile is faint.

"Go to the bank. *Now,*" I order.

Colin decisively stands and slips as he runs across the ice.

Let this be quick, I pray.

Several loud wails of grief carry through the icy air from the bank. Someone attempts to cross the ice. *Please don't let it be Colin.* But before they get close enough for me to see, the ice rips and river water spills upward, mixing with the blood.

Craackk.

My head snaps upward at the sound. People say time slows down when you're in imminent danger, like a car crash, but it slows even more for the poor girl bleeding out on the ice who is unable to move or scream or cry as she watches the free branch finally tumble down.

So I cry for her.

Showers of ice and snow stab the parts of me that aren't already numb as the branch breaks through the glass river and plunges into the water, pulling me down with it.

I fade fast. The loss of blood and the icy water quickly take me away into unconsciousness before I have to consider sucking in water to make it end.

I'll have to label it in my unknown category.

tuesday

"Hey, Emily."

Halfway to the parking lot, I didn't turn at the call of my name even though I'd recognize that voice during a hurricane. There was an exorbitant number of Emilys at my high school—at least twenty in the junior class alone. I rarely turned until someone said my name twice to avoid embarrassment.

Let her think I was deaf.

"Yes, Emily Chandler, I'm talking to you." I could hear the smile in her voice before turning to see it. She wore a lot more makeup than she used to, making her look almost airbrushed; and her hair was more platinum blonde and less strawberry. I almost didn't recognize her anymore.

"Arianna," I said, matching her pink-satin smile with a courteous one and pushing my glasses higher on the bridge of my nose.

"I realize we have too many Emilys at our school," she said with a hand on her hip. As my ex-best friend, she knew me well. "But I thought you'd at least acknowledge me."

"I didn't realize it was you," I said with a shrug. She narrowed her black liquid-lined eyes. She knew I was lying. "We haven't talked in a while," I countered. Plus, she used to call me *Em*.

"Look, I noticed you didn't join a group for the *Hamlet* project."

It was true. My recent social decline was part of the problem, but I'd spent most of my morning classes tuned out anyway. That tended to happen after experiencing death. "Yeah, I'll talk to Mrs. Tanner about that tomorrow." That was probably a lie too.

"We already have four people, but you can join my group."

"Thanks, Ari," I said. At least it would save me from standing in front of class while Mrs. Tanner asked for a group to take me as a charity case.

"Sure." Arianna shifted her feet. It was the first time we'd talked in months, and it was weirdly awkward. We should be talking about her new boyfriend while walking to my house to do homework. "Well, I'll talk to you later," she said instead, then walked away. So much had changed, but at least we were on speaking terms again.

My phone rang. It was Mom.

"Hey!" Her voice was extra peppy. "You ran out of the house quick this morning. Is everything okay?" Translation: Have you recovered from your night terror? You know, since you woke up screaming and all? That's what my parents thought the death dreams were. Night terrors. My psych too. *I wish.*

"Fine," I said in the happiest voice I could muster. Ari was one of two people in my entire world who believed the truth, and there she was—walking away with her too-thick eyeliner and platinum hair.

"Well, Josh is back from vacation and wants to work," she said. She'd mostly given up on prying if I didn't own up to my *feelings*, but I'd get more questions later if I couldn't convince them I was really okay. "We gave him the back sections to mow, so we don't need you today. But if you want to work, I'm sure Dad can find something in the office."

My family managed the Meadow Grove Cemetery. We sold plots, dug graves, coordinated with mortuaries, handled landscaping and maintenance, and offered other various services related to burying the dead.

"That's okay," I said. "There are some things I wanted to do this afternoon anyway."

There was a pause on the other line. If she guessed my lie, she knew I was headed to the flower shop. I could almost hear her internal debate on whether to press for the truth. "Okay." She didn't press. "I love you, sweetie."

"Yeah, you too, Mom."

<hr>

"YOU'RE EMILY, AREN'T YOU?" A GIRL IN HER TWENTIES asked. I'd been admiring the bouquet arrangements in the glass cases while Mr. Brewster was busy helping a customer. I nodded. She was a new employee. Her Brewster's Floral name tag read *Tiffany*.

"Mr. Brewster told me about you," she said. "So, what'll it be? The usual?" Tiffany flashed her customer service smile.

"The usual?" I wasn't ordering a burger and fries.

"Yeah, a single white rose?" She looked guilty, like she'd offended me. "Mr. Brewster keeps extras on hand. He says you come in all the time and that's what you always buy. He described you perfectly." I glanced at the owner; he was still busy writing up an order for his customer. "You know..." Tiffany waved her hands, flustered. "Shoulder-length black hair, glasses hiding pretty blue eyes, fair skin."

"Lots of girls could be described like that," I argued.

"He also said you might be wearing a black cardigan over a lacy white top and faded jeans."

I glanced down at my attire. It was true, but there was a good reason I wore my favorite clothes when buying white roses. "Anything else?" I didn't want to sound rude, but this girl seemed to know a lot about me and I knew nothing of her.

"Just that you always look—I think the word he used was *melancholy*—when you come in."

Did he also give you a copy of my mental health chart? Or do you want to go ahead and call Dr. Shew yourself? I wanted to ask. Or scream. Or stomp out because I hated being so predictable. It was Dr. Shew's fault. She'd recommended a strict routine and ritual to help cope with my *night terrors.*

On the other hand, it was endearing that Mr. Brewster was so observant. He knew nothing about my trials.

"So what'll it be?" Tiffany asked. "A white rose?"

"Yes please." I couldn't stomp out, I needed this. "Actually, make it two," I amended. *Just in case.* "And wrap them separately."

"Coming right up."

Maybe I would have to settle for grocery store flowers next time. No one got questioned by grocery store clerks.

A few minutes later with the flowers wrapped in clear plastic, I exited and made my way to the cemetery. Luckily my dad was on the phone when I walked into the office. He merely waved when I sat down at the computer and logged in. No questions today. Running out of reasons for researching people buried in Meadow Grove, I quickly conducted two searches and printed them, leaving before Dad got off the phone. I could have flipped through the plot book, but this was quicker.

It's funny that Dr. Shew thought the *rose ritual,* as she put it, was the best way to cope. The first time she suggested it I was ecstatic. After all, the cemetery was my favorite place to be. But the actual ritual was utter agony.

Despite what was coming, as I walked onto the grounds, I felt like I could finally breathe again. Like I'd forgotten how stifling every-where else was. Slowing my steps, I raised my head to the clouds and closed my eyes, feeling the breeze and heat of the afternoon sun against my face. The cemetery wasn't spooky, in my opinion. It was peaceful. Whenever I needed a break from schoolwork or from the stresses of high school and being a teenager—which happened a lot lately—I walked through the cemetery. I meandered up and down the rows or found a quiet corner to sit and read or think. The cemetery had been my sanctuary since I was a young child, but I'd only discovered my deeper connection to the consecrated grounds a few years ago.

It didn't take long to find her. Spending so much time with my family's business, I knew the plot areas like the back of my hand, but I stopped before approaching. After taking several deep breaths and counting backwards from fifty, I stepped forward and knelt down.

There was no flourish carved into the small white stone. Just simple block lettering: *Born July 5, 1832. Died February 12, 1849.* She was sixteen when she died. I always forced myself to verify the dates before reading the name because of what followed.

After one more deep breath I read her name: *Nora Violet Harker.*

A wave of emotions and sensations washed over me. The memory was strong and fresh, causing my head to ache and pulse like I had an open gash. My skin tingled from my crown to my toes with the pain of the ice and the freezing river water. Colin's voice, begging Nora to get off the ice, tore at my heart. His frantic babbling and mumbling and pleading rang in my ears. Within seconds it was over, the pain vanished and my skin warmed again. Only the sound of birds, a distant lawnmower, and my own thoughts filled my head.

With a shaking and sweaty hand, I leaned forward and gently laid Nora's rose on the stone.

"I'm sorry," I whispered. It wasn't my fault she died the way she did, I knew that. I felt bad for her, for them, but sometimes I wondered why I had to relive their memories and sometimes their deaths in my dreams. The burden was almost unbearable at times.

The rose ritual was utter agony, but the relief that followed was totally worth it.

"Emily?" An unfamiliar voice only two steps away interrupted my thoughts and startled me. I composed myself before looking at him and hoped the sweat on my forehead wasn't too noticeable. He didn't look familiar. "Sorry," he laughed. "I didn't mean to scare you." He looked close to my age, average height with brown hair. "You must've thought I was a ghost. They're all around us in the cemetery, you know." He winked.

"Visiting family?" I asked, ignoring the lame joke and pointed to the silk bouquet he held.

"Um, yeah. My grandma's buried back there." He hooked a thumb over his shoulder. "The cemetery cleanup is in a few days, and my mom didn't want the flowers thrown away." He smiled again. "But of course you know that since your family runs the place."

I nodded. He knew a lot about me, and I couldn't even place his face. It was déjà vu, this happening twice in one day. Flower-shop Tiffany and now this. Maybe he was new in school?

"Duncan Stewart." He gestured to himself seeing my confusion.

"Emily Chandler."

"Yeah, I know who you are." His smile lit up his face. It was the contagious kind.

His face still wasn't clicking in my memory, which was weird. It was normally pretty good. "Sorry," I said with a half-smile.

"We've never actually spoken," he offered with a shrug. "Check your yearbook. I promise I'm in there."

"I believe you."

"What about you? What are you doing here? Are you working?" He pointed to the flower I still held. "Has cleanup started early?"

"No," I said, pausing. "I'm... I'm visiting a friend." I managed a smile, which he returned.

"I'll leave you to it then," Duncan said, shoving his free hand into the front pocket of his jeans. "Nice talking to you. Finally."

"You too," I said and watched him walk away for a few seconds before returning to Nora.

Shuffling the printed pages, I located Colin's grave not far from his sister. His death date wasn't the same as hers.

He survived the accident, I thought gratefully. *Nora saved him.*

Doing the math in my head, I calculated Colin was seventy-four when he died. Though the white roses were supposed to be for the people whose deaths I experienced in my memory dreams, I placed the second rose on Colin's grave. He was only eight when Nora passed. It must have been awful for him to watch his sister die.

But at least she saved him.

CHAPTER 3

Lucy

I am engaged.

It is the first thought in my head when I awake. Stretching and smiling, I am so comfortable and content that my body will not allow me to arise. The magical memory of Charles—*my* Charles—on bended knee in the garden last night enters my thoughts. I happily let the memory play out slowly, but then my thoughts turn to Margaret, my dear friend. *How she will love to hear every detail! I must tell her the news!*

Not wanting to waste another minute, I ring for Betsy and sit at my writing desk. I pen a quick letter to my friend, inviting her to luncheon.

"Miss Lucy," Betsy knocks at my bedroom door and enters. "Shall I help you dress for breakfast?"

"Not now." I carefully fold my letter and seal it. "Have my family already gone?"

"Yes. Mrs. Eldridge and Miss Hannah left early."

Then I will have no one to eat with. But I do not regret the solitude. It will give me time to write my elder sister about my engagement. "Please have my breakfast sent to my room."

"Yes, Miss Lucy."

"And ask Drake to deliver this to Miss Wood." I hand her my

letter. "And then inform Mrs. Holt that Miss Wood will dine with me for luncheon today."

"Yes, Miss Lucy." Betsy curtsies and leaves my room.

———

MARGARET TAKES MY HANDS IN HER PRETTY WHITE gloves when she arrives. "Oh, Lucy, how lonely you must be!" she says, "Your guardians and sister gone for a fortnight!"

"Do not pity me, Margaret. I am happier than words can express." My smile is genuine.

A confused expression passes over her features.

"I am lonely only for someone to share my happiness." Still seeing her confusion, I gesture for her to sit. "Please, let us eat, and I will tell you all about it." In my elation, I am wearing my favorite blue dress even though only the servants and Margaret will see me today. We exchange pleasantries while our meal is served, then when the servants leave, Margaret leans forward.

"You are holding me in suspense, Lucy," Margaret says. "Please tell me the cause of your happiness."

I pause. "Charles proposed."

Margaret stifles a squeal. "When?"

"Last night."

"Oh, you must tell me all about it!" Her eyes sparkle with excitement. "And do not leave out a single detail." She takes a bite of her sandwich.

"I would not dare." I laugh once. "As you know, we had a farewell dinner last night."

"Yes, for your family." She provides. "And for Mr.—"

"And for *Charles*." It is bad manners to speak over her words, but she feels the effect and smiles. "Charles asked me to walk with him in the garden after dinner," I begin.

"Did you know why he wanted to walk with you?" she says before I can get another word out.

"Not until Hannah asked if she could join us and my aunt

rejected her." I am patient with my friend. Being friends—good friends—since childhood I forgive her interruptions. "She said Hannah must get to bed immediately since they planned to leave early this morning."

"So Mrs. Eldridge knew?"

"Probably." I smile. "Uncle Harry cannot keep a secret from her. Charles spoke to him first, of course." Saying his name gives me butterflies. I take a bite of my sandwich to build the suspense.

My technique works. "Go on," Margaret prods. "You walked together in the garden?"

"Yes. First we talked about his trip," I say. "He was excited to go. It will be a good opportunity for him, but he said he was dreading it for one reason."

"What? Missing you?" Margaret giggles.

"Yes, but I pretended not to know his meaning." I flash a sly smile. "Men are so fond of declaring their feelings. I didn't want to rob him of it."

"Is that true?"

"I read it in a book once." I take another bite, but quickly continue. "He became flustered and his face turned *crimson red*."

"What happened next?"

"He was speechless for a time." Pure joy fills me as I recount one of the happiest moments of my life. *I was right,* I thought. *This is much better than recounting my engagement alone.* "I wanted to ask him what was the matter, but the look on his face kept me quiet." For once Margaret allows me to speak without interruption. "I did not realize how desperately he would miss me until that moment."

"Oh, and will you miss him too?"

"Yes," I say. "He asked me just that, if I would miss him while he was gone, and I said I would. Then, Margaret—" I clasp my hands together and hear my voice change in my elation. "He told me how he adores me and that he thinks I am the *loveliest creature* he has ever seen. He said he planned to wait until he returned from his trip to tell me what he was about to declare, but could not wait a second longer.

"Let me tell you what he said: He told me that from the moment we met, he did everything in his power to be near me, to earn the privilege to be called my friend. He said he never dared to hope that I would see him as anything more than that, but he fell in love with me!"

Margaret sighs.

"Then he knelt down and took something out of his pocket." I continue. "'Now please,' he said, 'I must know your feelings. I must know if you love me even a tiny fraction of what I feel for you. If you do, and I desperately hope you do, Lucy, will you marry me?'"

"Go on!" Margaret urges when I again pause.

"Can you not guess, Margaret? I said yes!" I remove my glove and present my hand to show her my pretty ring. "I told him I loved him and that I would be the happiest woman in the world to be his wife."

"Lucy, how romantic!" She admires my newly decorated hand.

"It was his grandmother's ring," I add. "And now you know why I am so happy."

To my delight, Margaret asks me more questions about my enchanted evening, prompting me to divulge further details while we finish our meal. But all too soon it is time for her to leave.

"I am so happy you rescued me from an afternoon alone," I say, forcing a fake pout. "Thank you for coming."

"I only wish I could stay, dearest Lucy. Surely your beloved's absence will seem longer without a friend or family to pass the time." Betsy helps her into her overcoat. "When will he return?"

"Not for three weeks, but I will hardly be alone," I assure her. "Tonight a cousin of Charles's arrives and as his *future* cousin, starting tomorrow it is my privilege to divert him."

"Him?" Margaret's interest is piqued. "Is this *cousin* a bachelor?"

I laugh. "I believe so."

Margaret's face falls. "Is he old and gray with only a few hairs left on his head?"

"Charles said they were the best of friends as boys before his cousin moved to Savannah," I say. "I do not think he is old."

"Then he must be short and plump," Margaret says, her mood not shifting much. "And young men can lose their hair too."

I laugh. "Oh, Margaret, how you see the worst in every situation! And really, are looks the most important attribute a young man can have?"

"Perhaps he has missing teeth because he boxes and gambles," she says, ignoring my chastising words.

"Or," I say, with a wink, "he could be even more handsome than Charles."

"And cruel and unfeeling toward plain girls like me."

"Margaret Wood, you are anything but plain!" I exclaim. "I am sure that Charles's cousin is kind and considerate... and handsome."

"Well then," she says, her tone finally hopeful. "As my dearest, most-cherished friend, you should find out his character, then introduce us."

"Absolutely. And if you fall in love with this *cousin*," I mimic her inflection. "And decide to marry..."

Margaret's eyebrows rise with excitement. "Then you and I will be family!"

"What fun that will be!" I say, and we embrace before she departs.

I am all smiles in my solitude the rest of the day and find myself perfectly content reading in the sitting room after dinner. It is difficult to keep my mind on the pages as they wander to thoughts of my happy engaged state, but fortunately I am not reprimanded by anyone who demands my attention or cordiality since there are no guests at home and my family is away. And since books have no feelings, the one I pay horrible attention to has no reason to feel slighted—

"Excuse me, Miss Lucy," Drake says as he enters the sitting room. "A gentleman is here to see you."

"At this hour?" I put down my book and stand, noting the clock on the mantle shows the time is a quarter past nine o'clock. "Let him in."

Drake nods and leaves the room, re-entering with a young gentleman who looks not much older than myself.

"Would you like me to fetch Betsy for tea, Miss?" Drake asks.

"There is no need," the gentleman says, waving a gloved hand. "My visit will be brief so the young lady may get back to her evening." His voice is raspy and low, with a hint of a Brooklyn accent.

Drake bows and exits.

"Please tell me you are Miss Hannah." The gentleman approaches, removing a glove and extending his hand to take mine. "Younger sister of Miss Lucy who is recently engaged to my cousin Charles."

"News travels fast," I say, smiling. "I'm sorry, Mr.—"

"Harker, Andrew Harker." He presses his lips to my fingers, then releases my hand and crosses the room to the fireplace and turns again to face me. "Charles wrote me of his intended proposal weeks ago," Mr. Harker explains. "He left a note at the house telling me Miss Lucy's answer. I apologize for coming at a late hour, but I just arrived and wanted to offer my congratulations."

"Andrew Harker," I repeat. "I did not expect to meet you until tomorrow. You may congratulate me," I say, presenting him my left hand. "I am the future Mrs. Charles—"

"Then you are Miss Lucy." A hint of disappointment is evident.

"I am," I say, ignoring his rudeness in cutting me off. "If you wished to meet Miss Hannah, I'm afraid she's away at a funeral with our uncle and aunt, Mr. and Mrs. Eldridge."

Mr. Harker nods.

"But she will be back for her birthday in a fortnight," I add and give him a knowing smile "She turns eleven this year."

"Right." Understanding colors his features. "Forgive my forwardness, but when I heard of your beauty, which I must say is entirely accurate, and that you were intended for Charles, I hoped you had a sister I could meet." His half-smile only slightly covers his chagrin.

I feel my cheeks flush. "Hannah would be pleased to hear that, but please, Mr. Harker—"

"Call me Andrew," he interjects then bows his head and looks at me through dark eyelashes. "After all, we will soon be family."

"Yes, but we are not family yet." I laugh. "As I was saying, *Mr. Harker*, Hannah is too young for suitors."

"Of course, Miss Lucy." Mr. Harker again raises his head. His eyes linger on my face long enough to make me uncomfortable.

"Tomorrow," I say, causing his eyes to flit away. "Since Charles is gone, you will dine here with me."

"I look forward to it."

"I am sorry there is no one here but me to entertain."

"Nonsense. It is my own fault for insisting that I visit while everyone is away." He inspects a silver ring on his right hand, then loosens it and twirls it around his finger. "I intend to stay until autumn, so I will only be alone in the house until Charles returns."

"Well, as your future cousin, I will gladly do my best to make you feel welcome until then."

"I hope you mean it, Miss Lucy, because I intend to take you up on your offer." His smile is warm, but mischievous. "Saturday you can take me on a tour of your town."

"We can take a picnic and make an outing of it, Mr. Harker."

"And you will call me Andrew by the end of the week."

"We shall see, Mr. Harker." I do not hide my smile.

He pauses a moment as if deciding what to say then asks, "Could I pay you a compliment, Miss Lucy?"

"What an odd question, but yes." My smile does not leave my face. "Why would I refuse a compliment?"

"That dress." He gestures to my favorite blue gown. "If you look even half as fetching in your other frocks as you do in that dress, I am surprised Charles didn't secure your hand the moment he laid eyes on you."

My cheeks flame, and I turn away to hide my embarrassment.

"In fact, had I met you even a moment before Charles proposed, he would have had competition."

"Mr. Harker—" I turn back to face him.

"Do not take offense, it was only a compliment. I promise to act properly from now on in your presence." He tips his hat. "Good night, Miss Lucy. Until tomorrow."

"Good night," I say, and he leaves me.

While banishing the memory of Mr. Harker's compliment from my mind, I did not fail to note that he was indeed kind, handsome, and very likely in search of a wife.

Margaret will be pleased.

I determine to call on her first thing in the morning to see if she is not otherwise engaged on Saturday.

wednesday

Arianna tapped my desk at the end of chemistry class as I put my books and notes away. "We're meeting at Brian's house after school to start on our *Hamlet* project," she said. "Sorry it's late notice." I shouldered my backpack, and we walked out together. "Can you make it?"

She knew my social calendar was far from booked, but it was kind of her to act like it might be. "I'll be there," I said.

"See you later then," she said. "You too, Duncan."

"Will do," Duncan said. I didn't see him approach, but he stood behind me. "You're in Arianna's group too?" he asked after she'd left.

I nodded. "I'm a late addition." He didn't need to know all of the depressing details.

"Want a ride?"

"Thanks, but Brian doesn't live far from my house. I think I'll walk," I said immediately regretting it. Duncan was just being nice and rejecting him was not helping my loner label. I touched my purple frames as if to move them higher up my nose, though I didn't need to.

"It's a nice day. Mind if I walk with you?"

Inwardly I sighed with relief at the second chance. "That'd be great," I said, hoping my smile was as genuine as it felt. It had been so long since I'd had reason to smile for real. Part of my happiness was due to my Lucy memory-dream last night. Not all my memory-dreams were about death. But they were usually sad or painful. So Lucy's was out of sorts. In a good way. Nothing exceptionally exciting had happened, but she'd been happy. *Which was strange.*

That reminded me. "Duncan, I actually have to drop by the cemetery office before I go to Brian's." Honestly, it could probably wait, but who knew which Meadow Grove resident I'd be dreaming of that night? Maybe I'd have other research in the morning. At least I wasn't buying flowers today. "Is it all right if we stop there first?" I asked, not wanting him to think I was turning him down again.

"Sure."

As Duncan waited for me at the cemetery office after school, I felt even worse about not recognizing him yesterday. Everyone else recognized him. My dad apparently knew Duncan's dad and was theatrically telling him a story about a high school prank the two of them pulled *back in the day.*

Funny, he'd never told me the story.

"Come on, come on," I muttered under my breath. The cemetery database was running particularly slow. Dad thought I was getting on the internet for our school project, so I pulled up the browser and looked up a random Hamlet article to print while the program loaded.

"Are you about done, Emily?" Dad called back. "I've got a meeting with a family in a few minutes."

"Almost," I said right as the search screen popped up. I typed in her name: *Lucy.* The number of results was too high. A lot of Lucys were buried in Meadow Grove. The search had to be narrowed down. Unfortunately I never heard or saw Lucy's last name and unless a person said it, wrote it, or thought about it for any reason, there was no way for me to figure it out. People just don't think about their birth dates or full names on a regular basis.

Sometimes, like in Nora's memory-dream, I knew myself *in* the dream. When that happened, I could search the person's memories. But I'd had no such luck last night. My own consciousness remained silent until I woke up.

Lucy, Lucy, Lucy. Think, think, think. I tapped the keyboard keys while racking my brain. Lucy was engaged to Charles. His cousin was Andrew Harker. I easily remembered his last name since it was the same as Nora's. They were probably related somehow. *If Charles last name was Harker...* I typed *Lucy Harker.*

No results.

Frustrated and out of time, I cleared the screen and stood to leave with Duncan. *I'll have to check the journal.* Every morning I jotted down notes and details about my memory-dreams. Maybe there was something in there to help me find Lucy. Though it might be a dead end. I had a stack of dead ends.

"Everything okay?" Duncan asked as we left for Brian's.

"Yeah," I said and brightened my voice. He couldn't know why I was disappointed. Normally dead ends were nothing more than a fleeting annoyance. Sometimes I tried to convince myself that meant it was just a normal dream—a figment of my imagination. Although I hadn't experienced a normal dream since I was twelve. Besides, my subconscious wasn't good enough to make up Lucy.

It had been a long time since I'd had a pleasant memory-dream. It was too bad I hadn't found her.

I felt Duncan's eyes on me as we walked. I wondered what he was thinking, but didn't dare ask.

"What were you doing anyway?" he asked after a time.

He wasn't prying. It was an honest question, but I'd have to be careful.

"Something for our project." I waved the printed sheet.

He took it and glanced at it briefly. "Are you going to the football game Friday night?" He asked, handing back the sheet.

I looked at him out of the corner of my eye and twisted my mouth. "Probably not." Sitting on the bleachers by myself wasn't my idea of fun.

"Why not?"

"I'm not exactly Miss Popular." It was a stupid comment.

"Sure, but you and Arianna always go to games, right?"

Correction. Used to go. "Arianna and I had a sort of..." I paused. "Falling out."

"I noticed."

"Then why did you ask if she and I were going?"

"I didn't," he said. "I pointed out that you both went to games in the past. Your *falling out* shouldn't prevent you from attending. She still goes."

Yeah, but she has friends, I thought.

"What happened between you two?" he asked. We'd arrived at Brian's, but Duncan stopped on the front lawn.

"A guy," I said. It wasn't true, but I couldn't even begin to explain why Arianna decided she couldn't be my friend anymore.

Duncan raised an eyebrow and gave a sympathetic look. "Brian?" He hooked a thumb pointing behind him. I looked past him at the red brick house where Brian lived.

Were Arianna and Brian dating? I wondered. *Was that the reason for Duncan's sympathetic look?* My face fell, but not because I had any attachment to Brian.

Of course Duncan interpreted it that way. "I heard they've been together a few weeks now," he said. I nodded, my heart sinking with regret. Arianna had been crushing on Brian since the end of sophomore year, and I was hearing about her good fortune from a practical stranger. "Come to the game with me," Duncan said in a rush. "It'll cheer you up, I promise." He flashed me his contagious smile. I couldn't help but mirror it.

Still, I hesitated. It had been a while since my last appearance at a school event.

"I'd much rather go with Emily Chandler than *Miss Popular,* anyway," he said, rolling his eyes.

Laughing, I said, "Okay." I could always cancel if I was murdered in my dreams the night before the game.

I couldn't take my eyes off Arianna and Brian as we brainstormed our project. The way Arianna looked at him as he assigned parts to each of us was no surprise. After all, she'd pined for him from a distance for months. But now he reciprocated the look, stealing glances at her with a sparkle in his eyes. It gave me a bittersweet feeling. I was happy for her but sad that I'd missed out celebrating her dream come true. Duncan caught my eye as I wistfully watched the happy couple. He gave me another sympathetic look. From then on I pointedly kept my eyes on my book as we read act three of *Hamlet*.

"Any ideas about how we should parody this?" Brian asked when we'd finished. Our assignment was to condense, then perform act three in front of the class in a different genre, like *Romeo and Juliet* a la *West Side Story*.

First there was silence, followed by some weak suggestions. My creative juices were frozen, so I kept quiet.

"Emily has a good idea," Duncan said, keeping his eyes on a sheet of paper.

I stared at him with wide eyes. *I do?*

He looked up from the sheet and waved it to the group. "She printed this off before we came. It's a great idea."

"What is it?" Arianna took the sheet from Duncan, but looked at me when she asked the question.

"Uh..." I never read the article, only printed it, and had no idea of the content.

"It's a review of a *Hamlet* performance at a small theater," Duncan said, saving me. "They performed it Mafia style. You know, think *The Godfather.*"

Everyone muttered in agreement and quoted lines from the movie for several minutes.

"Thanks, Emily," Brian said.

"Sure."

"Okay, Ari and I will condense the act," Brian continued. "Sarah, can you and Emily find props?"

"Yeah," Sarah said. I nodded.

"I'll help Emily and Sarah," Duncan said, winking at me.

"Great, let's meet again next week," Brian said. "Tuesday good for everyone?"

We all agreed and stood to leave. Sarah left immediately, but Duncan and Brian began discussing the game Friday. Neither were on the football team but both had strong opinions on our team and their chances of winning. I would have left when Sarah did, but I didn't want to ditch Duncan since we had walked there together. So I was stuck awkwardly standing with my ex-best friend.

"Is Duncan your ride?" Arianna asked after a few uncomfortable moments.

"No, but we walked together."

"Ah," she said. "I guess we can sit. They could take a while." She giggled. I smiled, and we both sat back on the couch, falling into silence again. Arianna slowly folded a paper she held into smaller and smaller squares until the Meadow Grove logo ran diagonal through the top square. It was my *Hamlet* article. "You printed this at the office?" she asked in a subdued tone without looking up and slowly unfolded it again.

"Yeah," I said. "Duncan and I stopped there before coming here so I could look it up."

"So that was your cover for researching someone in the cemetery?" There was no alarm or accusation in her voice, just matter-of-fact. I didn't know how to answer. "'Cause you clearly didn't read it." She looked at me, but her expression didn't change. She knew me too well.

I opened my mouth, but nothing came out.

Arianna handed me the now-unfolded paper and leaned forward to talk to me with her back to the guys so they wouldn't hear. "Do you still have, you know, the *death-dreams*?" I nodded, not meeting her eyes. Since she had stopped talking to me, dealing with the horrific dreams had become harder. Arianna used to have my back whenever I tuned out in school after a particularly disturbing one. She had been my shoulder to cry on and my support when the flashbacks the next day were too hard to bear. My stomach twisted at the reminder that I was once again alone in my curse. Like yesterday's flashbacks from Nora's dream.

"Hey, uh," Arianna said in a lighter tone, sensing my darkness. "Brian really won't be good at the condensing part of our project. I think he is just excited to write the Mafia lingo. Could you help me condense it instead? Then we can let Brian Mafia it up?" She chuckled at her terminology. "I can help you and Sarah and Duncan with the props."

"Sure," I said. I stood up, seeing Duncan motion to me he was done talking with Brian.

Ari grabbed my hand, preventing me from walking away. "Honestly though," she said in a hushed tone and a sly smile. "I suspect Duncan will find a way to keep me and Sarah out of it, so he can help you alone."

"Why?" I asked.

"Em, he's had a crush on you for *forever.*" She smiled at me the way she did when we were still friends, then released my hand and stood as well. "You've been so oblivious to him for so many years. He'll take advantage of your attention now that he finally has it."

I smiled, but once again my guilt resurfaced over not even knowing Duncan existed until the other day. How had I been so blind to him?

"By the way, I'm happy for you," I said, nodding toward Brian.

She giggled. "Me too."

I smiled all the way home. A short chat about guys and our shared interest in a good grade weren't enough to make Arianna want to be associated with me again. She would probably stop talking to me after our project, but it felt good to have my friend back for those few short minutes.

CHAPTER 5

Secrets

"Miss Lucy, I am perfectly capable of making a picnic lunch without supervision," Mrs. Holt says for the fifth time. She tries once again to shoo me from her kitchen, but I am too anxious for my outing today with Mr. Harker to do anything else. After our tour around town, Margaret plans to meet us at the park for lunch so I can finally introduce them.

At dinner the night before, I made a point of speaking highly of my friend. My compliments so intrigued Mr. Harker that he suggested Margaret join us on our picnic. The thought of Margaret and Andrew falling in love at my matchmaking hand makes my heart warm.

"Mr. Harker has arrived, Miss Lucy," Drake says as he enters the kitchen.

"Perfect timing," says Mrs. Holt, putting the last items into the basket and folding a napkin over the top before clasping it closed. She then hands it to Drake.

"Thank you, Mrs. Holt," I say.

She nods and smiles. Probably only because she is glad to be rid of me, but I'm so happy I don't care.

Betsy helps me into my overcoat and I pull on my favorite gray gloves while entering the front entryway where Mr. Harker waits. He wears a gray suit and straw derby hat, which he removes when I enter.

"Lovely as usual, Miss Lucy." Mr. Harker gives a slight bow and a cordial smile.

"Thank you, Mr. Harker." Thoughts of our first awkward meeting vanish as I eagerly greet my new cousin. There was no sign of the flirtatious suitor at dinner last night. He was everything proper—my decorous future cousin. Though I wouldn't mind the suitor's return when I introduce Margaret. "Shall we?" I gesture to the door as our eyes meet.

His eyes darken, and his smile falters.

I cast my eyes down to avert his gaze and secure the hat Betsy hands me, slowly tying the ribbon under my chin as Mr. Harker replaces his hat. I lead the way out the door without looking at him again and attempt to dismiss the exchange.

Drake helps me into the open carriage and hands me our lunch basket while Mr. Harker climbs in and sits beside me. We ride in silence as we leave the manor, but I refuse to allow our uncomfortable greeting taint what I hope to be a perfect day.

"I love New England in the spring," I say, forcing my tone to mimic the comfortable, easy tone of our dinner conversation last night.

"It is beautiful." Mr. Harker's controlled voice and posture fail to hide his unease.

"Tell me," I lay a hand on his clenched fist resting beside me. "What is spring like in Savannah?"

The gesture helps, and he relaxes his hand, unclenching it to gently grasp my fingers. "Warmer than here," he says and meets my eyes. Only now do I notice his are a deep-chestnut color with flecks of amber. Charles's eyes are blue, like mine, only lighter, but Andrew's have a rich deepness—

I am forced to look away.

"Humid though," Mr. Harker adds, and releases my hand. "Where are we going?"

"Saint Marie's," I say. "The grounds are lovely. The chapel has the most-beautiful stained glass windows, and they ring the bells in the steeple at twelve o'clock every day. You can hear them almost a mile away."

Mr. Harker nods but doesn't say another word before we reach our destination.

I am pleased to walk around the grounds of Saint Marie's, enlightening Mr. Harker on the history of its construction and the people who built it. The shrubbery and landscaping are immaculately maintained, except on the north side, where there is only forest beyond it. A stone bench sits adjacent to the north wall, allowing its occupants a peaceful view into the trees.

"This is my favorite place," I say, leading Mr. Harker to the bench and taking a seat. "Whenever I come to town, I carve out enough time to enjoy sitting and reading or pondering in this very spot." I pat the bench with my gloved hand, gesturing for Mr. Harker to sit beside me.

He obliges. "It is beautiful," he says, his tone still guarded.

Mr. Harker is a head taller than me, so I tilt my head to look up at him from underneath my hat. He looks straight ahead into the brown-and-green maze. I turn to see what he sees, and my breath catches at the beauty of the sight—sunlight filters through the trees, creating warm patches of light, illuminating scattered sections of the forest floor.

I turn back to Andrew. My brotherly future cousin has yet to appear today. He seems to have been replaced by a guarded Mr. Harker. Envious of his long dark lashes, seen more clearly in his profile, I am again caught up in comparing him to Charles, whose lashes are short and light and almost invisible. Even mine cannot compete with Andrew's.

Mr. Harker meets my gaze, and I look away quickly. "Shall we go inside?" I ask and look at him again. "Morning is the perfect time to see the light shine through the stained glass." When he does not answer immediately, I continue. "I hope to convince Charles to have our wedding ceremony in the morning. We are getting married in this chapel, and I want the lighting to be perfect."

"Let us sit here awhile longer," says Mr. Harker, and he looks back into my forest.

I am happy to oblige. Even the beautiful ethereal light inside the chapel cannot compare with the naturally filtered rays of sun shining through the canopy of trees here behind the church. However, Mr. Harker's mood is unmistakably gray. "What is bothering you?" I ask. As future family, I feel the urge to pry and make him happy again.

A forced smile surfaces beneath Mr. Harker's guarded expression when he looks at me, but I also see conflicting emotions in his eyes that I cannot name. "Nothing is wrong. I was just thinking about our conversation last night," he says. "It has been a while since I have connected with someone so quickly."

"I feel the same, Andrew."

He laughs and looks down at his hands. "You called me Andrew, Lucy."

The realization strikes me as funny, and I laugh. "I did!" I say. "I had every intention of calling you *Mr. Harker* at least until Charles and I marry, just to spite you." I shake a finger at him and squint as I try not to smile. "But as you said, we have become close almost instantly, and I think of you as a brother. I cannot call my brother *Mr. Harker*, especially since I intend to marry a Mr. Harker." I lift my head to smile warmly at Andrew. "Even in my thoughts I cannot call you *Mr. Harker*." I shake my head and laugh again. "Not when you are clearly Andrew to me."

"Except for the last phrase, I did not understand a word of what you said." Andrew reciprocates my expression with an affable version of his own. "But I did warn that you would call me Andrew by the end of the week."

"You did, and you were right."

Our banter lulls a moment, and I am about to suggest we go to the park to meet Margaret when Andrew asks, "Is there a grave-yard on the church grounds?"

"No," I reply, fumbling my hands.

"Are you sure? I seem to remember one nearby."

"Perhaps you are thinking of Saint Phillip's. Just down the road."

"Is it far?" he asks.

"Not far," I say. An uncomfortable lump forms in my stomach. "Within walking distance."

Andrew stands and provides me a hand. "Let us walk then."

Taking his hand, I slowly stand, then grip his offered arm, somewhat tighter than intended as my legs weaken. It has been almost eight years since I set foot in the graveyard. "Margaret will be waiting," I say. "We really should go."

"We have time, Lucy." Andrew leads me around to the front of the church. "We will have Matthew meet us at the graveyard so we can promptly join Miss Wood afterward."

How can I protest more? If I tell Andrew my reasoning for not wanting to visit the graveyard, he will insist upon doing just that. I know that much about him. Most suitors do not find strolling through a graveyard a romantic outing, so it was never a concern with Charles. Of course, Andrew is not courting me.

"No more objections?" Andrew teases, lowering his head enough that he can look at me through his dark lashes.

"No," I yield. "But we mustn't stay long."

"Of course. We cannot keep Miss Wood waiting."

Our roles are reversed as we stroll down the road. Now I am distressed and withdrawn, while Andrew is happy and comfortable. He speaks about the beauty of Georgia in the spring and does not seem to notice my discomfort even as we walk through the ornate wrought iron gates. I involuntarily shiver, and my heart pounds faster with each step.

"Strolling through a graveyard is one of my favorite things to do," Andrew says, releasing my arm and walking backwards in front to face me as he talks.

I try to make my footing look steady without his arm as a

support. "Do you have family buried here?" My voice quakes slightly, and I clasp my fingers together to steady their shaking.

"Yes, the Harkers first settled here when they came to America," he says. "Many of them are resting here or nearby, but that is not my reason for wanting to visit." He stops walking to again offer his arm. I cannot be more grateful for the support. "It is peaceful and quiet."

Andrew pauses for effect, as if enjoying the sounds of birds and the breeze rustling through the trees. He probably does enjoy it, but I cannot hear any of it with pleasure. Feeling the pull of them at the far edge of the grounds overwhelms my thoughts. "There is a graveyard in Savannah I walk through at least twice a week," he continues. "It gives me time to think without distraction."

"How interesting. I suppose few consider a burial ground a good place to sort their thoughts." After all, *I* had never considered it.

"Precisely," Andrew says. I feel his eyes on me, but do not return his gaze. He ducks his head closer to mine and lowers his voice as he whispers the last words, "It is my little secret."

"You have my confidence," I say, meeting his eyes and attempting a smile.

"I appreciate it." Andrew's smile broadens. "I would hate to have crowds arriving in droves for picnics and socials, disturbing my sanctuary."

"My lips are sealed." I press a gloved finger to my lips and return his smile.

"Something is bothering you." Andrew sees through my attempted mask. "Please, what can I do to put you at ease again?"

I cannot tell him the real reason for my discomfort, so I offer another truth. "I am a little hungry," I say.

"Oh dear. It seems I have prioritized my contemplation over your hunger. Please forgive me." Andrew calls to my driver, Matthew, and we make our way back to the carriage. "Come, let us meet Miss Wood and have our picnic."

As hoped, my friend is enamored with Andrew as we talk and eat our cold sandwiches. I can tell Andrew has similar feelings toward Margaret as he often looks at me with a sparkle in his brown eyes and a smile on his face. I am sure he is seeking encouragement, so I gladly reciprocate.

"And where did Lucy take you this morning, Mr. Harker?" Margaret asks.

"Saint Marie's," Andrew answers.

"Ah, she has an obsession with the pretty stained glass windows." Margaret looks at me and smiles before her eyes flit back to Andrew.

"Yes, she told me."

"And what did you think of our little chapel?"

"I am afraid you will have to wait for my answer another time, Miss Wood. Lucy and I did not go inside."

"Why not?" Margaret is baffled. "Was there a wedding?"

"No, *not today*." Andrew's rasp is suddenly almost a growl. He glances at me then clears his throat. "Excuse me," he offers, then continues. "We spent some time sitting in Lucy's favorite spot behind the church."

"Behind the church?" Margaret's confusion grows. "But I thought your favorite spot was the third pew where you can best see the images in the windows?"

"Yes, that is my favorite place *inside* the chapel, Margaret." I glare at Andrew, but cannot hold it long. "For someone who asked my confidence not one hour ago about his secrets," I say, playfully throwing a piece of grass at Andrew, "you sure are eager to divulge mine."

"I did not know it was a secret." Andrew holds his hands up in surrender as I throw more blades of grass. "I am sorry, Lucy. To be fair, you are free to tell Miss Wood my secret."

"I promised I would not tell," I say. "I keep my promises." I fold my arms in a mock huff and shift half a turn.

"Fine, then I will." Andrew turns to Margaret. "But Miss Wood." He takes both of her hands and speaks in playful earnest. "You must *promise* not to tell another soul what I am about to tell you."

I roll my eyes at his melodrama. *Wait. Roll my eyes?*

"Of course, Mr. Harker." Margaret's face glows, and I can see the edge of her green eyes sparkle. I'm sure the sudden closeness of Andrew and his touch are having an effect.

"Lucy and I strolled through St Phillip's graveyard," he says. Margaret unsuccessfully covers a gasp, then looks at me. Andrew doesn't notice. "I enjoy the peace and quiet of walking through where the dead rest." I feel my playfulness vanish as I see the concern in Margaret's expression. "I asked Lucy not to divulge my secret so I can keep the solitude of the graveyard to myself."

Margaret takes her hands from Andrew's. "Lucy, you went to the graveyard?" Her voice is barely a whisper, but before I can answer, she turns back to Andrew. "Do you not know Lucy's history, Mr. Harker?"

Andrew's smile also falls, seeing Margaret's apprehension and whatever expression is plastered on my face. I avoid his gaze. Fortunately my friend enlightens him for me. "Lucy's aunt and uncle are guardian to her and Miss Hannah because their father and mother died tragically. They are buried in that graveyard."

I cannot help but meet Andrew's penetrating gaze. He is hurt. As if our intimacy should have made me tell him. "No," Andrew replies to Margaret. "She did not mention it." His voice is carefully controlled. I look away.

"Mr. Harker," Margaret says. "Lucy has not set foot in that graveyard since their funeral eight years ago."

"Until today," Andrew mumbles.

thursday

I slipped into my seat seconds before the tardy bell rang.

"Slept through your alarm?" Duncan asked. His contagious smile suddenly appeared.

"Not exactly," I whispered. It was still strange talking to him. We shared several classes together and were already two months into the semester, so I couldn't understand how he'd been virtually invisible until two days ago. It was like he didn't exist until Tuesday.

Class started, so I didn't have to answer Duncan's question, which was a relief. Sleeping in was not what had made me late.

Lightning had struck twice: I never dreamed the same person more than once. Determined more than ever to find Lucy, I read through my dream notes from the first night and was reminded that Lucy's guardians, her aunt and uncle, were named *Eldridge*. Hoping it was her last name too, I ran to the office before school to look up anyone named Lucy Eldridge.

Still no luck.

Eager to find any connection to her, I then searched for *Charles Harker*, *Andrew Harker*, and *Margaret Wood*. None of them were buried in Meadow Grove. None of them. I wanted to rip my hair out. Getting obsessive, I stayed at the office too long and was almost late for school.

"Wanna look for props after school, Emily?" Duncan asked when class was over. "Sarah can't make it today, but I think you and I can handle it."

"I can't," I said, standing to leave. "Not today. I'm helping Arianna condense the act this afternoon."

"I thought she was doing that with Brian."

"They are," I said. "They're going to add Mafia *lingo,* but Ari wanted me to help her condense it first." Duncan's disappointment was evident. "But we could go tomorrow after school."

"The *game.*" He smiled. "Did you forget already?"

"That's not until like seven though, right?"

"Yeah but the pep rally is right after school, *before* the game." He hooked an arm around my shoulders as we walked out of class. "And you, my friend, have been absent from school events for far too long. We're going to enjoy all of it."

"Okay. What about Saturday?" I asked, pretending to be indifferent to his plan in order to hide my anxiety.

"Saturday," Duncan agreed. "I'll tell Sarah."

———

Arianna drove me to her house after school. Her mother wasn't home, she'd assured me. In the past, we had always avoided her house when her mom was there. It made me even sadder that Ari and I were no longer friends. I hoped that she'd found another sanctuary from her home life after she stopped spending so much time at my house.

It was probably better that way. If we'd gone to my house, Mom or Dad or both might've given us the third degree about why we weren't friends anymore. Though I couldn't speak for her, I didn't want to hash out the truth right now.

We worked swiftly. Knowing each other's strengths and weaknesses, Arianna and I always worked well together on school work.

"Are you and Duncan going to look for props tomorrow?" Ari asked when we took a break to eat. She dug some cold fried chicken out of the nearly empty refrigerator. We were almost finished with our part of the assignment.

"No, tomorrow is the football game. We're going Saturday."

"Oh, are you going to the game?" Her interest was piqued. It was breaking news to her.

I nodded. "Duncan asked me to go."

"I told you!" Her eyes lit up. "I told you he liked you!"

"Why didn't you tell me before?" I asked, though I wasn't sure I agreed.

"I, uh…" She took another bite and chewed slowly. "I had other things on my mind."

"So it was when…"

She nodded. I knew exactly what she meant. Only Arianna and I knew the whole truth of why we stopped being friends. Everyone had their theory. Some were way off, like Duncan's, but that was my fault. Most involved some emotional-depression thing on Ari's part. Her sister died less than a year ago in an accident. That's what *when* referred to.

She and I stopped being friends several months later, and the most popular theory was that she cut things off because it was too painful for her to be around people who knew Carly. That's what my parents kept telling me. Obviously she couldn't divorce her family, but she could stop talking to me.

But Carly's death was only partially relevant.

"How's your family doing?" I asked, my eyes glued to the floor. I instantly regretted asking such a sensitive question.

"We're dealing." There was coldness in her voice. "It'll take time."

"Of course."

"Let's finish this."

Arianna's warm, friendly tone didn't return, and we finished our work in a cold, business-like manner. I almost wondered why she didn't get the broom out when she swept me out the door without even a hint of an offer of a ride home. Walking wasn't a big deal. It was just a long walk. But I couldn't very well call my parents and explain why they were picking me up around the corner instead of at Arianna's house.

Pulling my jacket tighter around myself, I pulled my pink mittens out of my pockets to cover my hands. The temperature seemed to have dropped since school let out. It had been a warm fall so far, but now in the second week in October, it felt like winter was close. I walked briskly to keep warm but soon decided to divert my route. It was out of my way, but two streets north and one block east would lead me straight to a steaming cup of hot cocoa.

Five minutes later, I walked up to one of my favorite places in the world. A small colonial house with a white-washed exterior, dark-blue shutters, and a fire-engine-red door. Out front, a large tree, now naked of its leaves, held so many memories. Swinging on the lower branches, climbing too high before falling and breaking my wrist when I was seven. Raking leaves every fall, including only a few weeks ago.

And my favorite little birdhouse hanging by a red cord.

It was depressingly beautiful. It was a pale-yellow color, intricately embellished with tiny black hand-painted birds. They reminded me of the crows that were always loitering at the cemetery.

"Get inside, girl!" Grandma Grace shouted from the front porch. "Don't stand there catching your death!"

I smiled. "Hey, Grandma," I said then followed her into the cozy home.

"What were you staring at out there?" she asked, as I trailed behind her to the kitchen. She was already heating up the water.

"Your birdhouse," I said.

"That old thing?" she said, opening her cupboard to retrieve two blue mugs decorated with fading purple flowers, her many rings clanking against the ceramic.

"Where did you get it?" I asked. "I've never asked you about it. Did you make it?"

"Oh heavens no," Grandma said. "Some young man—handsome too." She winked at me. "He was selling them door to door years ago."

"But you hate solicitors." I said. "You refuse to buy anything *door to door*."

"He gave me a good deal."

I raised my eyebrow at her as she scooped heaps of chocolate powder into each mug and added the hot water. "What do the letters mean?"

"Letters?"

"Yeah. *V. I.* What does *VI* mean?"

"Good question, but I don't think they're letters. They're Roman numerals."

"Well, I think they are ugly." I said. "They take away from the pretty birds. Why paint Roman numerals on it?"

She chuckled and tucked a piece of black hair behind her ear. Her hair was mostly gray, but she still dyed it close to my own color—her natural shade. It kept her young, she'd once said.

"I think they mean something," she said, her answers still vague.

I shook my head, a bit frustrated. "They mean four, right?"

"Six actually."

"Why would someone sell you a birdhouse with the number six on it?"

Grandma shrugged. She tried to keep her face neutral, but it felt like she was hiding something. "Guess that number means something to someone," she said.

"Who?"

She winked at me. "I'm not sure. It's fun to try to guess though."

"What?" I made a face. "Like they've been to Disneyland six times?" I rolled my eyes.

"Or they have six kids or six dogs."

"Or six months left to live," I said, though my mood was lightening. "Still, if it means something to someone, why sell it to a stranger?"

She shrugged again. "Maybe they're like you. Maybe they had the dreams for six decades." She noticed my face fall and amended quickly. "Or six years. Maybe you only have two more to go."

Grandma was the other person besides Arianna who believed my dreams were actually memories and not just night terrors.

"Who's died lately?" she asked quietly.

Nora. I didn't want to talk about my recent death-dream though. "It's strange," I said. "The past *two* nights have been days in the life of this girl named Lucy. It's amazing how two days of happiness has impacted me." A smile grew on my face as I spoke.

"Did you say two? In a row?"

"Yeah."

"Really? Well, what happened in the dreams? Were you, I mean Lucy proposed to? Did she get married? Was it her first kiss?"

"That's what's weird," I said. "The first dream started the morning *after* she was proposed to."

"Did something bigger than the proposal happen the next day? Did they elope?"

I loved how much Grandma liked to hear about my dreams. It made me feel like there was something exciting about them.

"No, she invited her friend over for lunch to tell her about it and met one of her fiancé's cousins. The fiancé had left town so I didn't even see him."

"That's odd. I thought memory-dreams *always* happened in the midst of heightened emotion." Her tone was authoritative, and she seemed almost angry. Before I could respond, she stammered, "So there was no kissing?"

"Nope, no kissing." I brushed off Grandma Grace's outburst.

"That's a bummer." She sighed. "I thought you always dream of big events, good or bad, that you were pulled in by extreme emotions. If you were dreaming Lucy, shouldn't you have experienced the actual *day* she became engaged? Not the day after?"

"Yeah, that's been the general pattern." I said. "But I shouldn't have dreamt Lucy twice, either."

"So what happened the second night?" She tried to sound nonchalant. It didn't work. "Last night?"

"Lucy's fiancé was still out of town."

"*Again*, no kissing?"

I shook my head. Grandma always liked the kissing dreams. I swear, she was more girlfriend than grandma sometimes. "She was just showing his cousin around town. They went to St. Marie's, then the cemetery."

"That sounds very dull."

"It wasn't bad," I said, thinking of Andrew and his brown eyes.

"Wait. This cousin was old, bad-smelling, and bald, right?"

I laughed, remembering Lucy and Margaret's almost identical conversation on the topic. "He was close to her age, actually."

"Which was…?"

"I don't know, eighteen maybe?"

"How old was Lucy? What year was she born?"

"I don't know. It's so frustrating," I said. "I can't find her. She never thinks or speaks her last name, and no one has mentioned the date. It looks like the late 1800s or early 1900s, but I'm not sure, because I can't find anyone. Not her fiancé, not her friend Margaret, not Andrew."

"Andrew?"

"The cousin, Andrew Harker."

Grandma Grace choked, then quickly regained composure. "Cute name. Is he cute?"

Without warning, my face colored. I nodded.

She laughed. "I don't think you should be crushing on people who are either dead or way too old for you. But too bad this Andrew isn't the fiancé. For your sake."

"Why? Because maybe then there would be kissing? *For my sake?*" I said.

"Exactly!" She giggled as only my grandma could.

"Actually, I think Andrew likes Lucy, but she seems oblivious to it."

"Then maybe there will be some kissing." She winked.

intentions

"Why is he here, do you think?" I ask while Betsy secures the last pins in my hair. She always does the loveliest things with ribbons woven through braids and curls to match the frocks I wear.

"I dunno, miss," says Betsy.

"I was not expecting him until this evening," I say, a bit distracted, admiring Betsy's work. "You know, when Drake first announced his arrival, I thought Charles was back." When Betsy does not respond, I continue, "He only said a *Mr. Harker* was here. My immediate thought was Andrew, but since he is not expected until dinner, my heart nearly jumped into my throat thinking Charles returned early." I laugh. "Of course he will not be back for another week." I sigh. "Oh, Betsy, how I miss him!"

"Of course, miss," Betsy says. "Perhaps you should tell Drake to give the full name when introducing a *Mr. Harker*."

"Good idea, Betsy." I turn in my seat and clasp her hands. "I think I will mention it. Now," I say and turn back to my mirror, "it is only Andrew, but how do I look?"

"Beautiful, Miss Lucy," she says. "As always."

"*As always*—that is what Andrew says!" I exclaim, amused. I stand and smooth the skirt of my lavender dress with my hands. It is simpler than some of my other wardrobe, but it belonged to my mother, and so is one of my favorites. With one final look in the mirror, I turn to leave.

"He has flowers," Betsy says before I reach the door.

I turn back. "Flowers?"

"Yes, they're pretty ones too. I saw 'em before I came to help you. Do you think they're for you, miss?" She looks down.

"It is not unseemly to bring a gift for a hostess," I say. "He *is* invited to dine here this evening."

"I beg your pardon, miss, but why not bring 'em this evening?"

"Maybe they are for Margaret," I say. "Perhaps he plans to visit her after leaving here."

"Or maybe they're for you."

"We will be family soon. Surely he can bring flowers to a cousin." I smile at Betsy. She seems uneasy, but determined to give her opinion.

"What if they're for you? What if he asks you to marry him instead of Mr. Harker?" She pauses. "Instead of Charles," she amends.

"What an odd idea, Betsy! Honestly! If that were the case, he would be very disappointed," I say with amusement. "I am marrying Charles, and no one can change my mind." I smile. "All this fussing over some simple flowers!"

"Beggin' your pardon, miss, but I've seen how he looks at you." Betsy's face flushes. "No one has ever looked at me like that. Even Matthew overheard him say—"

"That is enough, Betsy," I stop her. "I will not hear servant gossip, and you should not believe everything you hear. I intend to marry Charles. Andrew—Mr. Harker—knows that."

"Yes, miss." Betsy curtsies. "I'm sorry, Miss Lucy. It won't happen again."

"Andrew and I are friends, nothing more," I say. "We will be family soon."

"Of course, miss."

"Now, I mustn't make Andrew wait any longer," I say and leave.

I enter the library off the main hall where Andrew awaits. He wears a dark-blue suit, looking more formal than I have seen him before. His back is toward me when I enter, and he seems to be reading the titles on a high shelf on the south wall. He twirls his silver ring on his right hand and carries a bouquet of pretty spring flowers in his left.

"You are early," I say, announcing my presence. "Supper is usually served in the evening, not before mid-day meal." I tease as he turns to look at me.

"Lovely as always, Miss Lucy," he says, replacing his ring on his finger.

"Betsy just gave me that very compliment." I could not help but sound exasperated in the statement.

"Poor Lucy. Forced to endure compliments." Andrew mock frowns.

"I did not mean—"

"She is your servant and is obligated to say it," he says, cutting me short. "But that does not make it any less true." One corner of his mouth is turned up, and an eyebrow is raised as if he knows a secret. I am not sure I want to know what it is.

"One of these days it won't be true. Then you will no longer be allowed to say '*as always.*'" I place my hands on my hips, a gesture I have not displayed since childhood. My behavior surprises me. "And if I am beautiful again after that, you may only be allowed to say I am lovely. Nothing more." I probably should not have added that. Being so comfortable around him, sometimes I forget we are not yet related and should refrain from being so familiar.

"Yes, Miss Lucy." He salutes and stands at attention. "Of course, Miss Lucy."

I cover my mouth and laugh.

When my composure is regained, Andrew explains, "I know my presence is unexpected, but there is something I need to do today. My conscience will not allow me to wait another second." His expression is troubled, almost tortured. "Please, are you free to take a walk? Your lovely chapel is not far." His voice holds a hint of desperation.

"Those are pretty flowers," I say, allowing the beautiful daisies, peonies, tulips, daffodils and violets distract me from the uneasy feeling upon hearing Andrew's plea. "I'll have Betsy fetch a vase for them."

"No." Andrew says in a clipped tone. "They are not intended for that."

"Are they for Margaret?" I give an encouraging smile.

Andrew shakes his head, and his eyes darken as they meet mine. "They are not for Miss Wood," he says, then takes a few steps toward me. "Lucy, if you are otherwise engaged, I will go." He takes my hand in his free one. "But please come with me if you are not."

What else could the flowers be intended for? "I am not busy," I say, but my thoughts turn to my conversation with Betsy as I wonder whether he is hinting at another meaning of the word *engaged.* "Let me get my wrap." *Certainly he does not intend to propose marriage,* I tell myself.

It is a pleasant day, not too cold, and the sun peeks through puffy white clouds at regular intervals as we walk down the lane, my arm resting in the crook of Andrew's. We walk in easy silence for a while though my mind flutters with thoughts of the purpose of our walk and the reason for Andrew's determined air. When we are halfway down the lane Andrew says, "A carriage will meet us so we can dine at the Harker Manor afterward."

"Afterward?" I ask. "You have yet to tell me the reason of our spontaneous outing."

"Yes, I do not know how long we will be, but I promise not make you starve." He looks down at me with a smile. "Cook let it slip that you might be craving a slice of her pecan pie." He is well-skilled in diversion.

It is impossible to hide my pleasure. "Mrs. Carter makes the best pecan pie in the county," I say. "I haven't had any pie since Christmas."

"Yes, she told me." Pulling his arm closer to himself, he brings me closer to him in the motion. "She said she plans to make it for your wedding day."

On my wedding day? Andrew wouldn't propose an elopement between us this very day, would he? The bouquet, the church, the urgency to do something without waiting another second? It seems suspicious. Surely he would not do such a thing behind Charles's back. *Oh, Lucy, your imagination has run wild!* I tell myself, but am still unsure of Andrew's intentions. "Yes, I thought I would have to wait until then for another taste. It is kind of her to make it on a non-eventful day," I say, emphasizing the last words.

"Well, I hope you do not feel that way about today when it is over." Andrew's cryptic remark strangely makes my insides turn.

"Why are we going to the church, Mr. Harker?" I will not allow him to avoid the question any longer.

"What happened to you calling me *Andrew*? I thought we were finished with this *Mr. Harker* business since, as you said yourself, you are marrying a *Mr. Harker.*" He flashes a mischievous grin.

Do I sense a double meaning? Does he truly intend to be the *Mr. Harker* I marry? "I can differentiate between the two of you now, Mr. Harker," I say. Perhaps the familiarity of using his first name has encouraged his feelings. I am set on dampening it.

"Very well, Miss Lucy," he says, though I can hear the hurt in his voice. "But I will not tell you the reason for our outing until we arrive."

"Why not?"

Andrew pauses, gauging whether he should give his reason. "Because you might not agree to continue if I tell you now."

He is *planning to marry me! What do I do?* I release my arm from his and stop walking. "But I will agree if you don't?"

"I hope so." He holds out his arm for me to take again.

I don't. My heart pounds with anxiety. "I do not think we should continue," I say.

"Lucy, please." Andrew's face falls in an unhappy expression. "Please allow me this, I don't know what you are worried about, but I promise I will not ask you to do anything dishonorable or regrettable." When I don't answer right away he says, "Trust me."

Reluctantly, I take his arm again and we resume our walk. "How was your evening with Margaret's family?" I ask after several more silent moments. "I am sorry I could not come."

"The Woods are wonderful hosts," Andrew says with perfect cordiality. "Miss Wood is a lovely young lady. She is charming and accomplished and witty. I can see why you two are friends."

"She is my dearest friend," I say.

"This was actually her idea," Andrew gestures ahead with the hand holding the bouquet.

"It was?" I still have no inclination whatsoever why this journey is so important.

He only nods.

"If it is not too personal, might I ask a question, Mr. Harker?"

"We are future family," Andrew says. "Nothing is too personal. Please, ask away."

"Do you intend to court Margaret?"

"I hardly know her," he says, avoiding the question.

"That is the purpose of courting, Mr. Harker."

"Yes, but the heart must be willing." He seems to hide his frustration at my addressing him formally.

"Is it not?"

"Not exactly."

"And why is that? Does your heart lie elsewhere?"

"In a way, but enough about me. We are here," he says. As we pass the church I relax a little, but arriving at our destination causes my pulse to quicken again.

We stand in front of the graveyard.

"When Miss Wood learned I forced you to come here, she scolded me fiercely." His warm smile is a clear attempt to put me at ease, but it does not work. "She asked if I knew your history, how your father and mother died when you were a young child. I told her I was unaware of that. Although, in retrospect, I think I remember hearing something from Miss Amy when she came to Georgia last Christmas."

"I adore Charles's sister," I say, ordering my disobedient heart to slow. It does not. I should be embarrassed for thinking his intention was to elope, but my only thoughts are the anxiety of threatening emotions that will certainly flood and overwhelm at any moment.

"And she adores you," Andrew says. "What I did not know was that you have not set foot inside the graveyard since the burial. That is why we are here."

I shake my head. "I cannot, Andrew." Tears prick my eyes. "Please, now you know. I cannot go in there, I cannot see their graves." I pull my arm from his and back away.

"You must, Lucy. You were here only days ago." He holds a hand out for me.

I shake my head as the tears fall. "Yes, but I cannot. Please do not force me."

"You were already here. I cannot let your only memory of entering their graveyard be the mistake of a cruel gentleman who forced you to go in on a silly whim." He reaches down and takes my hand. "You have to see them. You have to make it memorable so you can forget about the last time you were here." Andrew holds up the flowers. "I brought these for you, to decorate their graves. Please let me right my trespass against you."

"All right," I say after several moments. My tears still rest on my cheeks. Andrew pulls out his handkerchief to dry them and gently leads me through the gate.

Though I have not been to their graves in so long, the path to them is etched in my memory. They rest near a poplar tree toward the back of the graveyard. My pace is slow as I lead Andrew, but he is patient and does not say a word or act with annoyance when I stop several times to take deep breaths.

And then, sooner than I thought possible, I kneel before Papa and Mama. I do not remember dropping to the ground. One moment my arm is linked with Andrew's and the next my fingers are running over the engraving on my father and mother's stone as tears fall from my face, leaving wet spots splattered on the letters of their names and the numbers of their lives.

Andrew hands me the spring flowers without a word, then disappears into the background, leaning in the shade against a tree.

Tears streaming down my face, every angry question from my nine-year-old heart screams in my mind at the parents who left my sisters and me orphans. *How could you? How could you?* But soon my seventeen-year old self takes over, and the years of suppressed anger and sadness dissipate. It was never their fault for dying. I forgive them.

After a time, when my tears have run dry, I adjust the bouquet one more time and stand to brush the dirt from my skirt. Andrew moves from his statue pose and offers a hand to help steady my shaky legs. I feel my hair has come partially undone, locks lying in dishevelment across my shoulders. I move to fix them, but Andrew stops me.

"Lovely as always, Miss Lucy," he says in a husky voice.

There is most likely dirt mixed with tears smeared on my face, but I look at him without embarrassment. "Andrew, you have no idea what this has meant to me. I do not know how to thank you for *forcing* me to come." I smile at the last part.

"Like I said, it was Miss Wood's idea." He bows slightly. "Let us go eat some pecan pie."

friday

"Where are you going again?" Mom asked.

"I told you, the pep rally for the football game," I said for the hundredth time. She was probably having a hard time believing I would willingly go to a non-compulsory school event. "And I'm going to the game after. Duncan might come by. Could you tell him I've gone on ahead and I'll meet him there?"

"Duncan?" Her interest suddenly increased.

"Yeah," I rummaged through the closet for my jacket to hide my reddening face. "He's just a friend though."

"Is he the boy Dad met?"

"Yep," I said, walking toward the door. I was in a hurry. She didn't ask any more questions, but I was sure to get the third degree about Duncan later.

A blue-and-yellow painted face met me when I opened the door. "Wow. I didn't even knock," Duncan said, dropping his suspended arm. "Are you ready?"

Trying hard to hide my disappointment, I nodded. My actual plan was to find Lucy—since I finally knew her last name, having seen her parents' headstone—then head to the pep rally. But Duncan was early, so I'd have to wait until later. *Why didn't I go find her this morning?* I scolded myself for prioritizing punctuality.

"Great!" His enthusiasm was a little much. Maybe the paint on his face soaked some extra school spirit into his skin. "Let's go!"

When we arrived at school, Duncan led me to the blue-and-yellow crowd, packed with what looked like the entire student body. I had a hard time keeping up with him as he weaved through the press of bodies and passed groups making banners.

"Duncan," a guy in a jersey nodded as we passed.

Duncan nodded back. "Good luck tonight, Scott."

"What does he play?" I asked catching up.

He looked at me with a raised eyebrow. "Scott? He's—"

"Duncan!" several girls yelped, interrupting him. "You're ba-ack!" they sang.

I turned to see a group of cheerleaders painting the faces of other students.

"Where did you go?" Allison Duke asked, throwing him a fake pout.

"I went to pick up Emily."

"Emily Monroe?" she asked.

Another girl asked, "Emily Sanchez?"

"No, Emily Chandler," Duncan answered.

I didn't fail to catch the collective, *Oh,* from the group. Some sounded disappointed, some sounded like they didn't recognize my name. I didn't let it bother me. Even when I had friends, I didn't run with the cheerleaders. It *did* bother me that so many people seemed to know Duncan. It appeared he wasn't invisible to anyone in the student body before this week. Just me.

"C'mon," Duncan said to me. "Get your face painted too."

"Naw, that's okay."

"You need to enjoy the whole experience, remember?" he said. "And since you aren't even wearing blue or yellow, the least you could do is have your face painted to show a little school spirit."

"Um... okay," I said, "But not my whole face."

He laughed then gestured to the seat in front of a pretty redhead. "Britt can just paint the school initials. That's what a lot of girls do."

Normally having blue and yellow paint decorating my cheek wouldn't seem like the best way to blend into a crowd, but seeing so many other identical faces, I realized it was *exactly* the best way to blend. I nodded and sat down.

"So, you're here with Duncan?" Britt said when another cheerleader stole Duncan's attention.

"Yean, I guess."

She began smearing the cold paint on my face. "Is it like a date?" she asked. Was there disgust in her voice? It was hard to tell.

"No." I didn't dare elaborate more than that. After all, Duncan never explicitly said it was.

"Oh good," she sounded relieved. "Because Clare has been on three dates with him, and she says they are super close to being exclusively boyfriend-girlfriend."

"Clare?" Duncan had never mentioned the name or that he had an almost-girlfriend.

Britt pointed to a petite, pretty blonde who had joined in on Duncan's conversation with the other cheerleader. "Clare Pickett. She's liked him for *forever*, and he's totally into her too." Britt reached for more paint and paused so I could turn my head. "Can't you tell they're totally *crazy* about each other?"

Honestly I didn't see it. He wasn't eyeing her in any special way, and though she kept laughing and touching his arm, he almost didn't seem to notice the flirtation. But I wasn't going to point that out to Britt. "Yeah, I can *totally* see it," I lied, mimicking her tone to sell it. "Duncan and I are friends; he just wanted to force me to be social." I tried to sound blasé.

It convinced her. "Good, because I'd hate to see you disappointed if he leaves with her."

"No worries." *Yeah, like she's concerned about my feelings.*

While Britt finished decorating my face, she prattled on about other couples: getting together, breaking up, then getting together.

"Did Britt catch you up on all of the school gossip?" Duncan asked when Britt was done, taking my hand to lead me through the crowd. Hopefully Clare and Britt didn't see.

"Don't ask me to repeat it," I said, though I was tempted to ask about Clare. "I don't remember half of it."

His laugh was cut off by a big guy who was on the football team. I recognized his face, but didn't remember his name. "Wish you were playing with us tonight, Duncan," he said.

"Me too, Matteo."

They slapped palms, and we continued walking to the field.

"Are you on the team?" I asked when the crowd thinned. I also slyly reclaimed my hand.

"I was, last year."

"What did you play?" I was borderline mortified for even asking. After all, I *had* gone to games last year. *Please say you were mostly on the bench...*

"Um... starting quarterback?"

I could physically feel the embarrassment etch my features and color my face. He quickly pulled me into a half-hug, one arm around my shoulder as we walked.

"Injured shoulder," he said in a tone that was attempting to console my guilt. "Doc says I can't play this year. Scott took my place."

"Duncan, I—"

"Don't worry about it." He looked me directly in the eye. "As long as I've got your attention *now*."

Before I could answer, he greeted several other classmates who were definitely in the "popular" crowd. This went on until we found some seats on the bleachers. "I'm hungry. Are you hungry?" he asked before we even sat down. "I'm going to get some hot dogs." And with that, he was halfway back down the stairs.

I didn't know what to think or feel. He was cute, sure, but

seeing him didn't bring butterflies, and I was pretty sure the only reason I was always excited to see him was because he was currently my only friend.

As if in sync with my thoughts, Arianna walked passed me and shot me a glare. *Yep. Duncan is pretty much my only friend.*

"What is *she* doing here?" a female voice said behind me.

"She's here with Duncan Stewart," another girl said. I didn't look.

"Well why is he here with *her*?" They weren't even trying to be quiet.

"Charity project, probably."

Ouch. Great, now I have haters? Maybe being friends with Duncan *wasn't* the best thing for my social game. Even if he was my only friend.

"Isn't she the strange one who comes to class totally high sometimes?" the second girl said.

"Oh yeah, she totally does."

High? As tempting as it was after a particularly horrific memory, I'd never touched any sort of illicit drug or even tasted alcohol. Why would they think I came to class high? Racking my brain for anything in my behavior that would look like—*wait.*

Every time I had a death-dream, school was the last thing on my mind. Accomplishing the bare minimum, I went through the motions but was clearly not present. Ari used to cover for me, but I was kidding myself thinking that no one noticed.

If they only knew...

I wanted out. I stayed in my seat for the longest thirty seconds of my life so it wasn't obvious that it was because of them, then I bolted.

"Whoa, where are you going?" Duncan caught my arm when I reached the bottom of the bleacher stairs.

"I, uh... realized I have some stuff I've gotta do." Tears pricked my eyes. It surprised me how much the conversation of the stupid girls hurt.

"You're gonna miss the game."

"Sorry." I fought back the tears. "Raincheck?" A traitorous tear escaped.

"Wait... did something happen?"

"No, it's fine." I hastily wiped the tear.

"Did someone say something to you?"

I sighed. "Not exactly."

"Let's go do something else." Duncan lead me toward the parking lot after handing me a hotdog.

"But you'll miss the game."

"*Eh.*" He shrugged then bit into his food. "I'll get a play-by-play from Matteo and Scott later," he said with a mouthful.

We ended up walking around the neighborhood and talking. We had a lot of the same interests, and the same tastes in music and movies. There was plenty to talk about. Eventually we made our way to Meadow Grove. I might've steered us that way.

"Do you mind if I check something real quick?" I said, hoping he wouldn't ask too many questions. He didn't object, so we went inside the office and I did a quick search for Lucy. I found her. Fighting back my excitement, I grabbed a notebook and pencil. "My dad wanted me to get some info from a headstone."

"Let's go then." Duncan smiled, buying my cover story.

It was hard to keep calm as we walked to her plot. I had never been *excited* to find someone, but Lucy's memories were happy. I hoped to have more dreams of her. We found it quickly. Out of habit, I took a deep breath before reading the dates and readied my notebook to sell my story to Duncan.

Lucy Marie Rhett. The name should be right. Her parents were named *Richard Edward Rhett* and *Hazel Tabitha Crawford Rhett.* They weren't buried in Meadow Grove, but I'd memorized their names immediately after waking up that morning.

In neat letters, I wrote Lucy's name before looking again.

Born January 12, 1884. The date also seemed right. The clothing and furnishings in her house looked like turn-of-the-century, and she was about sixteen or seventeen. I wrote down her birthdate. If I could find the date in the dream, I'd know exactly Lucy's age.

Died October 3, 1901. I froze.

"She was only, what..." Duncan pulled me from my thoughts. "Seventeen when she died?"

Hoping he didn't notice my small panic attack I wrote the date down.

No.

No. No. No!

"I wonder what she died from," Duncan said.

"They don't usually put that on the headstone," I said, trying to keep my voice steady.

"Then I guess we'll never know."

"I guess not." I forced a smile.

Now the thought of more Lucy dreams filled me with dread. She was my next death-dream. I was almost certain.

aware

My aching head pounds harder as a soft knock sounds at the door. Briefly my heart flutters with hope that it is my uncle. *No, he is not expected back for a few days.* Pushing my head further into the wings of the stuffed chair, I consider moving my legs so they no longer dangle over the arm. I care more about evading discovery than correcting my unladylike posture. If I move, the chair back will conceal me. Still, it is not enough to tempt me. I remain quiet instead. Perhaps they will leave.

The door creaks, and I remain motionless. "Miss Lucy?" There is no hiding my stocking feet now. "There you are!" Betsy rounds the chair to face me. "We've been looking *everywhere* for you, miss!" She says nothing of my crumpled state, but helps me to my feet. "You've been missing since breakfast. Are you all right?"

I nod, touching my forehead and say, "Just a headache." It is only partially true.

"You should be resting in your bed," Betsy scolds but then laughs. "Not in Mr. Eldridge's study!"

"Yes, I think I will go there now," I say and move to exit.

"But Mr. Harker is already here." Her eyes are alight.

"Charles?" There is no mistaking the hope in my voice.

"No. Mr. Andrew Harker. Do you want me to ask him to leave?"

I almost say yes, but after canceling our last dinner, it would be unkind to do so again. "No. Send a message that I will join him shortly, then help me dress."

"Of course, miss." She scurries down the hallway, and I turn the opposite direction toward my room.

"You know it was his suggestion to check Mr. Eldridge's study." Betsy says moments later, nimbly doing the buttons at the back of my dress. It is a light shade of green and out of style, but it does not require a corset, allowing me to dress quickly.

"Who?" I ask, frowning at the mirror. My hair is hopeless.

"Mr. Harker. *Andrew* Harker." She flits her eyes, catching mine in the mirror and smiles.

"You told him?"

"That you were missing? Yes." This time she keeps her eyes on the buttons. "We told him we looked everywhere. But he is so clever. He asked where was one place we would not expect to find you. And since you aren't supposed to be in your uncle's study..." Finishing, she moves her hands to my hair and quickly fixes a few of the worst spots. "There. Lovely as always, Miss Lucy," she practically sings. I wonder what has made her so giddy.

"Thank you," I say, looking at my reflection. I am not looking my best, but presentable enough.

"I am so sorry to have made you wait," I say to Andrew, finding him in the library.

"Not at all." He smiles, and we walk to the dining room. "Are you well, Miss Lucy?" he asks when we are seated.

"A headache is all." Lightly, I touch a finger to my temple as our first course is served.

Andrew takes a few bites and fidgets with his silver ring. It blinds me with a brilliant flash as it catches the light from the chandelier every few seconds. It is distracting and hypnotic, but Andrew is oblivious. He seems uneasy as he twists it around and around his finger. Finally he loses control and it spins like a top toward me. I lift a hand to stop it, but he stands and slaps it to the table before I can.

"Not the best dinner guest, am I?" Andrew forces a laugh. "It seems I have forgotten my etiquette."

I open my mouth to forgive him when he interrupts—

"It is only me. You needn't have the staff prepare such a formal dinner when I visit."

"I—"

"Lucy, *Miss* Lucy." He stands and moves to my side, kneeling near my seat with a hand on the armrest. "Please forgive me. I did not realize what I did *forcing* you into that graveyard—"

Surprising both of us, I grasp his hand. "No, Andrew, *Mr. Harker*." I smile. "*Thank you* for forcing me. I lied. It wasn't just a headache."

He smiles weakly and nods. "I know. A person does not hide out all day in her uncle's study because of *just a headache*." He does not meet my eyes.

"Andrew, I needed it. I needed to let it out. To let them go." I give his fingers a squeeze. "Eight years, and I have never properly grieved."

"You were a child. Children shouldn't have to grieve the death of fathers and mothers. They don't know how."

"Perhaps. But I never did. I never visited their graves because I never accepted their deaths. I think part of me expected them to finally come home from a... a very long trip, I suppose."

Expecting a smile or laugh, instead Andrew looks at me with concern.

"You did me a favor, really." With my expression, I try to convey the truth of my words, but he turns his eyes away from my gaze. "I kept everything inside," I continue. "Who knows what would have happened if... if—"

"Charles never would have forced you."

"No, he wouldn't have."

We sit silently with my fingers still clasping his. *Tick, tock, tick.* The sound of the clock, the thumping of my heart, and Andrew's shallow breaths are the only sounds in the room. Absently, Andrew spins his ring again, the polished silver glinting in the light of the chandelier. The entire room is hypnotic again, making my sleep-deprived eyes feel heavier and heavier.

In a split-second the ring escapes again and spins with a wobble on the table cloth. This time my reaction is quicker and I stop the spinning with my free hand.

And my heart speeds.

Not Lucy's, mine. Emily.

Finally I'm aware, and I'm holding Andrew's hand. I almost slip and let my giddiness show through Lucy's face. Andrew is... wow. Way better now that I'm seeing him with my own eyes... *Just... wow.*

Luckily Lucy regains control. I let her hand his ring back, and I resist the temptation to squeeze his fingers even tighter.

Instead, she pulls her hand away from him.

Confusion flashes across Andrew's face as he looks up at Lucy —at me—again. But it disappears in an instant.

Sadly, he moves back to his seat and continues to eat.

"Usually when a person hides out in her uncle's study all day," Lucy says with a smirk between bites, "in a place where only her uncle—who is currently out— would know to find her, it means she does not want to be found."

"I was only trying to assist your poor staff." Andrew holds his hands up in mock surrender without looking up. "They were worried. You could have asked me to leave you in peace."

"Of course not, I truly am grateful—"

"Excuse me," Drake interrupts. "Miss Lucy?"

"What is it, Drake?" Lucy asks. He approaches and leans in to tell her the most wonderful news.

Charles is here!

With scarcely a moment to brush away her anxiousness, her napkin flutters forgotten to the floor as she quickly stands and her beloved rushes into the room. Clasping both of her hands, his sparkling blue eyes full of adoration meet hers—well, and mine.

"You are back," Lucy whispers.

"Oh, Lucy, how I have missed you." He pulls her—*us*—close in an embrace, but then pulls away again to mirror the smile that has not left her face since the news of his return was delivered.

"Charles," Andrew says brightly. Lucy had nearly forgotten he was there. I didn't.

"Andrew!" Charles leaves her to embrace his cousin. "You are a glutton for punishment."

Did Andrew's eyes meet mine for that split-second? Or did I imagine it? Lucy doesn't seem to notice, having eyes only for Charles.

Charles nudges Andrew. "You couldn't wait even a few days for my return?" Andrew shrugs at the comment. "Instead you come to Harker Manor the moment I leave, just to be alone for more than a week?"

Another plate is brought in for Charles, and the three of us resume our meal. Lucy's beloved is now within arm's reach.

"I happen to like being alone, Charles," Andrew says after a moment, "which is why I came when I did." He gives his cousin a knowing smile.

"Andrew is the unfortunate brother of five lovely sisters, *all* of which are out in society." Charles explains.

"All? You must have balls and parties at your estate every other month!" Lucy says.

"Once a month at least," Andrew says. "Father has money to burn. Plus he thinks it will earn my sisters even richer husbands." His tone speaks annoyance at his father's wealth. "I believe exactly three events were being planned when I left: Rose's birthday party, Tessa's birthday party,"—he holds a finger up to count each one—"and a ball for Sage in celebration of her engagement, although she is *not* yet engaged."

"And you are missing these events?" Lucy asks. "Hannah would be devastated if I purposely chose to miss her party."

"Trust me, Lucy, they will not miss me." Andrew gives Lucy —me—a sad smile, but his expression changes when our eyes meet.

What is that *about?*

"Anyway, my solitary desires were foiled, Charles." Andrew's tone changes to forced cheer. "For when I found out that your betrothed was also alone, I felt I must take it upon myself to intrude upon and irritate her as much as possible." He smiles at me—at *her*.

Charles chuckles into his meal.

"You have not been a bother, really—" Lucy begins.

"Nonsense!" He winks. "I coerced Lucy into giving me a tour of town, insisted that she invite me to dinner at least a half dozen times, and *forced* her—" Lucy's heart drops when he pauses; she is certain he will mention the visit to her parents' graves. "I forced her to walk miles and miles in every direction." Andrew takes another bite, but glances at her—at me—through his lashes without moving his head.

"But Lucy likes walking," Charles says, his tone light.

"Not as much as Andrew does," Lucy says, then mouths *thank you* to Andrew when Charles is not looking. With Lucy's emotions still lingering so close to the surface, she does not want Charles knowing about her visit to the graveyard. Not yet.

"Besides, I had to meet your betrothed in your absence," Andrew says, "You know, determine that she is not an impostor posing as a blonde-haired beauty." He winks at me at that last part.

Wait. Does he know? He couldn't possibly know. My heart pounds again but for a different reason.

"Speaking of which," Charles says, looking at Lucy. "I think it is time to host a ball, for our engagement."

"Oh, Charles, that would be wonderful!" Forgetting her meal

for the third time that evening, she jumps from her seat to wrap her arms around him.

Charles pushes back, and she can see his beautiful blue eyes. He hesitates only a moment before bringing her face closer to his and pressing his lips softly against hers. After less than a moment, she slowly pulls away. "Charles, we are not alone," she says.

"Andrew doesn't mind," Charles says smiling, adding in a second quick kiss.

"Pretend I am not even here," Andrew says with forced cheer.

finally me

SATURDAY

A smile was plastered on my face before the fistful of wildflowers met me at the door. Duncan's smile fell slightly. Mine too.

"For me?" I asked. Duncan nodded and I took the bouquet, following him into his house. "What for?" A guy had never given me flowers, and I wasn't sure how to react. I'd have to tell Grandma about him.

"You were so upset at the game last night—by the way, you never told me why." Duncan said, leading me to the kitchen. "Then after we left the cemetery, you barely spoke a word. I wanted to cheer you up." He grabbed a handful of M&Ms from a bowl on the counter and offered me some.

"No thanks," I said. Then, "You did cheer me up. Thank you."

"No glasses today?" he asked, staring until I felt uncomfortable.

Out of self-consciousness, I reached to touch my absent frames, but paused. "Contacts." I shrugged, then awkwardly dropped my hand.

"I like it," he said. "I mean, you look great with them, but they hide your eyes."

Kinda the point. I thought to myself. I hid behind my glasses more than I should. I felt they hid my emotions from the world better, but I didn't feel that I needed them today.

"Anyway," he said when I didn't say anything. "I didn't cheer you up. Something or *someone* else already did." He pointed to my smile that hadn't completely disappeared.

"It's a new day." I shrugged. Feeling awkward standing in the kitchen doorway with Duncan clearly trying to read me, I examined my pretty flowers. Not at all like what Andrew gave Lucy for her parent's graves, but the reminder brought my smile back.

"Uh huh." His clear disbelief was interrupted by a ping from his phone. "Sarah texted," he said, "She can't come with us."

"Should we go another time?"

"Nah." Duncan grabbed another handful of chocolate, then motioned for me to follow him out. "Let's go. We can handle a few costumes and props on our own."

"Seriously, what's with the perma-grin, Emily?" Duncan shifted in his seat so his back was turned to the window and put his hand on top of my head rest. "Did you have a good dream last night or something?"

Luckily I'd offered to drive to the consignment store so I had the perfect excuse not to look at him and betray myself, but there was no way he missed me hitting the curb as I turned. "Actually, I did." He had no idea how close to the truth he was.

"What was it about?"

"I, uh…" *What do I tell him?* "I can't tell you or… or it won't come true." *Stupid, I know.*

"You're gonna play that game, huh?" Duncan moved the hand above my head to his knee. "You know that's not true, right? Dreams are just the subconscious trying to work out the crap in our lives."

Involuntarily, I sighed. "My crap must be pretty bad for my

subconscious to be making up *my* dreams." Of course my dreams didn't fall under the normal category. They weren't even mine.

Seeing out of the corner of my eye, Duncan was giving me a questioning look, but then shook his head. Hopefully deciding not to comment on my dark thoughts. "I thought you said you had a good dream last night."

"I did."

"Good. You look happy today."

Duncan thankfully changed the subject to the specifics of the football game we missed and prattled on about the play-by-play. I pretended to be more interested than I was and asked questions until we arrived at our destination so he wouldn't ask about my dream again.

Inside we split up to look for potential props and costumes for our group performance. My phone blared full volume, making me jump five feet.

"What's up, Grandma?" I answered.

"Did you finally have a kissing dream?"

My face flushed. "Uh huh. The fiancé came back," I said in a hushed tone.

"That's too bad."

"What? I thought you *liked* hearing the playback after a kissing memory." I absently shuffled through a rack of outdated dresses. "Even if it always leaves me a bit off-kilter."

"Is that why are you so happy?" she asked. "I can hear it in your voice."

I shook my head. It was confusing sometimes. "It's not just the kissing. I mean, that's great—there's probably some lingering happiness from her—but *I* was there. Like, as Emily."

"Really?" Grandma Grace squealed, definitely more like a girl-friend. "That could be fun if you have more dreams of her."

"I don't think I'm done having Lucy dreams." Saying it out loud gave me a jolt of terror.

"That's a gloomy tone. Shouldn't that make you happy?"

"Umm, if I'm right, Lucy will be my next death."

"You found her grave." It wasn't a question.

"It scares me, Grandma."

"How much time does she have?" she asked. It gave me such comfort that I could speak freely about this to my grandma.

"The dreams feel like springtime. If it's the right year, she dies in October."

Grandma didn't say anything for several moments. Then, "But you seem happy today." Her mood brightened. "Was kissing the fiancé that good?"

Lucy certainly thought so, I thought. Instead I said, "Why did you say it was too bad when I told you he kissed me?" I didn't want to go into detail about Lucy being kissed by Charles in the middle of a store with Duncan nearby anyway.

"Because you'd rather be kissing the cousin."

I quickly covered the speaker with my hand as my cheeks flamed. I wasn't expecting that.

"Andrew is his name, right?" she continued.

"You know, it's probably because they were talking about having a ball," I said. "What girl wouldn't want to attend an old-fashioned ball like that? It's probably better than prom."

"What's better than prom?" Duncan's voice came from behind.

"Grandma, I've gotta go." Honestly, I was glad for the interruption.

"Who was that?" she asked.

"It's... a boy." I kept my back turned as my face flushed again.

"A real boy? Oh, darling, you didn't tell me about a real boy!" She was shouting, and I really hoped Duncan didn't hear her comparing him to Pinocchio.

"Yeah, I'll tell you about him later. I gotta go, Grandma."

"Love you honey." She hung up.

"What's better than prom?" Duncan asked again. If he heard the "real boy" exclamations, he didn't mention it.

"A turn-of-the-century ball," I said quickly. I'd made my way to the costume jewelry section and picked up a gaudy gold chain.

"What do you think about this for our *gangstas?*" I turned to face him, and a name fell off my lips.

Duncan was decked out in a black fedora, a gray suit coat and a lighter shade of gray pants. If it weren't for his one shade lighter hair poking out from his hat and the t-shirt underneath his coat, I would have sworn...

"Who's Andrew?"

I shook my head. "A cousin," I said. "You a... kind of look like my cousin with that hat on. Which, by the way, the costume is great!" Duncan was... wow. He looked a lot like Andrew, which is why I blurted out his name, I'm sure. His hair was more of a honey-brown, whereas Andrew's was a darker shade of brown. And I hadn't gotten close enough yet, but I was certain Duncan didn't have the gold flecks in his eyes since they were more of a gray color from afar. Still, I had a strange urgency to look closer to see.

"Not quite the right time period." He beamed. "But I look great! Right?"

"You do!" My voice cracked slightly. "Just don't draw attention to your shoes." I was trying to divert attention from my voice.

"Hey, for this price, I won't complain." He held up his too-short pant leg. "There are a couple of blazers back there that I think will work for the other guys. I'm afraid your chain is a few decades off though..." He gave me a sheepish look.

I put the chain back and felt like an idiot. Still, I was relieved for coming up with a quick cover story for my momentary blurt-out.

We found some cheap floral dresses for Arianna, Sarah, and me. We paid for our purchases—which were to be reimbursed by Mr. Tanner, he was making a collection of costumes for future years—then headed back to Duncan's house.

Duncan resumed his posture in the car with his hand on my headrest. This time it made me feel self-conscious. *Why had I never noticed how... attractive he was?*

"So this Andrew person looks like me?" Duncan asked. It sounded like he was fishing for something.

We were at a stoplight, so I glanced at him briefly to reevaluate. Even without the hat and suit, Duncan's features were similar to Andrew's. They had the same nose, the same jawline, the same build. Andrew was slightly taller, if I remembered correctly—unless Lucy was shorter than me. And she was my vantage point.

Feeling my gaze, Duncan looked at me. In closer proximity, I finally saw emerald-green flecks that danced in the grayish-blue background of Duncan's irises. Comparable to the beauty of Andrew's eyes that I—I mean, Lucy—so often got lost in.

Or was it Lucy? She never thought about Andrew's eyes the way I did when I woke up. *Was it all me?*

"It won't get any greener," Duncan said softly. For the third time that day, my face burned. Eyes back on the road, I drove through the light and tried not to think about how long I had stared after the light turned green. "Don't take me home just yet," he said.

"Where do you want to go?"

"Drive to your cemetery."

"Are you one of those strange people who like to hang out in a graveyard?" *Please don't be some creepy Andrew doppelgänger.* I wondered exactly how much were they alike.

"No, but you are."

"Touché."

***

"You never answered my question," Duncan said after we'd parked and began walking the cemetery paths. It had grown chilly so we both shoved our hands into our coat pockets. "You think I look like... your cousin?"

I looked at him again, amazed how I never noticed the eerily close resemblance. We were headed in the direction of Lucy's grave, but I subtly redirected us, and we found ourselves at Nora's and simultaneously stopped. "You look a lot like him." A sad tone leaked from my voice, being at Nora's marker.

"Are you and this cousin close?" Duncan's eyebrows were furrowed, concerned.

I wish. "Not really." *He doesn't even know who I am.*

My eyes found his again. The green against the gray was striking. I was glad I didn't wear my glasses today so I could see them better.

"So it wouldn't be at all weird if I did this?" He closed the gap between us, pulling his hands out of his pockets and leaned down to kiss me with determination. Then he pulled back quickly. "Sorry, I didn't mean to—" Releasing my hands, I pulled him back toward me with a fierceness of my own. I'd been kissed so many times I knew what I wanted when it was finally for me.

After an incredible few seconds, we parted, and in one quick motion, Duncan pulled me into a hug. I felt him chuckle. "I've wanted to do that for so long. Sorry if I came off as too eager." He pushed me away slightly so I could look up at him, but when our eyes met, he seemed to lose what he wanted to say and kissed me again.

When we broke apart again, my eyes immediately fell on Nora's name. Nora *Harker.* Being so close to her, to a *Harker,* made me feel weirdly self-conscious, so I backed away from Duncan.

"How do you know her anyway?" Duncan asked, pointing to Nora.

"I didn't say I knew her."

"You put that rose on her grave the day I finally talked to you. You could say this is where we met."

"Right," I said. "It's a long story," I said without meeting his eyes.

"Call Grandma Grace," I said into my phone the second I walked into my bedroom.

"Hello, darling," she said. I could hear water running in the background. "Did you call to tell me about the boy?"

"His name is Duncan," I said, plopping onto my bed. "Grandma, I kissed him."

I heard the water turn off.

"Do... do you wanna hear about it?" I asked when she didn't say anything.

"Of course, honey," she said, but there was hesitancy in her voice. "But..."

"But what?"

She sighed.

"What, Grandma? Just say what you are thinking."

"You kissed this boy..."

"Duncan, yeah."

"But... you wished you were kissing Andrew?"

"*His* name you remember." I was mad. "Finally. *Finally*, I am kissed by someone. *Me!* Not Lucy, not Sarah, not Mary, or whoever, but me. You have insisted that I give you every last detail of every kiss I've experienced, but now that it is finally *my* turn all you can say is that you think I'd rather it be with a memory-dream guy? My kiss with Duncan was great. I think I might like him, and I know he likes me."

"I just think you like Andrew more," Grandma said firmly.

"Even if I did, it wouldn't matter." I lowered my voice. "Lucy is with Charles, and even if she weren't, Andrew would be kissing *her*, not me. What happened to you telling me not to have a crush on someone who was most likely dead or really old?"

I hung up before she could finish.

CHAPTER 11

revelations

I do not wish to move. With my head cradled in the nook of the wingback chair and my stocking feet dangling over the armrest opposite, I am absolutely comfortable and at leisure.

Without moving my head, I scan the room. A large mahogany desk in organized chaos is the center point, with piles of papers and books scattered haphazardly. Two large bookcases against the wall, behind the desk, stand as sentinels on either side, perhaps protecting the secrets of the room. Every piece of furniture is intimately familiar, even the faded wallpaper that has begun to peel in the corners. Her uncle's study.

The last memory-dream started exactly the same, with Lucy finding comfort in this exact chair while hiding from the staff. *Is this the same dream?* I have never experienced the same dream twice, but there's a first for everything.

Quickly I do inventory: No headache and my—her—eyes aren't puffy, so she hasn't been crying. The last dream was the end of a long day of mourning which had included a lot of sobbing. My head had pounded and my eyes stung until about halfway through dinner. Of course, the arrival of Charles helped Lucy forget almost immediately.

She is also wearing a different colored dress.

It's not the same dream.

Lucy feels content, so much that I almost don't want to scan her thoughts to find out what has made her so relaxed. I do anyway, but I don't find anything. Her mind is essentially blank.

We sit like this for a while, maybe a half hour before someone comes in the room. Immediately Lucy moves into a more proper posture and turns to greet her Uncle Harry.

"Lucy, I thought you were out," Uncle Harry says but doesn't look surprised to see her. "Don't you have a very important party to plan?" A smile emerges, and he winks.

"I needed a reprieve," Lucy says, smiling too. "Besides, the ball is almost planned anyway. Charles wanted to keep some things a secret from me, so he sent me away. But I am almost certain that his cook is making her delicious pecan pie just because I like it so much. Oh, Uncle, I am so excited. It will be just like Christmas!"

Uncle Harry chuckles and leans on the edge of his desk. "Well, Lucy, you should act surprised even if you are right about the pie."

"Pecan pie?" she says with genuine surprise, batting her eyelashes. "Oh, Charles, what a lovely surprise!"

Someone knocks.

"Yes?" Uncle Harry asks, inviting them to enter. Lucy stands as Drake enters.

"Mr. Eldridge," Drake says with a small nod. "I was actually looking for Miss Lucy."

"Yes, Drake?" Lucy asks, hoping her disappointment that Drake knew to find her here is not obvious to her uncle. "What is it?"

"Mr. Andrew Harker is here to see you."

My heart leaps at the mention of his name, even though it shouldn't. After all, I kissed Duncan yesterday. I shouldn't get excited over it. Charles is Lucy's fiancé, not Andrew.

"Yes, Drake. Tell him I'll be right down," Lucy says, then Drake exits.

"What do you think?" Lucy asks before Uncle Harry can chide her for her frequent visits to his office while he is not present. "Was I convincing enough?"

"It was good." Uncle Harry laughs. "You could have fooled me," he says with a wink.

"So I seemed adequately surprised about the pie?"

"No, about Andrew Harker coming to call."

"See?" Lucy's smile widens again to hide her concern about what he said. "No need to worry."

"CHARLES IS DRIVING ME TO INSANITY," ANDREW SAYS as we walk. "*The tables must go there, not here.*" He drops his voice and exaggerates inflection to mimic Charles' speech. "*Lucy doesn't like those flowers, we must use these ones. Dancing immediately, then introductions, then more dancing, then the food, then everyone clucks like a chicken and turns around three times.*" He becomes animated, waving his hand as if magic escapes his fingertips. "*Too much light, not enough light. No, too much light. Wait, not enough light. Too much light, damn it!* Pardon my language."

With a gloved hand, I cover my laugh. With the gesture, I realize I am in control.

"He wants it to be perfect, for you." Andrew's voice softens.

"He is so sweet." I keep my tone as even as possible.

We remain silent for a time as we walk to her favorite spot—the bench behind the church.

"I love it here," I say after we sit—mostly to myself since I'm saying it as Emily, not Lucy. The sentiment surprises me since I have only seen it one other time. But the filtered light through the trees is truly ethereal. I am happy to finally see it with my own eyes. In my darkened world, my dark life, the sight of it fills me with warmth and sunshine. And the quiet settles my subconscious—a constantly brewing and churning mess of hundreds of lifetimes of memories. If I had a choice, I would often visit Lucy's world just to sit here.

"I know," says Andrew.

I say nothing. Of course he knows. Lucy already told him.

"Can I tell you why I love it?" Andrew turns to me, the gold flecks in his eyes catching the light with a brilliant flash. They immediately warm when he sees my expression—which I'm sure resembles melting idiocy. He looks away, back into the trees before I can mask it again.

"You love it too?"

"Yes." He looks at me briefly. "The first time you brought me here, all I saw was a crumbling bench surrounded by overgrown foliage. But this is the perfect place. It is quiet, it is beautiful, it calms me." He clears his throat. "The company is not unwelcome either." *Did he nudge me when he said that? No. No. Keep it together, Emily.* "You see, there are things in my life that are so... *loud.* It is hard to explain." He clears his throat again, I think for a different reason. "So... *dark.*" He whispers the last part.

"What do you mean?" I ask when he pauses.

He gives me a pained, half-smile and seems to search my face before continuing. "I am burdened with the torture and ecstasy of others." Without looking away, he gauges my reaction to his words. To his existential crisis. He has no idea how much I relate to that statement, but whatever he is dealing with cannot compete with my death experiences. Torturous memories of mental and bodily injury.

I wonder if he sees the challenge in my eyes.

"I am cursed." His eyes drop to the ground. "And this place comforts me." He looks up at the light for less than a split-second before his gaze again falls to the ground, like he isn't worthy to enjoy it. "My sisters are so... cheerful?" He smiles. It's a strange change of topic. "They are kind and full of life and laughter. I cannot stand to be near them for long." His tone immediately turns bitter, but I can tell he dearly loves them as he complains. "And they're loud. Really loud." His chuckle sounds almost sinister, but I recognize it for what it is: a poor concealment of his agony. "I do not know why I am telling you this."

"Because I am family," Lucy says. "Whatever you are going through, whatever is going on, I am here for you Andrew." And just like that, Lucy takes control from me.

He glances at me sadly. Lucy has no idea what he is going through, and he knows it. Only someone who has experienced something similar—whatever it is—can truly understand. Someone like me. I have to say something to console him, something from one tortured soul to another. Though I'm not sure what the consequences will be for Lucy.

But seeing his face... to hell with Lucy right now. "You won't believe this," I say taking back control. "But I'm cursed too." A choked cough slips out. It doesn't escape me that we both label our trial as a curse. "My dreams are filled with nightmares. I've seen and experienced things..." *No, that's too much.* "The things I have to endure every single day"—I amend—"every night... I wouldn't wish them upon my worst enemy."

Something in his expression changes. "Does Charles know?"

Absolutely not since it's my curse, not Lucy's. I don't know how to respond.

"I cannot be around my sisters." Andrew stands and walks a few steps away. "It is beyond their understanding." He turns to face me. "That is why I came here to get away." He watches me for several seconds, an eternity, and I want to look away, but his magnetic gaze holds mine. "But you are just like them."

The words feel like a slap. "Like your sisters?"

"Yes. There are times that you are so happy and glowing—the effects of a soon-to-be-bride. And I cannot stand it."

"Then why did you ask me to walk with you?" I don't hide my sour tone.

"Because there are other moments that I see... a kindred spirit behind the joy." He is trying but failing at keeping his expression indifferent. "In fact, that is all I see now. You seem completely different from the lady who is betrothed to my cousin."

We sit in silence.

Kindred spirit? Sure, I feel it too. But there is no way... I am just projecting on him. I want to ask more questions, find out exactly what he means, but I also know that Lucy will be left to pick up the pieces after our conversation. I don't want to make things any worse for her.

"HOW WAS YOUR WALK?" CHARLES ASKS WHEN WE arrive at supper. Uncle Harry, Aunt Penelope, Hannah, and I have been invited to dine at Harker Manor.

"It was refreshing," Lucy says. "Andrew and I became good friends in your absence, and it was good to see him again. He enjoys walking as I do."

"I am happy you had a lovely time."

I take his arm as we move to enter the dining room. A gentleman with salt-and-pepper hair, wearing an outdated dinner jacket and a smile that puts the chandelier to shame, stands as we walk in. Andrew is also present and stands. The older gentleman looks familiar, but it's probably the resemblance to Charles. Andrew has his eyes, I note, as he moves next to him.

"Grandfather!" Charles says and quickens his step to greet the man. Briefly releasing me, he embraces him. "I did not know you were coming."

"And miss your engagement ball?" His booming laugh is contagious. "The most important social event of the season? Never!" He winks at Charles. Moving Charles aside, he motions to me. "And who is this beauty you have so carelessly tossed aside for an old man?"

Charles takes my hand. "Grandfather, this is Miss Lucy Rhett."

"Pleased to meet you Mr—"

The gentleman takes my hand. "Charles seems to have forgotten that I have a name other than *Grandfather.*"

"Right," Charles stutters. "Lucy, this is my Grandfather, Mr. Colin Harker."

...

Everything flashes purple. Then blinding white.

"Nora, wake up! Please wake up!" Young Colin desperately pleads. "We have to move! The ice is breaking. We'll fall through."

"Get off the ice, Colin," I say.

Colin decisively stands and slips as he runs across the ice... showers of ice and snow stab the parts of me that aren't already numb as the branch breaks through the glass river and plunges into the water, pulling me down with it... I fade fast. The loss of blood and the icy water quickly take me away into unconsciousness.

"Lucy! Lucy, are you all right?" Andrew's voice pulls me from the post-dream flash. I was surprised that I didn't wake in my own bed as Emily.

"I am fine," Lucy says. "A bit faint, I suppose." She places a hand to her temple. "May I be excused for a moment?" I ask, taking over for her. I could use a minute alone.

"Of course." Charles jumps up to help me from my seat and escorts me to the vacant parlor. "Go back, Charles," I say, hoping my tone sounds enough like Lucy. "Really, I am fine. I'll be in shortly."

Charles stares at me for several seconds as if trying to decide whether to believe me. "I can wait with you."

"You haven't seen your grandfather in a while," I argue. "I promise I will return soon."

Charles dithers for a few seconds before finally conceding and leaving.

I sink back into the chair with a humph, momentarily relaxing into my modern teenage slouch. Lucy's body isn't used to it, but I am finally comfortable. At last alone, I am left to wonder what happened. *Have I been in Lucy's memories too long?* It is strange to have a flashback not being... me. The only time I've ever had a flashback is the morning after, at the rose ritual, when I see the name of the deceased. Fortunately it has never happened like that. At dinner. In public. In my waking life.

I don't have time to sort any of it out. Someone walks into the room and slowly makes his way to my side. My first instinct is to tell Charles to go back, but I don't have the energy for that. Or maybe it is Andrew—my heart skips.

A rough hand covers mine.

"Are you quite all right, my dear?"

I flinch. I didn't expect their grandfather. Colin.

"It was just a spell." Hopefully I sound vague but not completely stupid. The flashback has left me completely out of sorts. I almost can't feel Lucy's presence... in fact, I can't feel her at all. *What does that mean?*

Grandfather Harker—*Colin*—nods. "I have those too." *Could he know?* He continues before I can ask. "Something happened to me when I was very young."

I know, I was there.

"Do you wish to hear it?" he asks.

I know the story of course, but I nod anyway.

"It was winter, and my sister and I were playing on a frozen river near our home. Most winters the river was solid from November to March, but that winter was warmer and the snow was heavier. A branch, heavy with snow, broke. My sister was directly underneath it when it fell."

I make an appropriate gasp.

"There was so much blood." Colin's eyes are haunted.

My stomach churns. How many times do I have to relive Nora's death?

"I wanted to stay with her, I would have stayed with her forever, but she told me to get off the ice."

"She wanted you to save yourself," I say softly.

"She just kept saying it over and over..." Colin's gaze penetrates mine.

"She loved you. She wanted you to be okay," I say. "She saved you."

"No, she didn't. You don't understand." He looks at the floor. "Someone else, *something* else, saved me."

"What do you mean?" I rack my memory. What did I miss? What did I forget?

"Since birth, Nora never said a word. Her first and last words were that haunting plea that I get off the ice."

"I... I don't understand."

"Nora was mute. Her words—her *only* words—saved me. But I am not entirely sure it was her. And that thought haunts me every day."

the calm

SUNDAY

He kissed me. Duncan kissed me. My stomach fluttered with butterflies thinking about the way he looked at me, the way his gray eyes, with flecks of green, held mine. I'd always imagined my first kiss would be light and soft—lips briefly brushing mine. On my doorstep, or stolen in a dark theater. Out in the bright daylight in the middle of the cemetery was a surprise, and he grabbed me so forcefully, with such passion. It was unexpected, but I liked it.

I liked Duncan. He was attractive and smart. A lot of girls liked him, but he had picked me for some reason.

"You never answered my question," Duncan said. I replayed the memory in my head. *"You think I look like your cousin?"*

I couldn't remember why I'd told him that. Duncan didn't look anything like any of my cousins, and even if it were true, why would I compare the guy I like to a relative? *"You look a lot like him,"* I'd said.

"Are you and your cousin close—"

"Emily... *Emily!*" Mom was trying to whisper, but the second time she said my name was almost full voice.

I shook my head to break from my sweet, sweet memory-replay. "Yeah?"

"Your dad isn't feeling well. I'm going to take him home. Can you walk home?" She had a strange look on her face. I must have still looked dazed. "Or, do you want to come with us?"

"No, of course I'll walk. I want to stay," I said. It's what I always did. I might not have been fully listening to the speaker that day or even hearing anything besides my own daydreams, but I loved church. It was my absolute favorite place to be. Even if I wasn't feeling well, I would stay through all of the lessons and meetings. No. Matter. What.

Mom smiled. She knew I'd stay. Quietly, she and my dad stood and walked toward the exit.

It seemed strange sometimes, how much I loved church, especially since I was a normal teenager who wasn't always fully paying attention. Some topics were boring. Some of the people who spoke or taught were dry. Meetings felt long. Sometimes the time dragged, but every week I was reluctant for the time to end.

I chalked it up to church being my sanctuary. No algebra questions, no essays to be written. No mean girls talking behind my back. No ex-best friends to run into. It was a little strange that I liked going to church so much, as that was the only time I thought about and questioned the reason Ari and I stopped being friends. It had happened after Carly's death, but I couldn't for the life of me remember why.

All too soon, church was over, and it was time to walk home. *I wonder if I'll see Duncan today...* I was daydreaming even before I left the building. *Should I text him? Or wait and see if he texts me? I hope—*

Nearly tripping as I stepped over the threshold—like always— my stomach filled with dread. Like it did every week when I left the building, when everything came back. My curse. The weight of so many awful and joyful memories that weren't even mine. I had to relive why Arianna stopped being my friend again as that memory came back. Suddenly Nora and Lucy and Charles were back. And Andrew...

In less than a breath, my feelings for Andrew came rushing

back, instantly complicating my feelings for Duncan. It was crushing, knowing with such certainty that my feelings for Andrew were deeper and more real than my fleeting attraction to Duncan.

And just like all of the Sundays before, the crushing weight was almost enough to make me not want to go back next week. But ditching church was so much worse.

Sunday was my favorite day of the week. It was the only time, those few hours at church, that my curse was absolutely forgotten. It was the only time I felt normal. It was the only time I didn't feel the weight of my burden. I felt it was God's way of giving me a reprieve from my heavy trial. The second I entered the building until the moment I left it, I experienced my very own blissful, memory-blocking Novocain. When I first realized what was going on, I tried to find any excuse available to stay inside the building. But the magic only worked during church services—and only while I was in the building.

Once I tried ditching, to see if that was better than the post-church crash. But not only did I lose the break from my misery, the dreams that week were *so* much worse.

Part of me wished I didn't have the break. That my curse was constant and never forgotten, so I wouldn't have to endure how I felt on the way home. But it was my life, and it happened every week. I quickened my step. *Just get on with it, Universe.*

My feet found the cemetery, and I was soon at Nora's grave. I sat with my legs crossed and picked at the grass next to me.

Nora Violet Harker. I read her name over and over. It was strange how connected to her I was. Being Lucy so many nights was obviously strange, but Nora's name kept coming up it seemed. I couldn't get her out of my head.

Still, I'd never had a flashback within a dream until last night, and it was Nora again. What could have caused that?

What causes your memory-dreams in the first place? I asked myself.

"Hello, Duncan," I said without turning. His creeping shadow gave him away.

"How do you know it's Duncan?" he asked. "For all you know, your cousin Andrew is sneaking behind you."

The mention of his name stung. *No, Andrew isn't sneaking up on me because he's probably rotting in his own grave somewhere.* "He lives out of state. I knew it was you," I said instead.

He laughed as he plopped next to me. Right next to me. "Got me," he said, immediately grabbing my hand and lacing his fingers through mine. "What are you thinking about?" he asked.

What? I looked at him.

"Well, you're sitting here by yourself at the grave of—" he cocked his head to read the tombstone—"Nora Harker."

So? my expression said.

"Any passerby probably assumes you are sitting at the grave of your grandmother or uncle or some other random family member and thinking about how much you miss them."

"Maybe she is my grandmother," I retorted, taking my hand back.

"She's not."

"How do you know?"

He pointed at the stone. "She died in 1849. Even if she gave birth to your mom the moment before she died, that would make your mom way over one hundred and fifty years old."

"My mom ages well." I let a smile leak.

His laugh made me laugh, and he held my hand again. It felt nice holding his hand. It reminded me of our kiss on this very spot the day before.

From the corner of my eye, I studied his face. It was very clear why so many girls were infatuated with him. He was attractive and smart. I liked him, even if my feelings were complicated. Duncan was here, in my world. Andrew was not. Andrew didn't even know me; he thought he was in love with Lucy.

It was hard to admit it, but it was true. Andrew loved Lucy, it was very clear. If Lucy (*real* Lucy, not me) didn't have Charles, I'm sure Andrew would make a move or whatever they called it back then.

Although sometimes I wondered if that still would be true without me behind Lucy's face. Andrew was in love with someone who wasn't real. Not exactly Lucy, but not me either. Without me, he might see Lucy only as his future cousin-in-law. Without Lucy's face, he might not even be remotely interested in me. Of course, that was assuming one of us could actually time travel and we could actually meet.

Stealing me from my thoughts, Duncan turned my chin toward him and kissed me. I'd been staring too long.

"I was thinking about yesterday too," he said when our lips parted. I didn't respond, so he kissed me again. I didn't tell him he was wrong. He probably wouldn't like to hear that I was daydreaming about my "cousin."

"So, really. Who is this Nora Harker person? I hope she's not really a relative."

"Why?"

"Because then..." He gave me a quick peck. "You really would be kissing your cousin." He smirked with a knowing smile.

"Huh?" I asked.

"My mom is a Harker."

"Really?" I made sure my tone said *wow, what a coincidence!* instead of what actually wanted to fly out of my mouth.

"Yeah, I don't know who this Nora person is, but Mom's maiden name is Harker."

"Do you have a relative named..." I sucked in a breath, hopefully discretely. "Charles?" I couldn't bring myself to ask about the other one. That would mean that he lived happily ever after... with children... and...

"Um... I don't know, but Grandpa's name is Adam Harker."

"What about your great-grandfather?"

"Bill? I think? Or William?" Duncan paused and cocked his head. "Sorry, I didn't bring my family tree with me."

I shook my head and forced a smile. "Of course, I'm sorry."

"What's this about?"

"Nothing... it's nothing."

"You're really not going to tell me?"

I shook my head and studied my dirty shoelaces.

"Or maybe." Duncan rose to his knees and took both of my hands. "Maybe this is *our* spot. Where we first met... and where we had our first kiss."

"And second..." I said, feeling my cheeks redden. Perfect alibi. "You got me." I smiled up at him, and he moved down to kiss me again.

"How'd you know I would be here?" I asked.

"Good guess?" Duncan shrugged. "Actually, your mom said you might be here."

"You talked to her?"

"I stopped by your house."

I looked at him expectantly. Clearly he'd been looking for me and hadn't just happened by. "What's up?" I said cheerfully, hoping to break the sudden tension.

He shifted uncomfortably for a few seconds before saying, "I have something for you, actually."

"S-something for me?" I said, my insides twisting.

"Yeah, I know we've only been..." He paused again. "Hanging out for a short time..."

"Like a few days."

"And don't worry, this doesn't have to mean anything." An unspoken *yet* was evident. "I couldn't help but notice you have interest in..." He gestured to Nora's grave.

"Headstones?"

"Well, yeah." Duncan looked down, self-consciously. "N-no, I mean..." he stammered. "This is going to sound stupid, okay? But it's no big deal, really." His confidence returned as he dug into his front pocket and pulled out a silver ring and held it out palm up.

"What is it?" I asked, not daring to touch the object for fear of what it meant.

"I told you my mom is a Harker."

I nodded.

"Well, this is a sort of Harker heirloom."

My heart thudded loudly in my ears. *A family heirloom?* A *Harker* family heirloom?

He raised his hand slightly, silently asking me to take it. I lifted it from his palm to examine it. It was delicate. Swirls of leaves and vines wrapped around tiny diamond-looking stones. The detail was exquisite.

"It's beautiful." I said, then tried to hand it back.

He shook his head and hands. "You keep it."

"No, I can't," I said. "It's a family—"

"Borrow it then."

My expression was clear confusion, I'm sure. "But why?"

He grabbed my hand and shoved it on my middle finger. I felt a jolt of something, almost like an electric shock when the metal circled my finger.

"You okay?" he asked when my hand jerked.

I felt a buzzing, lingering sensation, but it wasn't unpleasant.

"Yeah," I said. "Thank you."

Duncan's smile was wide and knowing. I tried not to dwell on the meaning behind it.

As soon as we parted, my thoughts were consumed with Nora again. And what bothered me even more was my conversation with Colin. *Nora never said a word.* Meaning I was the one who ordered Colin to get to safety. I was the one who pleaded and asked him to save himself. *Me.* Emily, twenty-first century Emily. Somehow my dream-actions saved someone. Did that mean that I could change the past somehow? There was really no way to know the consequences of changing the past, unless it triggered different events in the future. So far I had no proof of that.

Almost immediately my next thought was Carly. What if I could have saved her when I dreamed of her? Would things be different?

Carly was the last thought in my head before I fell asleep that night.

déjà vu

Her eyes are open, but she doesn't see. She doesn't see the posters on her wall, the nondescript images and letters. All gray. Her blackout curtains are still drawn, but the damned sliver of light the duct tape just won't keep out doesn't bother her anymore. Not anymore.

Briefly her eyes focus on the texture of her ceiling. A tiny spider scales the peaks and valleys of the plaster. She envies its obscurity. But trading places would only drive her for that crack in the corner. Disappearing. Into the dark.

It's too much effort and bother to let her eyes look, so she closes them again.

...

...

...

...

The door is forcibly pushed open and swings until it slams against the wall.

"Carly. Get. Up." Mother spats but doesn't linger, stomping down the hallway as soon as the words fly out of her mouth.

When she sits up, she clutches her chest. It hurts so much. The deep lump in her chest, the heavy hard rock of a lump that saps every scrap of whatever she has left. Her eyes flit to her bathroom door. She can see the drawer from where she sits. The drawer where she hid it. Instinctively her fingers reach for the hidden scars. Maybe she should go for the wrists next and just end it.

Instead she throws the discarded sweatshirt over her head and tunes everything out as she heads for the front door.

Her sister and her dark-haired friend are blocking the door. They won't stop her. She shoves past, head down.

"Carly?"

Surprised it wasn't her sister who said her name, she looks up at Emma? Or is it Emily? The smallest smile is on Emily's face. Not pity like everyone else. Not fake like Mother's. The smile looks a lot like empathy. Empathy is even worse. It means Emily knows.

Everything flashes purple. Then blinding white.
No. No. No!

She pushes the door open before Emily can say another word. Quickening her pace.

Oh no! I can't do this again. I can't. I've already done this. I've already lived Carly's death.

Carly, don't do it! I want to scream at her as her lead feet are suddenly light enough to stumble instead of drag down the street. Her head is void of thought. She's checked out, letting her muscle memory take her to her destination.

Carly, stop! Carly, stop. Please stop. The weight of her depression seeps into me. It isn't as heavy as the first time I lived it. Emily was completely forgotten the first time, but the pain and despair were potent enough to sap the will I had to scream at her.

Squelch, squelch.

The mud suctions onto Carly's thin flats. It has rained for days, soaking the forest floor. It is sunny now, but that makes everything so much worse. She is sinking deeper and deeper. The squelching of Carly's shoes is the only sound I hear, but I cling to it, fighting to keep my fight.

Carly, stop!
Squelch.
Carly, please, don't do this!
Squelch.
Carly, your family loves you!
Squelch. Squelch.
I barely have enough energy to keep my broken record going.
Carly, stop. My plea fades.

The call of a horn in the distance sends a figurative jolt to my heart. Carly's heart doesn't feel a thing, even as her heavy feet carry us to the tracks. Her initial intention wasn't to throw herself in front of it, but the sound of the whistle gives her the idea.

Carly, stop! I try to take control, I try to speak through her lips. Maybe she'll hear it and snap out of the despair. But it won't come. I can't get through.

Not even a trace of fear is evident in any part of her as she calmly steps over the ties and kicks her toe underneath the metal. So hard, a toe or two might have cracked, but even the throbbing pain and overwhelming exhaustion doesn't bring her to her knees. She stands, looking at the oncoming engine straight on. Forty-five seconds.

I need to take control, I have to! I feel a brief opportunity when she resigns herself to her fate. I am able to slip in and take the reins.

Finally! I have control over her trapped foot. I pull and pull, agony and sharp pains shooting up her foot as I try to pull it free.

Thirty-five seconds.

Pull! I internally shout at Carly. Maybe a combination of both of our wills can pull her foot out. But her will is nonexistent. *Carly, pull!* I have to save her. *Carly, they love you!* What else can I say? Colin said Nora saved him because she spoke—something she had never done before. But there is no one else here! And Carly isn't mute!

Twenty-five seconds.

"Carly, pull!" I scream.

She freezes. I have her attention.

"Carly, you can get through this! I can help you!"

"Why am I talking about myself in the third person?"

"It's... it's not you. It's Emily."

"Wait. I didn't say that." She is confused. "My name isn't Emily."

"It's me, Ari's friend. Emily Chandler."

Fifteen seconds.

"How are you in my head?" She cries and tears at her hair.

Please, we don't have time! I lose control again.

Five seconds.

Four.

Three.

Two.

it never happened

MONDAY

"No!" I shouted, tears streaming down my face as I shot straight up in bed. Keeping my eyes closed tight, my breathing shallow, I sucked in a few sobs to muffle the noise. If Mom and Dad hadn't heard my initial outburst, I wanted to be as quiet as possible to prevent them from rushing in. I focused on my breathing to calm myself down, but my thoughts couldn't be controlled.

I'd repeated Carly's death. That had never happened before. Not until Nora. Why now?

Why did I repeat Carly's death?

I tried to compare the two Carly dreams as my emotions recovered. I tried to note any differences, but the first dream had been so long ago. Instead, my memory went back to what happened in my real life right after the first dream:

"Em! What is it?" Ari opened her door surprisingly fast for a 4:00 a.m. pounding.

My lungs ached. I couldn't catch my breath. Sweat streamed down my face even though it was so cold out.

"Em, what's wrong?" She gripped my shaking hands and

guided me to sit on the porch step. "You're scaring me. Was it another dream?"

I nodded, then put my head between my knees and tried to breathe through my mouth.

She patted my back for a few seconds. She knew how deaths affected me. Suicides were even worse, especially enduring the mental pain and suffering that came before.

My breathing slowed as minutes passed. Ari was the best friend someone like me could ever have. She knew that sometimes I couldn't talk about it. She knew that sometimes I needed silence, that sometimes I checked out to forget everything.

But I had to tell her.

"It was Carly," I whispered.

"What?"

"Carly."

"My sister?"

"Yes."

"Oh, Ems!" She pulled me close and started to cry. "You had to go through that awful train accident? I can't even imagine how horrible it must have been. How scared she was!"

It had been ruled an accident. Ari and I had seen her run out of the house for her walk. She always walked along the train tracks, but her shoe had gotten stuck in the tracks and the oncoming train had killed her. They ruled it an accident.

Now I knew it wasn't an accident. I had to tell Ari.

"She must have been so scared." Ari's face was tear-stained and leftover mascara smudged her cheeks. "Which means you were so scared too." She hugged me again.

"Ari, I have to tell you something," I said between my own sobs.

She stiffened but didn't let go. "Was the pain horrible?" she asked. "Or did it happen instantly?"

"That isn't... this is really important."

"Just for my peace of mind." She ignored my question again.

"It was instant," I said quickly. "Could you please listen?"

She sighed in relief. "Okay, yes. What do you need to tell me?"

"Carly's accident... it wasn't..." I took a deep breath. "It wasn't an accident."

"Of course it was!" Ari let go. She slid over and pulled her strawberry-blonde hair up, securing it with an elastic. "Her foot got stuck. She couldn't get it out and the train..."

"Ari, she..." I couldn't look at her. "She shoved her foot under the rail. She forced it until it got stuck." I omitted the part where Carly had broken some toes doing it. She was so determined.

"Why would she...? What are you saying?" She moved her hands back to her hair and pulled the pony tail out again, feathering her hair back over her shoulders.

"I'm saying..." I forced myself to look at her. "She was miserable. She was sick." I choked, my tears flowed again.

"Like she had the flu?" She shook her head in disbelief.

"Like she was depressed. I think that she had depression. Like she committed suici—" I couldn't finish the word. "It was bad."

Ari shook her head again. "No, Mom is horrible, sure. And everyone has bad days."

"Ari—"

"Sure, she had a lot of bad days, but her boyfriend broke up with her."

"Ari, that was a year ago."

"She was fine. She just went for a walk—"

"Ari!" I didn't mean to snap, but she had to know the truth. She stopped rambling and looked at me. "Arianna, Carly committed suicide."

She stared at me for several uncomfortable seconds. "How did you even dream of her? Don't you usually dream of people who died before you were born?" Her eyes glazed. Her features hardened. Her lips pursed and eyebrows furrowed.

"I dream of those buried in Meadow Grove." I whispered. "I don't think there are specific rules..."

"I don't believe you."

"What—?"

"I think you made it up."

"I would never—"

"I don't know why you would put me through this, Emily." she said, practically spitting my name. "But I will not let you taint the memory of my sister."

The front door was opened and slammed before I could react.

THE TEARS FLOWED AGAIN, EVEN AS I KEPT MY EYES squeezed shut. The reminder of my fight with Ari all of those months ago still stung.

I had to pull it together. Quicker than I thought possible, I–again–regained control and opened my eyes. It was time to get ready for the day.

"More Andrew juiciness?" Ari rounded the corner into my room wearing a towel on her head, sporting my bath robe, and smelling of peachy shampoo.

I sat up quickly and grabbed my glasses, blinking at her a few times. What was Arianna doing in my bedroom? *Correction:* What was she doing in my house? Less than ten feet away?

"Oh no!" She rushed to my side. "Not another death dream, was it? I swear, you are having more and more of those lately. It's only been like, a week, since the Nora dream, right?"

"How do you know about Nora?" I shifted away, still baffled by her sudden appearance.

Ari pulled her wet hair out of the towel, threw it on the floor and ran her fingers through her damp hair. "Uh... you *told* me."

"I did?"

"Yeah, I'm your best friend. You always tell me about your *dreamymemories.*" She whispered the last two words, so quickly that it sounded like one word. "It makes you feel better, especially the bad ones like Nora's death."

Again, all I could do was blink.

"Spare me the details if you must, but you always feel *so* much better after you tell me. Remember?" She straightened her back, as if bracing herself. "I'm ready. Tell me what happened."

"Carly died." I kept a straight face. "*Again*. I tried to save her this time, but she died *again*."

"Carly who?" she asked. Then recognition dawned. "My sister?"

I nodded.

"This is great!" She clapped her hands and reached over for a side-hug.

"Have you lost your mind?" I pushed away. "It was a death-dream." I couldn't bring myself to say the s-word. "It was a repeat, a *deja vu* of your sister's *death*. This is not great."

"It was a nightmare." She spoke slowly as if I were hard of hearing. "Night. Mare."

All I could do was stare.

"Nightmares can seem really real. Trust me," Ari said like an expert in an effort to console me. "Tell me, how did my sister die?"

"No, I uh…" Tears pricked my eyes

"Just tell me. Talking about it might help. Okay, so it felt like a death dream. What else?"

"Er…"

"*How* did my sister die?" she repeated in a very casual, nonchalant, like-her-sister-wasn't-dead, sort of way.

"It was a train." I braced myself for Ari to step out of her momentary memory block and remember.

"Like she was on a train? Or was hit by a train?" she asked.

"She was hit by a train."

"That's horrible, Ems! But maybe your curse is going away."

"What on Earth led you to that conclusion? I. Lived. Carly's. Death." *Not to mention our subsequent breakup about Carly's death.* Confusing.

"Exactly. Night. Mare." She met my tone. "Bad. Dream. How many ways do you need me to say it?"

"I don't know. I don't even know why you're here."

"Mom's out of town. You know that." She shrugged. "I stayed over last night because Carly couldn't stay home past the week-end. She had to get back to school for some big statistics test this morning."

"*Carly?*"

"Yes. My. Sister. Man, that dream really rattled you, didn't it? Carly is not dead, Ems. You just had a bad dream." She stood up and rummaged her bag for her clothes. "You know, most people are relieved when they wake up from a nightmare and realize it wasn't real."

My thoughts slowed. I couldn't quite process what she was saying. "Well, mine are real, so yeah, I'm relieved that it's over, but the things I dream really happened to someone."

"Except Carly." She smiled at me. "Look, if it will make you feel better, we'll drive up to see her after school."

I nodded. I attended Carly's funeral. How could she all of a sudden be alive? I'd need to see it to believe it.

"Great! She forgot her flat iron anyway. She texted me this morning and asked me to bring it later."

"She's alive?" I whispered.

Ari returned to sit on my bed. "Ems, it was just a nightmare. Carly is alive and well. You'll see." She stood again. "Now, get dressed! Your boyfriend will be here in less than fifteen to pick us up."

My boyfriend?

Fortunately my wardrobe looked the same, though there were a few shirts I didn't recognize. I picked a red ruffled one and joined Ari in the bathroom to do something with my face and hair.

"You look a-maz-ing in that shirt, Ems." Ari said while applying mascara. "Aren't you so glad I talked you into buying it?"

That answered the new-shirts question. "So glad." I smiled.

"And you know it's Duncan's favorite." She winked at me in the mirror.

"Duncan?" I pulled out my own makeup and began to apply,

hoping it would distract me from the fact that I knew essentially nothing about my life.

"*Your boyfriend,* Duncan Stewart." She capped her mascara and turned to me. "Man, what's wrong with you? It's like you were abducted by aliens and had your memory wiped or something."

"It's that stupid dream." I rolled my eyes and focused on the mirror to apply my own eye makeup. "It's like I've forgotten everything that happened this past year."

"Everything?"

"Well, not *everything.*" *I hope.* "But, like, tell me about Duncan. How long have we been dating?"

"Six months."

"What about you, are you dating anyone?" I'd never taken that long to apply mascara, but I couldn't look at her.

"Brian." She was smiling when she said his name, I could hear it.

"For a few weeks now?"

"See! You do remember! Although it's kinda weird that you remember my boyfriend and not yours."

"I remember mine." I capped the mascara brush, and started to apply some powder. "He kissed me Saturday after the game. And again yesterday." Although he wasn't my boyfriend yet.

"No offense, Em, but that's not really a big deal considering what I've walked in on." She laughed once.

I was mortified. "What have you walked in on?"

"Not that!" She giggled. "No, no, no. No, just some pretty heavy make-out sessions."

I closed my eyes and covered my face with a hand. *Make-out sessions. Plural.*

"Don't worry." She put an arm around me. "You two are so cute together. Everyone thinks so."

I looked at my best friend. It finally hit me that for whatever reason, I had her back. Ari looked the same, but different. She still wore more makeup than I did, but a ton less than what she wore the last time I saw her... a few days ago. No caked-on foundation or Pink Satin lipstick. Her hair was starting to dry, and I could tell it was her natural strawberry-blonde color, not the box-platinum-bleached. I wrapped my arms around her.

"I've missed you so much," I said.

Tentatively she hugged me back. "I'm right here, Emily. I'm not going anywhere."

DUNCAN HONKED A FEW MINUTES LATER. CHECKING MY reflection one last time, I hoped the alter-me looked sufficiently happy to be greeting her—*my*—boyfriend.

I'd never been in his blue Corolla before but acted like I'd climbed into the passenger seat a hundred times.

"Good morning, beautiful," he said after I shut the door.

"Hi, Duncan." I said sheepishly.

"Hello, Ari," he said to her when she climbed in the back. "How are things with *Brian?*"

Her face was flushed when I looked back at her. "Things are great," she said.

He peeled out of my driveway and immediately grabbed my hand. The sudden movement made me jerk away, surprising both of us.

"Everything okay?" he asked quietly.

"Yeah, you just startled me." I took his hand and tried to calm my racing heart. This was our thing, I guess. Hopefully my hand didn't get sweaty.

"I really wish you could come to the game Friday," he said, his voice again loud enough for Arianna to hear. He squeezed my hand when I didn't reply.

"Me?" I asked.

"Yes, you silly." We were at a red light, so he leaned over and kissed me on the cheek. *In front of Ari?*

"Remember, your parents won't let you go 'cause it's an away game?" Arianna prompted.

"Right." *Just play along, Emily,* I chastised myself. I'd have to ask Ari the reason later. "I wish they'd let me go. But hey, why don't you stay home too?"

Both Duncan and Arianna laughed.

"What?" Sure, he was a great spectator, but the team could play without Duncan.

Duncan squeezed my hand again. "The team needs their quarterback."

Quarterback? What about the injury? "I know, but can't your backup quarterback play?" Being a needy girlfriend was the first thing that came to mind to cover my tracks. Probably not the best idea though.

"I'll miss you too." He lifted my hand to his lips and kissed the back of it.

"Are you going to be okay?" Ari asked as we walked to class, after Duncan gave me a very-public kiss before heading the opposite way. Like the hand-grabbing, the PDA surprised me, but no one else seemed to notice. I guess it was another part of the new alter-me.

"Yeah, I'm still just having a hard time remembering things." We had homeroom together—at least that was the same. When I sat down, Ari sat next to me. A couple of people were sitting in different spots, but everything else looked the same. Same classmates, same posters, same teacher. "Why won't my parents let me go to the game?"

Ari laughed. "I'm not the only one who has walked in on you two."

"My dad?" I was mortified. *Please don't say it was my dad.*

"Your mom actually."

I could breathe again. Mom I could handle. "Don't we have *any* self-control?"

"I know it sounds bad, but you really are crazy about each other." A strange smile appeared.

"What?"

"It's like you've got amnesia or something."

"Sorry, I know." I shook my head. When she didn't say anything else, I asked her again. "So my parents won't let me go because Mom caught me kissing Duncan?"

"Yeah, they thought it would be good for both of you to be apart occasionally. I think the team is staying overnight anyway, so they were worried—"

"Got it. Thanks," I interrupted, then turned around as class started.

Fortunately we were going over the same material in class that I did remember. Unfortunately the homework I'd finished last night after getting home from meeting Duncan at the cemetery was not finished. Ari's sleepover had probably distracted alter-me last night. Quickly, I filled in the answers I remembered and turned it in. Hopefully the questions I didn't remember wouldn't hurt my grade too much.

My thoughts drifted. Part of me understood. I liked Duncan and things were definitely moving forward with him before this—whatever it is—happened. It made sense that despite whatever had happened to change things, I still ended up with him. But it didn't seem very much like me to be caught in more than one make-out session with him. Was I really *that* into him? I'd have to pay attention the next time I saw him.

"Why weren't you in chemistry this morning?" I asked Duncan when we met for lunch. "I mean, I'm sure you told me. I just forgot." I double-checked with Arianna that Duncan actually was still in our chemistry class, like before.

"Coach wanted to talk to me," he said, hooking an arm around my shoulder. I still wasn't used to all of the physical attention, but I focused on remaining relaxed so he wouldn't notice.

Until I figured out what was going on, I needed to act normal. So I allowed Duncan to lead the way while we got slices of pizza and cartons of milk and sat at what I assumed was our "usual" spot. Arianna, Brian, and Sarah soon joined us at our table. It was the *Hamlet* project group. *I can handle this*, I thought.

But then half of the football team joined the table too. I'd barely taken two bites of my lunch before I was assaulted—along with Duncan—with greetings, questions, and high fives. But the packed table wasn't full yet. Allison Duke, head cheerleader, gave me a hug before squeezing between two linebackers. Britt, the girl who painted my face Friday night complimented my shirt. And even Clare Pickett, the girl who had a "major crush" on Duncan (according to face-painting, pep-rally Britt) greeted me warmly with a silver lipstick tube that apparently I'd loaned to her for a date with "Chris." She winked and whispered that the date had gone "very well."

By the time I got back to my lunch, the cheese on my pizza was rubbery and the entire thing was cold. I moved it aside and peeled my orange, picking at the strings inside while I internally caught my breath from so much socializing.

I guess being the quarterback's girlfriend made me the exact thing I once told Duncan—or rather the *other* Duncan—that I wasn't. *Miss Popular.*

Ari was the more outgoing of the two of us. Why wasn't she the girlfriend of the football star? Surely she would revel in the attention. I glanced at her as I took a juicy bite of my fruit. She dreamily looked at Brian as he quietly talked to her. She looked absolutely happy, and even though I didn't recollect the moment when she excitedly told me they were dating, I knew in this version of me and her that it had definitely happened.

"What are you thinking?" Duncan whispered a breath away from my ear.

Involuntarily, I flinched. I turned toward him so our noses were almost touching and immediately kissed him. Like a moth to a flame. Our chemistry was obvious; I could feel myself being pulled toward him, as if I could never get enough. *Okay, so the make-out sessions sort of make sense...* It was hard to pull away. Fortunately he did it for us.

"We get in trouble for things like this." Again he whispered, our noses still only a few inches apart. "And we're in the middle of the cafeteria." His smile was so infectious. His eyes creased in a smile that matched his mouth. My limited memories of him flooded my head: our meetings in the cemetery, the way he ditched the game he was so excited to watch because I didn't want to stay, our talks, and walks. Our first and second kisses. This was still the Duncan I knew, just a happier one.

I could easily guess one of the reasons for his happiness.

"Can I ask a weird question?" I asked after he returned to his meal. Apparently cold-rubber pizza didn't bother him.

"Sure," he replied with a mouthful.

"Did you ever have an *accident*?"

He stopped chewing and looked at me strangely. "Like... I didn't make it to the bathroom in time?"

"No! No. Like, did you ever injure your shoulder doing anything?" I couldn't remember if Duncan ever told me how he injured his throwing-arm.

"Not that I remember." His expression didn't change.

When did he say it happened? I racked my brain for the conversation we had about why he no longer played, *before*. All I could remember is that he was starting quarterback last year, but his shoulder never healed properly so he couldn't play anymore. Or at least this year.

"What's going on, Ems?" Arianna looked at me strangely too.

"Em asked if I ever injured my shoulder?" Duncan filled her in.

"Why would you think that, Emily?" Ari asked, but her expression said that she knew it had something to do with the strange way I'd been acting all day after my memory-dream of Carly.

How do I cover this one? Clearly it never happened.

"When would I have been hurt?" Duncan asked. His tone changed from skeptical to soft. "I'm with you when I'm not at practice or an away game." He winked at me. "I think you would know if I was ever injured."

"Right. Right, of course," I said and shook my head. "It must have been a dream or something."

"*Nightmare*, Emily." Duncan chuckled. "Injuring my shoulder? I assume it was my throwing arm?"

"It was."

"Injuring my throwing arm would have been a *nightmare.*"

I gave him a courtesy smile then shook my head. "My dreams are really vivid. Ask Ari," I explained. "Obviously it never happened."

breathing and heart beating

MONDAY

"I'm surprised you didn't *beg* Duncan to come with us," Ari said after school on our way to see Carly. *I still couldn't believe Carly was really alive.* I guess I'd believe it when I saw her. "Especially since it's the only day this week he doesn't have practice after school."

I shrugged. "We don't need to be with each other every second."

"Could've fooled me."

"Maybe I'm trying to appease my parents," I lied, but it was plausible. "They won't let me go to the game Friday, so I need some brownie points."

"True."

Honestly, I didn't want more prying eyes when I finally saw Carly. If it was true and she really didn't die a year ago, my reaction could prompt questions I might not want to answer. I'd been intentionally ignoring the obvious while trying to get through my *Twilight Zone* day. It was still unnerving that Ari was actually talking to me, let alone letting me tag along on an hour-long drive each way.

I changed the subject to her and Brian for the rest of the drive.

It almost worked, distracting me from my own churning thoughts. At least until we were pulling up to the dorms.

After we hiked two flights of stairs to her door, I took a deep breath. I braced myself as Ari knocked.

"Thanks, Ari. My hair has been a complete *mess* today, and I've got a date tonight." Carly didn't bother with greetings when she opened the door and took the flat iron from Arianna. Unlike her traditionally beautiful, blonde sister, Carly was fair-skinned and had plainer features, green eyes, and brilliant red hair. She was also very confident and upbeat—completely different than the last time I saw/was her.

I caught myself staring. The last time I saw her, besides *being her*, she was rushing out the door for her *walk*. The accident was so bad they had to have a closed-casket at her funeral with a blown-up picture that was at least two years old. It was the only one they could find of her actually smiling.

And now here she was. Smiling.

"Oh hi, Emily," Carly said.

I averted my eyes. "Hello, Carly."

"See, I told you she was fine." Ari whispered to me, but it was loud enough for Carly to hear.

"Why wouldn't I be fine?" Carly asked in a high, happy tone as we followed her into her room.

"Oh, Emily just had a nightmare about you last night," Ari explained, plopping down on Carly's comforter. "You were hit by a train or something. She's been pretty shook up about it all day."

"It was just a nightmare," I said, joining Ari on the bed.

"Yeah, but you've, like, forgotten stuff because of it," Ari continued.

"Forgotten stuff? What kind of stuff?" Carly asked.

"Weird stuff, like the fact she has a boyfriend and that he's the quarterback." Ari playfully rolled her eyes, but I knew there was concern behind it. She was trying to play it off like it was no big deal for my sake.

"Ari, I could really use some caffeine," Carly said. "Would you mind going to the machine downstairs and getting us some sodas?"

"Okay." Arianna took the handful of change Carly handed her and left.

"Thanks for not razzing me for forgetting my boyfriend," I said. "I've had an off day."

"No worries," She said. "So you had a dream that I was hit by a train?" Carly asked.

I nodded.

"It might sound weird, but can I ask you something?" Carly said.

"Sure?"

"So, here's the thing, and you might think I'm crazy like you did the last time I asked you about this, but I think you saved me."

"Saved you?"

"From myself. From the train."

"So, you pulled your foot free?" I asked in disbelief, despite the fact that she was sitting here breathing, heart beating and all, in front of me.

"It's true then." Her eyes lit up. "I never told anyone the details of my attempted suicide except my therapist."

"W-what did you tell your therapist?"

"That my depression was bad. So bad that I couldn't stand the pain anymore and I wanted to end my life."

"I know," I said softly. "I remember."

"But," she said, "I felt like something or someone was there telling me not to do it. My therapist suggested it was a higher power—and I think it was—but the voice said it was you."

I didn't know how to respond.

"The next time I saw you, I was convinced that it was you and that you were there somehow. But you looked at me strangely when I asked you about it. I guess you remember now?"

"I guess," I said. "I mean, yes, I was there. I remember."

"How did you do it? I mean, how did you project yourself like that?"

"I don't know."

"Well, you saved me." Carly said. "I got help, I went to therapy, and I'm on medication. I'm healing and feeling so much better. Because of you. However you did it."

I looked at her in disbelief, tears swimming. "You pulled your foot out?" I asked again.

Carly nodded. Alive and well, Carly. "Broken toes and all."

new information

"I cannot believe your engagement ball is the day after tomorrow!" Margaret is in an extra-peppy mood, I note. Lucy doesn't seem to notice the difference.

Covertly, I look around. We are in what looks like a parlor. It is smaller than Lucy's and the cream wallpaper is faded, but the furniture is plush and actually kind of comfortable—unlike the furniture in Lucy's parlor. Margaret is playing host, so I conclude we are in her home.

"I cannot wait!" Lucy says, gushing about plans for the ball and her upcoming nuptials. I hang back and listen. It distracts me from the recent complications in my own life. "And Uncle ordered the lace from *Paris*," she continues. "Oh, Margaret, it is so exquisite! I cannot wait for you to see it!" Inwardly, I breathe a sigh of relief and let her brag to her friend. It's comforting to be in a world I know again.

I don't miss the irony in that thought.

Thunder rumbles in the distance. It's a cathartic sound, and with the dark gray sky to accompany, the promise of rain is a sure thing. But my thoughts return to my world flipped on its head: the boy I knew less than a week suddenly has six months of memories as my boyfriend. Arianna is my best friend again. And Carly is alive.

I saved Carly. Maybe I can save Lucy.

After I saw Lucy's death date that day in the cemetery and realized it fell *before* her wedding date, all her talk about wedding details felt pointless. I couldn't get excited for her when she thought about or talked about it. She would not experience it. I would not experience it.

Now, I realize, if I can save Lucy, she can have her wedding. I finally listen in on the excitement.

"Lucy, your wedding will be the event of the season!" Margaret squeals. "Everything is coming together so perfectly."

"I do not know about that," Lucy says, but clearly she thinks so too. "And I want you to be a part of it." Lucy pauses for effect. "I want you to be my—" A familiar figure passes the doorway, surprising me so much Lucy loses her train of thought. *So much for finally listening in.*

Margaret's eyes are alight. "Yes?" she prods. "Please do not tease me as you always do!"

I shake my head and close my eyes with a smile on my lips. "Yes, forgive me," I say. "I just thought I saw someone..." *Who couldn't possibly be here.* "I am sure it was just your maid."

"Oh," Margaret laughs. "It wasn't Andrew then, was it?"

"No, she—"

"Because he will be here soon." Her eyes sparkle again.

"Oh?"

In one swift motion, Margaret takes my hands in hers and leans closer. "Lucy, I have the best news!"

"Miss Wood?" Her butler enters the room and interrupts.

"Yes?"

"Mr. Harker is here."

Before his name is spoken, Andrew struts into the parlor. Wearing his favorite gray suit and bowler hat in hand, his eyes find mine the instant his feet hit the threshold. We exchange smiles. His brown hair is swept across his brow. His cheeks are slightly flushed and the tips of his ears and distinguished nose are bright red from the cold.

Margaret springs from her seat and rushes to him, taking both of his hands. My chest tightens. "I was just about to tell her the news!" She speaks to him more intimately than Lucy expects. Lucy guesses something I don't dare think about.

"But I was about to ask you a very important question," I say, changing the subject.

Margaret moves so she is standing next to Andrew, linking her arm through his. "Of course," she says, grinning from ear to ear.

"For my wedding," Lucy takes over. "I wish for you to be my maid of honor."

"Lucy, oh absolutely!" She releases her grip on Andrew and bounds toward me, squeezing me in a tight embrace. "I would be so honored! Now let me tell you of our wonderful news," Margaret continues. "Andrew wanted us to wait until after you engagement ball to announce, since we know how excited you are and we do not want to steal your special day, but—" She pauses and looks at him with an expression full of adoration.

I avert my eyes from Margaret's potent doe-eyed look. "Could you excuse me a moment?" I ask and dart from the room before anyone can protest.

A hand grabs my arm before I am a few steps out of the doorway. "Lucy," Andrew says, stopping me.

My hands sweat, and my heart thumps loudly at his touch. It shouldn't happen. I'm the one with the impossible crush. Lucy shouldn't have to endure the physical symptoms too. She loves Charles, I know it.

"I, uh... is everything all right?" he asks.

"I am feeling a little faint and want some fresh air." Lucy takes over. "I will be only a moment." She gently removes his hand from her arm, and we walk down the hall to the exit leading to the garden.

I want to look back. I try to look back, but Lucy won't do it.

She is surprised at herself for wanting to leave at that exact moment. She forces my heart to slow and my breathing to calm.

What is the matter with me? Lucy thinks to herself. *Certainly any happiness Margaret wishes to share should also bring me joy.* She puts one hand on her forehead and the other braces against a nearby pillar at the garden entrance. *No fever.* She thinks, though her skin is slightly warm to the touch in the chilled air. Stumbling a few steps onto the paved path, Lucy keeps a hand on her head and the other on her hip.

She walks past neatly manicured hedges and pruned rose bushes. The flowers are a myriad of color, but in the ever-darkening light, everything looks like a muddled shade of grayish red. She stops at a lone stone bench toward the back wall and sits.

"Oh! Is everything all right?" a small voice says, rounding the corner. A young woman, a little taller than Lucy, with curls a familiar shade of brown sits next to me on the bench. Her pretty pink dress can be seen under her thick burgundy cloak adorned with polished silver buttons.

Lucy doesn't recognize her. "Yes, thank you," she says. "I do not know what has overcome me." She is embarrassed to be found this way by a stranger.

"Anything I can help with?"

Lucy studies her face for a moment: flawless skin, chestnut eyes framed by thick lashes, and a full mouth. But she looks familiar somehow. "I am sorry, have we been introduced?" Lucy asks.

"Oh no!" The girl chuckles and covers her mouth with a gloved hand. "Where are my manners?" She gestures to herself and says, "My name is Tessa Harker. You must be Lucy Rhett?"

"I am."

"We will be family soon!" Tessa's enthusiasm is contagious. "You are engaged to Charles, my cousin."

"Yes," Lucy says. "It is a pleasure to meet you, Tessa."

"And I believe you have met my brother, Andrew Harker?"

Lucy pushes down my thrill at the sound of his name. "Yes.

Andrew and I have spent some time in one another's company these past few weeks."

"He has spoken of nothing but you since I arrived, which is why I neglected to introduce myself sooner." She laughs. "I felt I knew you already."

Lucy is immediately put at ease. And so am I. Tessa's personality and demeanor is so pleasant and endearing our thoughts are in unison. We could be very good friends with Tessa.

"Now that we are the best of friends, could I ask you something, Lucy?"

Lucy smiles at that. "Of course, Tessa."

"What could possibly cause you to rush out of a warm parlor without so much as a shawl in this bitter weather?"

Lucy thinks for a moment. Part of me wants to answer for her, but I have caused so much trouble already I don't want to make it worse. "I really do not know. I..." She stops herself.

"Yes?"

Lucy narrows her eyes at the girl. "Well, as you know, I am engaged to Charles."

"But you do not love him?" The smile that had adorned her pretty face from the moment she sat down vanishes.

"It is not that," Lucy says quickly. "I *do* love Charles. I *want* to marry Charles. It is just..." She shakes her head again. "Never mind."

"Don't worry. It's not you, dear." Tessa says in a slightly lower-pitched, matronly tone. She reaches out to touch Lucy's hand.

And Lucy falls back.

Not physically, because I am still standing on my feet. But it's as if she is forced to step back... and falls.

"I only have a few minutes to speak with you, Emily." Tessa looks behind her to see if anyone is within earshot, but doesn't release my hand.

"Wait, what—?"

"Just a second," she interrupts, her accent flipped to a modern one I am familiar with. "Let me get this out."

"All right," I say slowly.

She winks. "And I'll make it quick so that you can get back to Andrew."

Red flag.

She tsks a finger with her free hand at me before I can even respond, then smiles. "Although you really should be careful about him since you are engaged to his cousin."

Clearly this is not Tessa. Someone is wearing Tessa just as I wear Lucy. "If you know that I am Emily, then you know I am not engaged." For being in such a hurry to tell me something, Tessa, or whoever she is, is sure taking her time teasing me. *Who is she?*

She sobers, then takes a deep breath. "It's about your curse."

"My curse. My memory-dreams?"

She nods. "Your curse is not a curse. I mean it's unpleasant, but so are crooked teeth and bad eyesight."

"I am not following."

"Have you ever heard of guardian angels?"

"Sure," I say. I want to rub my bare arms against the cold, but the hold Tessa has on my hand makes me suspect that Lucy will immediately emerge if I let go.

"That's what you are," she says. "I mean, you aren't an angel, but you have the ability to connect your soul with another's in a time of great emotion. You are the guardian angel who is with someone during their last moments on this earth as they meet death—even in violence. You help contain the joy when a girl so in love has her first kiss or gets engaged. You hold onto the child during a traumatic event such as losing a parent. You tell the girl how much she has to live for and talk her off the cliff... or the train tracks."

Tears well in my eyes at the rush of emotion. I've borne all of those things. "So, you are saying that I am actually *there* with a person during a memory dream?"

"Yes. Haven't you ever had a moment where you felt like

someone was there with you, watching over you or comforting you at a moment of great sorrow or pain?"

I nod.

"Guardians have helped you too."

My thoughts immediately turn to the time I broke my leg falling out of a tree and waited in agony for almost twenty minutes until my dad found where I'd wandered off to. The bone hurt, bad, but I swear someone was singing a soft lullaby in my head the entire time. I was eight.

"How is it possible?" I ask. "How do I travel back in time to be with them? Every person I have 'guardian-angeled' or whatever is dead in the cemetery."

"That's how it works. You help those who came before you. Future generations help you and your generation." She smiles Tessa's smile. She looks relieved to get it off her chest. Like she's been waiting a long time to tell me, whoever she is.

I mull over her words until the temperature drops again and tiny raindrops make the rosebuds twitch.

"Why have I never seen you before?" I ask. "Why has no one ever told me any of this until now?"

Tessa is hesitant. "Because..." She pauses. "Things have taken a turn."

"Well, if you had told me all of this a week ago, I would have believed it..." My stare is locked on the leaves and petals.

"But you don't now?"

"Most of my dreams are just as you described: emotionally charged—important life moments good and bad."

She remains silent at my pause.

"First kisses, birthday parties, engagements, weddings, births." I lower my voice. "Injuries, break-ups, deaths, murders... suicides."

"Oh, and did I mention it's hereditary, like crooked teeth and bad eyesight?" She forces a smile and a chuckle. There is something very familiar in her mannerisms. Like I've known her my entire life. Mine. *Emily's* entire life.

I shake my head. "But how do you explain Lucy?" I ask, ignoring her last comment. "I was thrust in *after* her engagement to Charles. Every moment with her has been boring stuff." *Except Andrew. Not the point, Emily.* I chastise my wandering thoughts. "Not to mention the fact that I've been living her for a week."

"I don't—"

"How do you explain Carly?" I interrupt. "I assume you know about Carly?"

She nods.

"She was dead," I continue. "Buried in the cemetery. Gone. But then last night I dreamt about her again and when I woke, she was... well, miraculously *not dead.*"

"I know. I know!" The girl controlling Tessa throws her hands in the air and turns to walk a few steps away. It shocks me. I had assumed that physical contact was necessary to keep Lucy suppressed. "I don't know what is happening." She continues anyway. "It's like you're *changing* things. Changing the past, the future, all of it." She truly looks at a loss.

"Lucy?" It is Margaret's voice.

What am I still doing out here? Lucy wonders, awake again.

"Come inside, it is freezing!" Margaret says, coming around the corner and seeing the two of us. Andrew follows close behind.

"Oh! Tessa!" Margaret's tone brightens.

"I see you have met my sister," Andrew says with a guarded expression.

"Yes, Andrew," Tessa says, her tone is higher pitched again, so I assume she really is Tessa now. "Lucy is delightful." She turns and winks at me. The other girl is still present too.

"Please tell me your good news," Lucy says to Margaret, confused by the entire exchange. I brace myself for the news.

"Let us go inside." Andrew moves forward, reaching for me. I take a step back. "Come inside and warm up. Then we will tell you." His hand is palm up, inviting me to take it. I don't.

"Please be kind," I say, though Lucy wants to get warm first.

"Do not delay the news a moment longer." My voice becomes breathy as my lungs lose wind.

As if she knows, Tessa links arms with me. Steadying me.

Andrew's half-smile is apologetic as he says, "Margaret and I are engaged to be married."

Tessa leans in and whispers in my ear. "Look happy for them, darling. I'm right here." Then quickly she adds, "It's me, Grandma Grace," before letting go so that I can embrace Lucy's friend in feigned joy.

CHAPTER 17

that is the question

TUESDAY

"Another migraine?"

I groaned. It was easier to let her think that was it. I'd only had one migraine in my entire life, but once had been enough to sear the symptoms into my memory. The debilitating head-pounding, nausea, and sensitivity to light and sound. I used the excuse only for special cases: the more traumatic deaths, the murders, the suicides. The ones when I knew I absolutely couldn't go about my day as normal with the memories so fresh. In a lot of ways, my symptoms weren't a lie: head pounding, nausea, sensitivity to *everything*.

I pulled my pillow over my head.

"I'll call the school," Mom whispered, but I could hear her through the fluff. Then quietly, she shut my bedroom door.

A small amount of guilt crept in. I hadn't died last night, but the heart-wrenching emotion felt immensely more potent. *What is my problem?*

C'mon, Emily, I chastised myself. Lucy clearly loves Charles. But still, news of Andrew's engagement bothered her... or me somehow.

And it didn't seem like he was in love with Margaret. Not like—

I shook my head, banishing all other thoughts.

If the dreams weren't enough to justify feigning a migraine so I could skip school, then let's add the fact that I was still totally freaked out by my new life.

My invisible status was gone. Sure, I had Ari back and my boyfriend was cute, but I had lost six months of my memory. I groaned again.

I tried to collect my thoughts. The facts were these. It had been one week since Nora's death. I'd had so many Lucy dreams in a row that Nora's death was still pretty fresh. Under normal circumstances, I should have had a birthday, a broken leg, a proposal, a snake bite, and a handful of other things to dull the pain. Instead, Lucy's boring life had taken me over.

Okay, so it wasn't boring.

Fact number two: Duncan and I met one week ago. Yet he had six months of memories of us dating and who knows what else.

I couldn't keep this up. He was going to figure out something was wrong.

I couldn't face Ari and her questions about seeing Carly yesterday.

And I couldn't face putting on a smiling happy face, pretending nothing had changed overnight. Because for me, it had. It literally had.

"Are you going to stay in bed all day?" Grandma Grace asked, barging into my room.

"Ugh... did Mom call you?"

"I called your mother." She threw the comforter completely off me and left it in a pile on the floor. "She said you were in bed with a migraine," Grandma said, sitting near my feet. I still hadn't moved. "I knew that was code for 'I don't want to face the world after a memory-dream' and since I was with you in your most recent dream, I thought I could help."

I sat up. Grandma showing up in my dreams had fled my thoughts. There were *other* things that were taking up space in my head. "How?" I asked.

"How what?"

"How were you there?"

"Because I am like you."

My eyes widened. "You mean, you have the dreams too?" I asked. "How is that possible?"

She chuckled. "Hereditary. Like crooked teeth and bad eyesight."

"That's what Tessa said!"

She gave me a knowing smile. "Let's go for a walk." She stood, pulling my arm for me to join. "It'll clear your head and prevent us from being overheard."

"Overheard about what?"

"Super-secret dreaming-dead-people's-memory stuff."

I rolled my eyes but was glad that there was finally someone who not only believed me, but knew exactly what I'd been through. "Fine," I said, standing. "Let's go."

Stepping into the warm afternoon sunlight, I realized I really *had* been in bed all day.

"So... are you going to tell me more about this guardian angel business while we walk?" I said after ten paces.

"What do you want to know?"

Mostly, I wanted to know why she'd kept it a secret that she was just like me. Why make me suffer through it like I was all alone... when she knew exactly what it felt like?

"How does it work?" I asked instead.

She remained silent for several moments. At first I thought she was collecting her thoughts. But when a minute, and then two minutes, went by and she still hadn't said a word, I wondered if she hadn't heard me.

"Grandma? How does it work?" I asked again.

"I wasn't entirely truthful before."

"Okay..." I prodded.

"I'm not exactly like you."

"But you were there." I argued. "With Tessa."

"Yes..." She paused again. "But Tessa was the first time for me."

My heart sunk. So she wasn't cursed. She didn't really understand. Not really. If Tessa was her first, and Tessa seemed healthy and happy, then Grandma hadn't experienced much. Definitely nothing painful and obviously not a death.

"I've been doing a lot of family history, as you know." Grandma said.

I nodded, but stared at my well-worn boots with scuff marks on the toes as we walked. I didn't look at her.

"I came across a series of journals from my grandmother, Juliet Cole."

"That would make her my..."

"Great-great-grandmother."

"Wow," I whispered.

"She was like you," Grandma Grace said. "At least I suspect she was, by her writings."

"I wish I could have met her."

"Wonderful lady. She died when I was eighteen. Whew!" Her voice caught. "I still miss her."

Grandma's sentiment jolted my heart. I hoped I didn't lose *my* grandma when I was eighteen, only two short years away.

"Anyway," Grandma continued. "With her journals there was a silver ring." She held out her hand for me to see the rings on her fingers and motioned to a mostly dull, but beautiful one with tiny braided strands on her smallest finger. "Her journals said her mother was able to 'piggyback' into her dreams by wearing this ring."

"And you wore it last night?"

"I wore it last night."

Terror filled my chest. What if Grandma had "piggybacked"

into something terrible? What if she ended up in one of my multiple-casualty dreams? The ones where many people died?

"Grandma, you can't—!"

"Hush!" She cut me off. "Now, let me tell you my theory after reading Grandma Cole's diaries."

I wanted to protest more but was extremely curious about her findings. I'd bring up her "piggybacking" later. "Tell me your theory," I said.

"I suspect that you go to sleep every night," she started. "And your spirit energy essentially connects with someone else at a marked moment in their lives. An important moment for one reason or another."

"Like, I travel back in time in my sleep?"

"I know it seems strange, but I suspect that your spirit visited those people, connected with those people during their time."

"How—?"

"*Before* you were born. While you were still just spirit energy."

My brain was going to explode. "So, why do I have to experience them again in my sleep?"

"I don't know." Grandma Grace stopped and plucked a browning leaf from a low-hanging branch and studied it. "But the connection is so seamless and imprinted that they are your memories too. You remember them as you dream."

"Is there a way to stop the dreams?"

She shook her head. "Grandma Cole experienced them her entire life."

"Her entire life?"

"She wrote that she met a few guardians throughout her life," Grandma said. "And some of them only had the dreams occasionally…"

"Lucky," I mumbled.

"Others had them very often. Grandma Cole was one of those. And a few like you…"

"Have them every. Single. Night." I began walking again.

"Why didn't you tell me all of this sooner?" I asked after a pause. "When did you read these journals?"

Grandma sighed, then fell into step with me still holding her leaf. "Because I hoped you'd grow out of it. I hoped you'd have less and less until the dreams finished."

"Why would you think that would happen for me if it never happened for Grandma Cole?"

She shook her head. "I guess it's never been done, but I hoped that my granddaughter," she choked on the word, "would somehow be able to stop them."

We walked in silence for several steps.

"Instead," she began again. "You have it worse than most."

"When did you read the journals?" I asked again.

"Well…" She wrung her hands as we walked. "I've been re-reading them these past few weeks."

"When did you read them the first time?" I asked slowly.

"Several years ago."

"So you thought four years of torture was enough for you to finally tell me about them?" There was bitterness in my voice.

"I have regretted that decision every day," she said, her steps slowing. "Especially since your mother…" She stopped.

"Mom doesn't believe my dreams are anything but night terrors, and Dad just goes along with her."

"Perhaps I'll lend her the journals," she said half-heartedly.

I huffed. We both knew that wouldn't change anything.

We arrived at the park. A welcome change from the cemetery where most of my walks lead to.

"A place of the living," Grandma said, nudging me with her elbow and resting on a nearby cast-iron bench.

A pickup Frisbee game had started now that school was out. I recognized a few of the players from my high school, including a few of the football players. Duncan being one of them. I hoped he wouldn't see me and interrupt.

"Did you know that I have a boyfriend?" I asked, motioning to the group.

"Duncan," she said as she nodded.

My heart fell. I had hoped that one person might remember my previous life before I saved Carly. "Yes, Duncan," I said. "We started dating six months ago." I didn't dare ask if she'd ever met him.

"But you weren't aware of that until..." She closed her eyes tight in concentration. "Yesterday?"

I looked at her with wide eyes and a question I couldn't formulate on my lips.

"I've actually been wearing the ring for a few weeks," she admitted.

"If that's true, then how many dreams have you—"

"Enough," she interrupted.

"So you lied to me about Tessa being your first," I said with accusation in my tone.

Grandma looked caught, but not guilty. "Tessa *was* my first," she insisted, "But I have piggy-backed as Tessa more than once."

"Wha—?"

"It's not important," she interrupted again. "You changed something sweetheart." As if calling me by an endearing name made everything better.

It didn't exactly, but I nodded anyway.

"That's the real reason I decided to tell you the truth as Tessa."

I looked at her steadily. "You only told me because I changed things? That's why you didn't tell me sooner?" I hoped she could see how much that fact bothered me.

She returned my gaze and took a deep breath. "I didn't tell you sooner because I *don't* think you should be changing things."

"But I did anyway."

"By accident," she said, "I hoped that if you didn't know it was possible, you wouldn't do it."

"Was that in Grandma Cole's journals too?"

She nodded. "Grandma Cole thought it was her duty to change things if it was for the better."

"But you don't agree?"

Grandma Grace shook her head. "It's not right."

I wasn't sure I agreed with her, but didn't voice it. I couldn't see anything bad about saving Carly, other than some strange changes that somehow only affected me.

Our presence drew the attention of one brown-haired, gray eyed boy with a goofy smile on his face. Duncan walked toward us away from his Frisbee game.

"When I saved Carly," I said quickly before he was within earshot. "Do you—do you remember both versions?"

"Bits and pieces," she said quickly. "We might have to continue this conversation later, dear."

"Emily!" Duncan called before quickening his step into a jog.

"Oh hey, Duncan," I said and managed a genuine smile. I was grateful for the interruption anyway. I'd need time to process what Grandma had said.

And have time to forgive her for lying to me and keeping things from me.

"Ari said you were sick?" Duncan asked when he stood right in front of us.

I nodded. "Migraine." It was hard to look at Duncan since his face was so much like Andrew's. *Engaged Andrew.*

"But you're feeling better?" Duncan asked.

"I slept it off," I said as he pulled me up from the bench for a hug. Even his arms felt like Andrew's and were surprisingly comforting. "The fresh air is helping too. Have you met my grandma?" When I briefly glanced at her, her face—which was slack-jawed—instantly flashed a smile. *What was that about?*

"Grandma Grace," he said, reaching a hand out to shake hers. "Only once."

I didn't miss Grandma's sigh of relief. She must not have remembered much of my alternate life. Which made me think she still wasn't telling me the truth about how long she'd been wearing the ring. "It's nice to see you again, Duncan."

"Likewise," he said. "Are you up for some *Hamlet*?" he asked, turning back to me. "Our group performs Thursday, and I've got practice tomorrow for the big game, so we are meeting at Brian's in about ten minutes to go through our act."

"Go ahead, dear," Grandma said before I could protest. "I think I'll rest here a while longer. You go on ahead."

"All right. See ya later, Grams." I said, and Duncan and I left for Brian's.

***

"Feeling better, Ems?" Ari asked, hugging me tightly the second I walked through the door.

"Yes," I assured her.

"You know you can tell me anything, right?" she said, eying me.

"Of course," I said, but I didn't want to get into the Grandma Grace *thing* or the Andrew is engaged *thing*.

"O-kay," she pulled back and gave me a forced smile. She knew there was something I didn't want to share with her.

"The costumes look great!" Sarah said when we joined the group. "Sorry I couldn't come, but, Duncan and Emily, you did great!"

Everyone mumbled in agreement except for Ari, who looked irritated. No one seemed to notice except for me.

"Let's read through," Brian said.

We began our read-through, and Arianna seemed to settle. I relaxed, hoping she was appeased and wouldn't give me the third degree when we were finished.

"*How now! A rat!*" Brian said as Hamlet, pretending to draw a sword. "*Dead, for a ducat, dead!*"

Ari snickered and said something I couldn't hear.

"*Oh, I am slain!*" Duncan was dramatic, acting out Lord Polonius's death from behind a sheet acting as a curtain.

"*Oh me, what hast thou done?*" I said, acting as the queen, right as Arianna said something else I didn't catch.

"*Nay,*" Brian said, then paused. "Doesn't sound very gangster-like, does it?" He asked, looking at Ari, who was still snickering. "*I know not: Is it the king?*" he continued anyway.

Ari chuckled again.

"What is it, Arianna?" Brian asked, shooting daggers at her with his eyes.

"What?!" She laughed again.

"Your little comments." Brian looked exasperated. "I *need* this grade Ari, okay? Coach will kick me off the team if I don't bring up my grade in English."

"Sorry," she said but still had a smirk on her lips.

"What's so funny?" I asked.

She straightened. "He thought it was a rat? C'mon, Hamlet *knew* Lord Polonius was behind the curtain."

"He didn't," I said. "He wouldn't have killed him had he known."

"But then Hamlet tells the queen—his mom—that his killing Polonius was no worse than her killing his father to marry Claudius," Ari said. By her tone I could tell she was upset, but I wasn't sure what she was trying to say.

"Hamlet thought he was killing Claudius," I said, keeping my tone even. It plainly wasn't *Hamlet* she was upset about, but I didn't want an outburst in front of the entire group. "He never would have killed Ophelia's father if he had known."

"Exactly," she said, her tone even. You could've heard a pin drop—and the floor was carpet—everyone remained so quiet. "If he had *known.* But no one bothered to let Hamlet in on the fact that Polonius was there!"

Brian reached next to him for Arianna's hand. "That was the point," he said in a calming tone. "Polonius was spying on Hamlet. He didn't *want* him to know."

She glared at me. "Is that it, Emily? Do you not *want* me to know?"

"What?" *Yeah, definitely not about* Hamlet.

"You used to tell me *everything!*" She threw her hands in the air and stood up. "It's like you're a different person! Like I don't know you, or... or you don't trust me." Frustrated tears filled her eyes.

"Ari, I—"

"What *happened*, Emily?" she interrupted in a shout. "Why do I feel like you are a stranger now?"

"Because I am," I mumbled under my breath.

"What was that?" she said louder.

"Because I am!" I matched her volume. "And I can't tell you because you don't remember!" My feelings rushed to the surface quickly. "You don't remember *abandoning* me. You don't remember the horrible things I endured practically alone after that." I hadn't meant to get into this, especially not in front of everyone. I didn't need to glance at the confused expressions to know they were there. "I am having a hard time trusting you." Two tears escaped down my face. "Because you weren't there."

Suddenly I was levitating from the floor.

"We'll be right back," Duncan said, carrying me out of the room.

"Put me down!" I squirmed so he had to drop me just outside the door. Being that close to him in his arms felt too intimate. I hardly knew Duncan.

Gently, he pressed me against the wall and leaned in for a kiss. My anger melted. In this version of my life, I'd apparently had a plethora of make-out sessions with my boyfriend, but in the version I remembered, the one where I had only met Duncan exactly one week ago, we really did kiss on Saturday. I really did feel an attraction to him. You could even say that I had a crush on him. So I kissed him back more intensely than expected.

But he pulled away.

"Feel better?" he asked.

I nodded.

"Let's get some fresh air," he said.

He took my hand and led me out to the back patio, sparsely furnished with a cheap table, a dirty umbrella, and four matching chairs. He pulled out a chair for me, but I refused and walked away, moving further into the yard with my arms folded. Duncan followed with his arms behind his back.

"Emily, what was that about?"

"What? Back there?" I gestured to the house. "It was nothing, probably just a result of my headache earlier."

"It didn't sound like nothing."

"What do you want me to say, Duncan?" I was getting heated again. How could he possibly understand what I was going through?

"Did you dream a death last night?" He moved to embrace me, but I stepped back.

"What did you say?"

"A death dream. Is that why you had a *migraine*? Is that why Ari is upset? Because you didn't tell her this time?"

"How do you know about that?" I whispered.

"You told me." He laughed nervously. "Last spring, when we started dating. You relive the memories of dead people. Don't you remember?"

"My parents don't even know." Well, it was more that they didn't *believe*. But that was beside the point. "Why would I tell you?" I couldn't help the venom in my tone.

"You told Ari."

"Yeah, but she's my best friend."

"And I'm your *boyfriend*." He sighed. "What is going on, Ems? We've been friends since the fifth grade." He stared at the ground, insecure about something. "I agree with Arianna. You kinda feel like a stranger right now."

"I thought you were too shy to talk to me in the fifth grade."

"I was at first—but that's beside the point." He looked at me again, the insecurity gone. "What is going on?"

"I..." I hesitated. "I don't know."

"That's a lie," he said, frowning. "I can tell when you lie, Emily Chandler. What. Is. Going. On."

I stared into his gray eyes for several seconds. He knew a lot about me. What was the harm in telling him more? I wanted to trust him. I felt I could trust him. "I changed things," I said finally.

"What do you mean you changed things?"

"I saved Carly. Ari's sister. She was dead, and I saved her. And that changed a lot of things."

"Is that why you were with Grandma Grace today?"

It irritated me slightly that he called her Grandma. As if she was his too. But I nodded and said, "The dreams are supposed to be residual, not actual."

"Okay..."

"Apparently, I supposedly visited people before I was born. At least that's what Grandma says. But that doesn't explain *any* of my Carly dreams."

"You've lost me." He smiled and gave me a quick kiss on the lips.

"But how could I have changed something further in my past? Before the Carly pivot point?" I stared off. Trying to work this out.

"What do you mean?" Duncan said, being a sport and helping me talk through it.

"Well, you said we've been friends since the fifth grade."

"We have." Duncan agreed.

"But when I met you a week ago, you said you were too scared to talk to me until then, until last Tuesday," I said, half speaking as if he wasn't there.

"I what?" Duncan said.

"I don't remember ever meeting Duncan until last Tuesday," I repeated, but now talking about him as if he wasn't there.

"What?"

"Then when I saved Carly, he was suddenly my boyfriend of six months. So I figured since Arianna knew he liked me before Carly died, that she told me and introduced us because Carly hadn't died and we never stopped being best friends."

"I am still not following," Duncan said, but I'd all but tuned him out now.

"And now he's saying that we've been friends for six years." I half expected Duncan to say "*we have*" again, but he remained silent, so I continued. "How could my saving Carly change something further in the past?" Then a thought flickered.

"What?" he asked, reading my expression.

"I don't think I am the only person who is changing things."

an epiphany and a confession

Clusters of beautiful people cover the polished ballroom floor. Colorful dresses evenly matched with dark suits create a pleasingly aesthetic view from the balcony. All of society have come to the event of the season.

But Lucy is uneasy.

Still poised and in perfect posture, she leans slightly toward the rail with intricate-laced gloves griping the iron. She is supposed to remain out of sight from the guests. Instead she stands in full view, prettily packaged in her corseted, full-length burgundy gown. If anyone cares to look up, that is.

Being, well *her,* I can only guess how beautiful she is tonight.

Looking around, I try to figure out what is bothering her. A few people notice her presence on the upper floor and covertly point in her direction. She barely notices.

"Lucy, you are supposed to remain out of sight." There is a cheerful tone in Charles's voice as he chides her.

"I am being discreet," she says.

"But you are in full view." He laughs. "Are you ready to make our entrance?"

"Almost," she says. *Not everyone is here,* she thinks. "I need another moment." She finally looks up at him and gives him a genuine smile.

"Another minute then." Charles gently grasps her hand, then releases it and walks away.

She flits her gaze back to the awaiting party.

And then I see him. Andrew has arrived. Involuntarily, I smile. He looks amazing. I've never seen him dressed up like this. He's wearing a tuxedo—if that's even what they call them here. His eyes are alight and take in the room. Of course, pretty Margaret is on his arm. Perfect auburn curls frame her face and her full-length emerald-colored gown perfectly sets off the coloring of her skin. It's not her party, but she looks elated. She could be the belle of the ball.

But my smile is overridden by Lucy's accompanying frown. I step back internally.

What is wrong with me? she wonders. *I love Charles, I am marrying Charles. So why do I smile when his cousin enters the room? Why does my heart flutter when he touches my hand? Why was I so devastated when he delivered the news about marrying my friend?*

Wait, she was devastated? I thought that was just me.

I am so happy that he has chosen Margaret, her thoughts continue, *so why was my initial reaction unhappiness?*

I try to suppress my own thoughts and emotions about Andrew and the engagement so Lucy doesn't find them. I never realized how much influence my feelings have on her. I will back off, let Lucy take the lead. Hopefully my infatuation with her fiancé's cousin won't cause problems for her and Charles. Does she wonder and agonize over my conversations with Andrew when I am not around? Does she worry about ruining things? I have to back off and let her have her magical night.

Does she know about me? That a girl a hundred years in the future is a parasite in her life? I mentally make a note to ask Grandma Grace about the possibility. Maybe she is here again.

Persuading Lucy's gaze, I turn our eyes that had drifted high above the crowd back to the party. Scanning the groups, my eyes soon fall on him again. He looks distracted.

Margaret hasn't left his side, and with a smile plastered on her face, she greets people as they pass her. He barely says a word to any of them and seems to be searching for something or someone.

Again, I look around the room, but even searching Lucy's thoughts doesn't give me a clue about who he is looking for. Hopefully it's not the one person I desperately *don't* want him to think about. Andrew leans down and whispers to Margaret. She giggles and without being obvious, she points at me—at us. His eyes immediately follow and like a physical force pushing me, I stumble back and let go of the rail.

And into Charles' arms.

"Do you feel all right, my dear?" he asks. "You don't feel faint again, do you?"

"No." Lucy places a gloved hand to her temple. "I am fine, really." She makes sure her smile is exceptionally genuine.

"Then, shall we?" He gestures toward the grand staircase

"Yes," Lucy says and secures herself with her hand tucked in the crook of Charles's arm.

"Ladies and gentleman," the Harker steward announces. All conversation is silenced. All faces turn toward the staircase. "I am pleased to introduce the celebrated couple of the ball, the newly engaged Miss Lucy Rhett and Mr. Charles Harker."

A tasteful applause follows, and Lucy concentrates on simultaneously breathing, slowly taking each step, and smiling.

"Are you sure you are all right?" Charles leans in after they are stopped by a few for congratulations. "You seem uneasy."

"I guess it was having everyone watching me—watching us," I say. Lucy seems speechless.

"But that is what you wanted. I suggested we greet each guest as they arrive. It was you who wanted all of our guests here before we made a grand entrance. Remember?"

"Of course," I say.

Luckily, Lucy regains her wits and I let her take over as she converses with people. After all, it is her night. I'm just hijacking her life. Still I can't help but watch for him in the crowd.

"Please save a dance for me, Miss Lucy," a balding gentleman asks after a short conversation about beets. Lucy has eased into her party and is enjoying all of the attention.

"Absolutely, Mr. Everett," she says.

"But can I have this one?" A low, familiar voice asks from behind as soon as Mr. Everett steps out of hearing range. Andrew. My heart jumps as I turn to see him holding a hand out.

"Certainly," Lucy says and takes it, now filling in for my speechlessness.

Let her take the lead, I tell myself, *don't mess things up for her and Charles.* I chide myself because Andrew couldn't possibly know about me, Emily. Any feelings he may or may not have are for Lucy—unavailable Lucy and only Lucy.

"That was quite an entrance," Andrew says, taking me—umm, Lucy—in his arms. "Was it your idea or Charles?"

"It was mine," Lucy says. "It felt regal, did it not?"

"It did."

"But you did not like it?"

"For you, it was stunning, however, Margaret and I will be having a traditional dinner so her father can announce our engagement."

His words stung Lucy. "Margaret is blessed to have a *living* father and since I do not..."

Andrew's face paled at his faux pas.

"Charles and Uncle Harry agreed," Lucy continued. "That going against tradition and having a ball instead was a happy substitute."

"Lucy, I did not mean—"

"Never you mind," Lucy interrupted. "You love tradition, and Margaret will give you that. It is fortunate that I am marrying Charles instead of you." Her tone is light; his inadvertent insult is helping her with her confused feelings about him.

Without warning, Andrew grips me—her tighter. "It is fortunate." His words don't match his tone. I feel a twinge in my chest. He *is* in love with Lucy, and he bitterly regrets his mistake.

He is in love with Lucy.

Remaining in his arms is suddenly agonizing. *Please, someone cut in!* I groan inside. Did they do that in 1901? I can't wait to find out.

"Excuse me," I say and let go, dashing to an exit before he can stop me. Closing the door behind me in a small side room, I hope no one will follow.

Almost immediately the door opens again.

"Seriously, is there no peace here?" I say, not caring that my modern accent is nothing like Lucy's proper speech.

"Emily, darling?"

I turn to see the Tessa—well, Grandma—dressed in a deep-blue gown and feel instant relief. "Grandma Grace," I say and throw my arms around her.

She holds me briefly, but quickly pushes me back. "Lucy won't like it if you rumple her dress too much."

"Right." Nervously, I smooth the skirts. "Sorry."

"What's going on, Emily? This is Lucy's party, you know. Not yours."

"I know, I know, I just…" I want to rip the pins from her hair, give my head space to breathe, but Lucy would be upset about that too. "I was dancing with Andrew and… and—" I can't finish.

"You like him," she finishes for me.

I nod.

"Emily, Lucy is engaged to Charles. You shouldn't mess that up for her."

"I know, I know," I say. *But wait.* Now she's acting all responsible? "Why are you telling me this?"

"What do you mean?"

"Less than a week ago you were teasing me about wanting to 'kiss the cousin.' Normally you would be encouraging me to do things like that if I had the opportunity."

"That was before you began changing things. You know, before you were bringing people back from the dead?"

"Right," I say. "And that's why I had to leave. I've been thinking the same thing." Something dawned on me. "But I looked at Lucy's records in Meadow Grove. She dies *before* her wedding date, so does it matter who she is with if she dies anyway?"

Tessa/Grandma stares at me for several seconds. Her petite face is hard and unreadable. She appears to be mulling my point, but she looks conflicted.

"I think something else is going on," I say. "I wonder if someone else—"

But we are interrupted before I can finish. It is Andrew.

"Lucy, is everything all right?" he says, "Truly, I am so very sorry." Then his eyes flit to Grandma and they widen. "Tessa?"

"Hello, Andrew," she says, looking like she's been caught red-handed. Which is strange.

"I thought you were halfway back to Savannah," he says.

"There is something you both should know," Grandma says.

"Both of us?" I ask. "What is going on?" I eye Grandma. *What are you doing?* I try to ask with my expression.

Andrew is confused too. "What are you trying to say, Tessa?"

"Grace, actually." Grandma admits.

I expect Andrew to look even more confused, but understanding suddenly smoothes his features.

"Grams!" I hiss.

Her expression is apologetic. "I've been visiting him, dear," she says. "I am afraid you're right. Something else is going on and you aren't the only one changing things." She eyes Andrew and gives him a knowing look.

"Why are you telling me about this in front of him?" I ask, talking through my teeth though he probably hears anyway.

She ignores me and looks at him full-on in the face before saying clearly, "She is like you, Andrew."

Andrew's slack-jawed face matches mine, I'm sure. Then he

smiles. "Lucy?" He rushes to take my hands. "You have the dreams too? You are a guardian angel—er, something like me?"

My heart races, but words don't form so I nod.

"Lucy, you cannot—" He pauses, I can see the wheels turning in his head. "You cannot marry Charles, you mustn't! You should be with someone who understands what you are going through. Someone who knows your trial and can comfort and be with you when it gets bad."

Tears build. *Why didn't you tell me?* I silently ask Grandma. If I thought he was the perfect guy for me before, I am completely convinced of it now. But a blonde-haired girl and a hundred years stood between us. I let go of his hands and back away.

"Lucy," he holds his hands, palm up. "I love you. I am in love with you. Please do not marry my cousin."

"Andrew," I say as the tears flow. He takes it as an invitation and suddenly I am back in his arms with a kiss on my lips so fierce, so passionate—more so than any other kiss I had experienced in my dreams or real life. I am absolutely certain that he will kiss me awake and it will suddenly and finitely end.

unbreakable friendship

"Em!" Arianna shouted, but then chuckled. "Wait up!"

I stopped in my tracks. "Sorry."

"That's the third time you've done that." She caught up, and we walked out of the store together. "Seriously, why are you so distracted today?" She laughed again and shoved me playfully. Apparently we weren't talking about our recent fight.

"I, uh..." Honestly my excuse wasn't the greatest. *Yeah, sorry. I forgot we were friends since, you know, you hated me until, like, two days ago. But this version of you doesn't remember that since I guess your sister didn't really die and all...* That would go over well. I was foolish to even bring it up in my recent outburst. There was another reason to be distracted though. Even the thought gave me butterflies. "I had another Lucy dream last night." I didn't even try to hide my goofy grin. "Do you want to hear about it?"

"Would I?" she squealed and yanked my arm, dragging me down the common area of the mall toward the food court. "C'mon. I need caffeine. Then you are spilling!"

We found a small table out of the way after getting some sodas and chili-cheese fries because you can't tell a good story without chili cheese fries according to Ari.

"You had another Lucy dream?" Ari prodded, reaching for a fry.

I took a swig of my Coke and nodded.

She clapped in excitement. "After your nightmare about Carly I was worried I wouldn't get any more Andrew stories." Her tone told me exactly how my alter-self must have been describing him.

"Ari, I have a boyfriend?" I was testing her, but it came out as a question.

"I remember." She winked. "Besides, it's not like you're cheating. You only see Andrew in your dreams. And it's not like Lucy will ever kiss him or anything."

I could not, for all of those cheese-covered fries, keep my face neutral.

"Wait, no way..." She eyed me. "Did you—? I mean, did she—?"

I gave a pained smile. That turned into a real one.

"Okay, I'm shutting up." She shoved two more fries in her mouth and quickly swallowed. "Every. Detail."

"It was Lucy and Charles' engagement ball..." I began.

"Ooh!" Ari squealed again.

"I know, but Lucy was distracted—"

"Tell me about the dresses!"

I suddenly remembered that Ari was a sucker for anything Jane Austen and mentioning a ball must've sounded *very* Austen. "I thought you wanted to hear about Andrew," I ventured, teasing.

"I do, but dresses first."

So I described the dresses and the hair and the candles and the food and everything else as best as I could remember, and I realized how amazing it was that I had the privilege of experiencing different lives, different times, different places. I met new people without the awkwardness of meeting new people, because they thought they already knew me. I experienced full immersion into a different time and culture without expensive props and clothes. And no one broke character or ruined the atmosphere by pulling out a cell phone. It was like free travel. Without the hassle of security lines, long flights, or hours in a car.

My curse was actually kind of cool sometimes. Maybe I shouldn't call it a curse anymore.

Too bad not all of my dreams were exciting and happy. *Maybe I can only change them if I'm aware.* But that train of thought only reminded me of the way Lucy felt last night—confused because my emotions, thoughts, and actions were affecting her life.

"I'm afraid I'm ruining things for Lucy," I said when Arianna seemed satisfied with my descriptions.

"What do you mean?"

"Well, I'm aware when I am Lucy."

Her eyes grew large. "You are? Do you have any control?"

"I think so."

"This is getting even better!" she shrieked.

"It's not! I'm afraid the way I've been thinking and feeling about Andrew is confusing Lucy. She loves Charles, I know it, I feel it. She absolutely thinks of Andrew as nothing more than a friend."

I paused because Ari was staring at me. When she didn't respond after a moment, I raised an eyebrow, silently asking why she was staring.

She still didn't explain.

"What?" I looked away, self-conscious.

"Nothing." She broke her stare. "Go on." Her giddiness was replaced with a more serious mood.

I dismissed it.

"Anyway, fast forward," I began again. "I—Lucy—danced with Andrew, but the way he was talking, the things he was implying was too much so I... I bolted."

"Too much for her or too much for you?" she asked, eager to hear more.

"For both of us... I think?"

"Anyway." I left out the Grandma Grace part since it was a

whole other confusing complication. "Andrew finds me—us—and I learn that he's just like me."

"Like Lucy?"

"No, like me. Emily."

"What do you mean, *like you*?"

"He has the dreams."

"Shut. Up." Her eyes went wide. "You mean…"

"Yeah, there is someone else like me." Well, besides Great-Great-Grandma Cole who I never met and can never talk to about this.

"And he knows about you?"

"Well, yes… er, not exactly. He thinks Lucy is like him."

"When did this kiss happen?"

"Right after he found out. He confessed that he is in love with Lucy, and that she should marry him instead of Charles."

Arianna didn't comment and looked at me worriedly.

"What?" I asked again. "Do you want to hear details of the kiss? It was pretty magical."

"You're in love with him," she said softly.

"Lucy? No, she really does love Charles."

"No, you, Emily. *You* are in love with Andrew."

"I am not in love… besides I am with Duncan. I like Duncan." I said. But did I? My alter-self consented to be Duncan's girlfriend, but I never did.

"So my sister is alive," Arianna said almost in a teasing tone after we discarded our trash and left the food court. "We never talked about it, but are you glad we drove out to see her? I mean, that must've been a pretty real nightmare that you thought she'd died, right?"

I shrugged, grateful for the subject-change. "When all of your dreams are real events, it's disconcerting to have *just* a nightmare."

I'd let her think it wasn't real. But it made me curious. "Can I ask you a question though?"

"Always." Her answer was overly enthusiastic.

"What if your sister had died? What if she committed suicide because of her depression? Would you have believed me if it was ruled an accident and I told you the truth I'd lived in a memory dream?"

"Well, yeah, she was sick. She spent like a month in the psych ward. She's on meds now."

"But you didn't know she was sick until after the accident—the almost accident."

"I still would have believed you. We're best friends. Of course I would have believed you." Her voice was confident.

But she didn't. How do you tell someone that they didn't react the way they should have? If it never really happened?

I was a glutton for punishment but I had to ask. "Hypothetically, let's say it happened, that Carly died—"

"Please, why are we hypothetically taking about my sister dying?"

"Just... just listen."

"Okay, so if Carly had died?" Ari prodded.

"And let's say you *didn't* believe me... about her death."

"Okay, let's say I didn't believe you. But you know I would, Ems." I could hear her internal eye roll even though I didn't look at her face.

I took a deep breath. "Would you stop being my friend?"

She stopped and grabbed my arm to turn toward her. "Is that what yesterday was about?"

I couldn't look her in the eye. The memory of our friendship breakup was so painful and fresh. I'd relived it in my own weird memory dream just two nights before. "Would you?" I asked again.

"Emily Chandler." Her voice was serious and firm. She meant what she was about to tell me. "There is nothing—Look at me."

I obeyed.

"There is nothing in this world that would make me stop being your friend. I repeat. Nothing." She hugged me tightly. "We are best friends forever. I love you. You know that?"

I nodded into her shoulder and tried to hold back the tears as we broke from our embrace and continued walking.

CHAPTER 20

Escape

My heart lurches. He is standing right in front of me. It's a good thing I am wearing Lucy's face.

"You summoned?" Andrew asks. His expression is stone cold.

My pulse thuds with the memory of the last time I saw him fresh in my mind. It annoys Lucy, and she shakes the thought and replaces it with the memory of the moment immediately after the magical kiss:

I shove him hard. Immediately breaking his hold on me.

"Mr. Harker, you will refrain from ever touching me that way again!"

His expression is bewildered and something else I do not bother to name. He knows I am intended for his cousin, and even if I weren't, he should not assume such advances would be welcome.

"Leave. Now." I command.

He obeys and exits.

. . .

LUCY DOESN'T ACKNOWLEDGE THE HURT ON HIS FACE, but I do.

"Yes, I need your help." Her tone is different. Repentant and kind, but she hides her thoughts about this meeting from me.

Wait... that means...

Lucy must be aware of me.

Andrew doesn't respond or make any movement. He stands as still as a statue, waiting to hear what she has to say, but is clearly ready to bolt as soon as she says it.

"I have run through the events and thoughts—and actions—of the past few weeks." She then turns and walks to look out the window. It's gray outside. Dark clouds roll overhead. It will start raining soon. "And I am at a loss." She turns to face him again.

It hurts me to look at him

Andrew does not react.

"And the *only* person I can even talk to about it is you."

Lucy sees the spark in his eyes.

"I am going to tell Charles what happened the other night. I must. I am going to marry him, but I need to understand some things first."

The spark extinguishes.

"Miss Lucy, I apologize for any impropriety on my part," he says, his voice devoid of any emotion though he is sincere. "I clearly was misled by your—"

I feel one of Lucy's eyebrows raise.

"By *my*," he amends, "perception of your actions."

"I cannot talk to Charles," Lucy says, ignoring the apology. After everything, she doesn't even trust her feelings enough to be kind to him. "I mean, I will tell him about the—about the other night. But if I tell him that... that I think..." She takes a deep breath while Andrew patiently waits. "Andrew, you once told me that you have to endure horrors, the kind that no one should endure. Is that true?"

He nods. "That is true." I hear a tremor in his voice. If Lucy hears, she doesn't make a sign and hides her thoughts.

"And I told you that I have nightmares or a curse or—well, I do not remember what I said precisely," Lucy pauses. "But that is not true."

"What do you mean?" His voice is even, but he is angry and takes a deep breath. I have never seen him angry. "What purpose would you have to be untruthful about that?"

"I do not think I was being untruthful."

Andrew throws his hands in the air and turns to place his hands on the mantle, his back toward me. I realize we are in the sitting room where we—where they first met. "You lie." He grumbles almost inaudibly.

"It is not a lie." She sits at the edge of the settee, hands carefully folded in her lap.

Andrew continues to hang his head, facing away.

"Please do not think that I am insane," she continues. "For a while now…" She takes another breath, afraid to continue. "I have felt like I am being watched."

Andrew turns around, still clearly angry and skeptical, but curious.

"At times I feel like someone is watching me or is *with* me."

"What do you mean by *with* you?"

"I do not know. It is like someone is in here." Lucy gently taps her temple.

And points right at me.

I cower back even though it isn't really possible. She closes her eyes. "It sounds crazy, I know. And I cannot tell Charles—I am afraid he would refuse to marry me."

"So you decided to tell me?"

I can't read his expression.

"Yes. We have had conversations. You told me that you are cursed, and I told you I was too, except it was not *I* who told you that."

She doesn't know how to react to his slack-jawed expression. Neither do I.

"I think maybe it is connected," Lucy says, her voice breaking.

She is close to tears, afraid something is wrong with her and that it was a mistake to tell Andrew.

"Impossible," he whispers and runs a hand through his hair, messing it until some parts point in different directions.

"You do not believe—"

"Stop talking," he interrupts. "I have not met anyone like me. Not waking or asleep." There is clear awe in his tone.

"But I am not—"

"Lucy! Please stop." He walks from the mantle to the door as if to leave, but then pivots and walks back toward the mantle. "This whole time I thought it was you who is like me." He says the last part to himself, still pacing. "It would have made things much easier, but it all makes sense now. Your actions and words make sense." There is unbridled hope on his face and in his voice even as his feet wear the rug.

"What makes sense?" Lucy asks. I feel her walls of defense rising.

"Never you mind. Can I talk to her? I mean, is she with you now?"

He... he wants to talk to me. My heart thuds louder. *Andrew wants to talk to me. To Emily. Finally.*

"For the longest time I thought I was the only one. Of course until Tessa—until Grace—started cryptically explaining... but I never expected..." He stops pacing and abruptly pulls me to my feet. "Please let me talk to her."

And I feel her step back.

Charles will be here any minute. She warns me, directly thinking at me.

"We don't have much time," I say. Those are the first words I say to him. The first words Emily says to Andrew when he actually knows he isn't speaking with Lucy. I could rip my hair out.

"Is she threatening you?" His tone is different, warm like I've heard so many times, but before was directed toward Lucy.

My heart soars. I feel Lucy's cheeks flush. "No," I say with assurance. "After what happened at the ball—"

"Our kiss." He smiles.

"She doesn't trust you. She told Charles to drop in without announcement, and he will. Soon."

"This is so strange," he says taking my hands in his. "I have never met anyone with the dreams. Except for Grace, I suppose."

"She's not like us." I say quickly. "She piggybacks into my dreams."

His is clearly perplexed by that statement.

"Another explanation for another time," I say.

Andrew's face brightens.

"I haven't met anyone else like me either," I say steering our conversation back.

"And here you are, dreaming, while I am awake." He leads me to sit next him.

But I stand quickly. "Andrew, if Charles walks in it could ruin things for them."

"We could explain."

"How? We can't tell him the truth! He would assume Lucy is lying and being unfaithful." *Unless...* "Does he know about you? About the memory dreams?"

"I like that. *Memory dreams.*" He has a goofy, dreamy expression. "It is almost poetic for such an awful condition."

"Andrew!" I snap. "Does he know?"

His face falls. "No. No one knows except you and Grace."

"Lucy loves Charles," I say softly. "We can't mess things up for her. She is happy." Even though she's technically going to die before her wedding, but I don't mention that part.

"So everything that has happened between us, the looks, the gestures, the bone-tingling emotions... none of it was her?"

"No, that was all me." And with that, without any hesitation at all, I admitted my feelings.

By the look in his face, he tricked me into saying it. My cheeks burn.

Might as well own it. It's not my face isn't saying it. "Yes, Andrew I have... feelings for you."

"Are all women of the future so blunt?" he teases.

"It's not like we'll ever actually meet," I say softly, but I'm sure he can hear.

"The feeling is mutual. I absolutely adore you—"

"How can you?" I shout, interrupting. "Until just moments ago, you thought you were being slighted and rejected by your soulmate *Lucy*."

"How many times have you memory walked with her?" He ignores the question. "It could not have been a constant thing, which explains her sudden shifts in temperament. At least six times? I have never dreamed a person more than once." He is slightly winded from talking so quickly.

"It doesn't matter," I say. "How can you adore—?" I practically choke on the word. "How can you say that about a person whom you haven't actually met?"

"Because I know you."

"You don't. You don't know what I actually look like. You don't even know my name."

"I am sure you are beautiful."

"I look nothing like Lucy."

"I prefer dark-haired beauties."

I try to ignore the fluttering of my heart and vow to try with all my might to stop the Lucy dreams. I will somehow find a way. I have to.

"Tell me your name," he pleads.

Suddenly I need to get out. "I'll tell you," I say, "but answer a question for me first?"

"Anything."

"Do you know how to wake up?" My heart pounds in my borrowed chest.

He eyes me suspiciously. "Why?"

"You know, sometimes the especially painful ones would be nice to escape. The ones you just can't endure anymore?"

"No." He didn't lie very well when he said it.

"Please, Andrew." I give him the best Lucy pout I can muster.

He studies me for several uncomfortable moments. "I did it by accident once." He finally says. "At least I think that is what happened. Sometimes I am yanked out for no reason."

"I think they push us out sometimes," I say.

He has a thoughtful expression, and then continues. "I was burning. The man was being executed and being burned at the stake. The pain was excruciating, so I tried to distract myself by thinking about my own life." He pauses and studies my face. "But it backfired. All I could think about was a painful memory of my own."

"A previous memory-dream?"

"No, an actual, real-life, painful moment." He looks at me a bit too intently before averting his eyes.

"My name is Emily," I say quickly, then close my eyes, clear my thoughts, and focus. *Here goes nothing.*

"Carly's accident... it wasn't..." I took a deep breath. "It wasn't an accident."

"Sure, she had a lot of bad days, but her boyfriend broke up with her."

"Arianna, Carly committed suicide."

"I don't believe you. I think you made it up—"

"I would never—"

"I don't know why you would put me through this, Emily," she said, practically spitting my name. "But I will not let you taint the memory of my sister."

The front door was opened and slammed before I could react.

It worked. I woke up.

dr. shew

THURSDAY

The street lights passed in streaks of fuzzy orange flashes through the cold window. My elbow rested against the door, and the ring on my finger clicked against the glass as I tapped it with my knuckles. The ring that Duncan had given me, at least in one version of my life. My hand was cold, but I hardly noticed.

Mom didn't say a word as she drove me the familiar route. She didn't even mouth the words to her favorite 80s station. She was deep in thought and probably wouldn't have even turned the wiper blades on if I hadn't mentioned the rain. She had a way of seeing through the raindrops unless it was a major torrent, I guess.

I should've acted normal at breakfast. I should've hid the regret from my face and pretended nothing was wrong. I could've yammered on about Duncan or something. Or I should've lied and said I was upset about a fight with Arianna. Of course I would've had to lie about the reason for the fight too, and I wasn't exactly talented at improvisation, so it would've blown up in my face anyway. Really, I should've skipped out before Mom or Dad suspected something was wrong.

"Everything okay?" Mom said. I didn't catch on quick

enough, but she had definitely used the tone reserved for anything involving me seeing my shrink.

"I'm fine," I had said. "It was just a bad dream." And that was my first mistake.

She had that look *on her face.* Nothing I could've said would have prevented what would come next.

"I know it's been a while," she had said. "Maybe we need to make an appointment with Dr Shew?"

"A while?" That was mistake number two. I had seen Dr. Shew only a few days before my Nora dream, so a little over a week ago... that is, *in my other life* I had seen her.

Mom walked from the sink and slowly pulled the chair out next to where I was eating my Lucky Charms. I hated when she moved like that, like she was worried that if she didn't move slowly and carefully, she'd spook me like a startled animal. "Emily, you've been doing great lately, but the night terrors haven't stopped, have they?"

Internally I cringed. They weren't night terrors. Still, I shook my head no. Another mistake. I should've lied.

"I'll make an appointment. Hopefully she can fit you in soon."

When she got back to making dad's omelet, I asked. "Mom, how long has it been?" I shrugged when she turned to look at me, then I made a face like I was trying to remember even though I was actually clueless.

She stared at me long and hard before saying, "It was before your trip to New York, so three months or so?" New York trip? Three months or so? What *didn't* change from saving Carly?

Mom got a hold of Dr. Shew and was able to get me in during last period. At least I got to skip some school for it. But I was really more grateful for the excuse to avoid my "boyfriend" and "best friend" after the final bell.

"It's been a while, Emily," Dr. Shew said.

"That's what I've been told," I said, digging my fingernails into the armrest of the deep chair, trying not to react. There were worn indents in both armrests. I wasn't the first to attack the soft tan leather.

"Do you remember our last session?"

Of course! It was last week! But I didn't respond.

"You smirked when I said that," she said, flipping through my file.

"I remember," I said, "but I know you don't." Dr. Shew always brought the honesty out of me.

"The Rose Ritual. Has it been working?" She hardly glanced at her notes, probably trying to prove she remembered our session... from three months ago.

"It was the only thing that got me through the terrors, especially after losing my best friend."

"Did something happen between you and Arianna?"

"Yeah, her sister died, and I had a memory dream of her *suicide*. Ari didn't want to hear it so she stopped being friends with me."

I almost smiled as Dr. Shew frantically flipped through her notes.

"Why didn't you come see me after it happened? When did she die?"

"Over a year ago. And I did come see you. It's been one of our main topics of discussion lately."

Dr. Shew tried not to react.

"But of course you don't remember. Because I changed things." My voice cracked. Saying it out loud broke the tension inside me that had been building ever since I saved Carly. I was certainly glad she survived, but the burden of remembering the version where she didn't and trying to pretend to move on in the version where she did, but I didn't remember, was a lot to handle.

"You changed things." It wasn't a question. Dr. Shew set her notes aside.

"Yes." I couldn't look her in the eye, focusing instead on a stain in the mostly-white carpet. It was a familiar shape. "I was given a second chance. I relived Carly's death. I saved her—well, I helped her save herself—and everything changed."

"You saved her?"

I nodded. "I even went to see her. You know, since Arianna and I are friends again. But it changed more than just her not dying." I continued. "In fact, I was actually here in your office about a week ago, but apparently that was in the alternate universe. The original universe."

"And what did we talk about?" she asked, intrigued. "Last week?"

That question was easy, since I actually remembered living it. "The usual," I started. "Have I made any friends? How I am dealing with losing Ari? The fact that my parents don't believe that I experience real people's memories."

"Okay. Let's try something. Pretend that nothing has changed. Talk to me the way you would have if things were exactly the same... in your *original universe*."

"Okay." I don't know why I always resisted coming to see her. When she said things like that, when she validated me, it reminded me why I liked talking to her so much.

"Let's start at the beginning," she said. She always got all excited and animated when she found a new way to *shrink* me. It was something else I strangely liked about her. "Hello, Emily. Tell me, what has happened in the past week since we last saw each other?"

"I made a friend," I said, playing along.

"Oh?"

"Yeah, his name is Duncan," I said. "I guess we've been going to the same school our entire lives, but I didn't know who he was until several days ago."

"Duncan. Is that your boyfriend Duncan?"

"I thought we were pretending like nothing had changed?" I began to shut down.

"So Duncan was a change?"

"Yes. He was my new friend before I saved her. Then after... he was suddenly my boyfriend." And just like that the balloon popped, and my euphoric feeling of actually talking about what I remembered vanished.

"Why do you think that happened? Or was different?"

"Because Ari and I never stopped being friends in this version. I think she must've introduced us."

"Do you want him to be your boyfriend?"

I'd thought about that question many times over the past several days. "I like him, but I don't know him well enough yet. I'd rather have made the choice myself."

"Some people don't need longer than a little time before becoming involved."

"I'm not one of those people."

"Did you break up with him? Since you aren't ready to be his girlfriend yet?"

"No."

"Why not?"

"Because I've been pretending like nothing has changed. Because for everyone else, it hasn't."

"Have you talked about this to your parents?"

"No, they don't believe anything I tell them anyway." *They just make me come see you if I say anything about anything,* I wanted to add but didn't.

Dr. Shew jotted down some notes. I studied my cuticles and my prettily polished nails. They were painted my favorite pearl-pink color, and the paint was chipped in places, but it was clearly the work of a professional.

Since when did I start getting manicures? It was like I didn't even know myself. Like I was a stranger in my own life. Like I was dream walking one of the Meadow Grove residents and was scrambling, trying to pretend to be the person I was walking. Pretending I knew everything I should.

Except I wasn't. And I didn't.

My eyes burned. I blinked several times but it wasn't enough to hold back the traitor tear that escaped and dropped to my cheek.

"Emily?" she said. Her tone softened when she noticed me crying.

I took a deep breath. "I don't even know who I am anymore."

"Because of the changes?"

"Yes." I showed her my nails. "Look at how perfect they are. If I'd done it myself you would see the mistakes. Someone else did it. Why did someone else paint my nails?" I was becoming hysterical.

"Let's back up," she said. "Take a deep breath."

I obeyed.

"Tell me again how things were before you changed them?"

"Okay... I had a new friend, *not* a boyfriend." I said with emphasis on the *not*. "Ari and I were barely beginning to speak to each other again."

"Explore that. What did you talk about?"

"A school project mostly. She was nice enough to let me into her group. Duncan was in the group too, but like I said, we'd barely met.

"Did you have any other friends?"

"No. You kept encouraging me to try to make friends." The memory made me smile.

"Were you happy?"

"Not exactly, but things were getting better."

"And now things have changed: you have a boyfriend; you are friends with Arianna; and, from the sound of it, you are pretty popular at school."

"Sounds right."

"Are you happy?"

I had to think. My life sounded like a teenager's dream, but I wasn't with the person I wanted to be with. How I wished I could talk to Andrew about all of this. *Did he ever change things so drastically that his entire life was virtually unrecognizable?* I wasn't *unhappy*. I was definitely grateful to have Ari back, but...

"I just don't feel like me," I said.

———

DR. SHEW MET WITH MOM FOR LIKE A HALF HOUR after our session. It'd been a long time since they'd had a long consultation without me present.

"I hate the idea of you being on medication," Mom said on the drive home. It was still raining, but she had remembered to turn on the wipers this time. "But Dr. Shew really feels that it is necessary to get you well."

"Pills aren't going to change things back," I grumbled. Dr. Shew had prescribed me an antipsychotic, I think. Maybe it was an antidepressant. Either way, I wasn't going to take it.

"I still don't know why you didn't tell me and your dad how you were feeling."

"You would have made me see her sooner."

"Probably," she admitted, "but only to get you better sooner."

"I'm not going to take some stupid pills!" I shouted.

"You will take them," Mom was trying to keep her voice even. "Because otherwise you might need to be hospitalized." Her voice cracked at the last word.

I was speechless. Dr. Shew didn't believe me either. And why should she?

"Besides, she says they will help you to sleep without dreaming." Mom strained to sound cheery. "No more night terrors? It could be worth a try, right?"

"Fine," I said and folded my arms over my chest. "I'll try them."

If they worked, it could be my answer to staying out of the Lucy dreams.

reprieve

FRIDAY

Something was different. I didn't dare move, not even to scratch the sudden itch on my nose.

What is different? I racked my brain. It was Friday. Another game day. Duncan mentioned that when he called last night to ask about my appointment.

My appointment. With Dr. Shew.

My nose really itches. I thought, trying to concentrate on the task at hand. *Oh great, and now my neck itches too.* I gave in and scratched both.

Moving my eyes around my bedroom, I noted that the pastel-purple paint color that I'd chosen when I was ten was still the same. My dark blue carpet was the same. Those had never changed. It looked like morning. Still, I didn't dare push open the curtains to double-check.

My bulletin board looked different, but that had changed when my entire life warped after saving Carly. The once sparsely filled space (containing only a school calendar and a couple of holiday cards from my other grandparents who lived across the country) was now crowded with pictures, ticket stubs, dried flowers, and other mementos, from what I assumed were good memories in the alternate-life. I was happy to see it full of memories, but sad because I didn't remember any of it. Part of me would've felt relieved if I'd woken to my school calendar again. But I was grateful because it meant Carly was still alive.

I backed up in my thoughts. I had been thinking about that appointment yesterday. Dr. Shew prescribed me pills... My thoughts mulled over that. I didn't feel loopy like I did after taking narcotics when I broke my wrist last year. I slowly moved my wrist around to check if *that* had actually happened. It was still slightly stiff, but my wrist was broken *before* Carly's death, so I was sure that had happened.

Wait. No dreams.

Absolutely *no* dreams.

The pills had worked.

I was relieved and sick at the same time. No more dying. No more breakups and broken arms. No more first kisses and proposals—they could be nauseating or depressing sometimes. No more drowning. No more freezing. No more deadly sickness or car crashes.

No more suicides.

No more Lucy dreams. *No more Lucy dreams.* I didn't allow myself to think about the other person I could no longer see because of that truth.

And I wouldn't have to live Lucy's death.

With that last thought, I busied myself with getting ready for the day and took two steps at a time down to breakfast.

"Is that just you, Emily?" Mom asked from the kitchen right as I poked my head around the corner.

"Just me." I smiled. "Who else?"

"I don't—" She stopped and turned off the water from the faucet so she could study me. A slow smile crept up her full lips. "Did they work?"

I allowed my grin to widen. "No dreams."

She squealed and ran to hug me, causing Dad to look up from his paper. "You mean, you didn't have another—"

"Nope." I interrupted him and walked over to squeeze him too.

Dad thought the dreams had stopped long ago. Mom didn't want to worry him, but after my appointment, he was pretty broken up that I'd still been suffering and he didn't know. "They're really gone?" he said, his voice cracking a little.

"Well, it was only one night," I said. "I guess we'll see if they stay gone."

"I'm sure they will," Mom said. "As long as you keep taking the medication."

I nodded. I didn't like the thought of taking meds, but if it meant no dreams, I could use the break and be… just a teenager.

WEEKS LATER

"Brrrr." Arianna shivered again. We were huddled together, standing on the bleachers. It was the last home game of the season. "Aren't you fr-fr-freezing?"

I smiled and shrugged. It really was cold and was snowing huge flakes, but I couldn't be bothered by it. Not when life was so different these past few weeks.

The first few days I'd held my breath, waiting for another dream. There was a time early on when I didn't have the dreams every night. So I remembered what it was like to have a break for several days. There was a couple of times when I woke up screaming, but since I had no recollection of why (and my parents believed me when I said it wasn't a memory-dream), we all figured it just my body adjusting to the medication. Or maybe perhaps a residual effect of not having the dreams anymore. But when the dreams didn't come and didn't come, I was able to breathe easy and mainly focus on getting used to my new life.

And I liked it.

I had my best friend back. I actually had friends, and I didn't feel like a freak anymore.

I was still trying to get used to the boyfriend thing. When we were together, I tried to covertly ask him questions to get to know him better, but it was difficult. He got suspicious sometimes. I missed the old Duncan. There was no pressure, and he was just getting to know me too. No awkward instances where I couldn't remember some great memory we had.

The announcer's voice boomed over the loudspeaker as the bleachers began to shake from the excited student section, jarring me from my thoughts.

"Wahoo!" Ari called through cupped hands covered in purple cotton gloves.

I was so distracted by my own thoughts that I didn't realize we'd scored. I clapped along with my peers anyway so no one would notice.

"What's up with you, Ems?" Ari asked when the crowd settled.

"Hmm?" I answered. "Nothing, what's up with you?"

"Um… your boyfriend just scored and you just acted like you were a polite spectator at a golf tournament."

Duncan scored? Whoops. "I, uh…" *I uh* didn't know what to say.

"Were you thinking about another attractive boy from your life?"

"Huh?"

"Andrew. You haven't told me any juicy Andrew dreams in a while." She nudged me. "Although you probably shouldn't think about your dream boyfriend when you're supposed to be watching your real-life boyfriend's big game."

Andrew. I'd been very deliberate about not letting myself think about him.

"He's not exactly *in my life*," I said. "And it's been a while since I've had a Lucy dream."

"Oh, right." She pointed to her temple. "The meds. So, still no dreams?"

I shook my head. "It's been so nice. I feel so normal." *Other than the medication adjustments,* I thought, but didn't think it was important to tell her I'd still woken up screaming a few times.

"But don't you miss it?" she asked.

"The deaths? The injuries?" I said. "Not even a little."

"But the dresses? The lacey gloves? The curled and pinned hair? Andrew?" She pretended to swoon. "You must miss him?"

I did. I achingly did. But I couldn't go back. Still the thought of *accidentally* forgetting to take my pills so I could go back had crossed my mind more than once.

"Right. You have a boyfriend, so you can't talk about your feelings for a certain *dream*-boy."

"Even if I didn't have a boyfriend, how could I ever be with Andrew?"

Ari shrugged. "The dreams are your thing. I never said I understood it. But I guess it's over now."

"Yep. It's over now." Even Grandma Grace was on board with the meds stopping the dreams. I noticed that she'd stopped wearing the ring too. Probably because there was no point.

The clock ran out soon after, so trying to play the part of girl-friend and normal teenager, I rushed the field with my classmates and sought out Duncan.

"You did great!" I said, a bit out of breath as Duncan lifted me off of my feet in a hug. Then he surprised me by kissing me. Hard. He tasted of sweat and dirt. He'd played rough tonight.

"Everything okay?" he asked, pushing me back.

"Fine." I smiled. "What a way to end the season, huh?"

Duncan looked at me quizzically, and then tilted his head. "Can we talk later?"

"Of course. Everything okay with you?"

He paused before responding. "Yep, just want to talk."

Duncan was pretty adamant about leaving as quickly as possible, so it was only a handful of minutes before we were driving out of the parking lot. Fortunately the snow had stopped.

"Was Ari okay finding another ride?" he asked.

My eyes didn't leave the road. Driving in snowy conditions always made me nervous. Fortunately it didn't seem to be sticking to the road much. "Yeah, Clare's taking her home." Because apparently we were friends with the girl who was in love with Duncan in another world. I wondered if she was in love with him in this world too. Maybe she wasn't broadcasting to me, because... well, *girlfriend*. I still wasn't sure I'd ever get used to all of the changes.

Still, I wouldn't want to go back to the life I remembered. Not if it meant Carly would be dead.

"Are we going to A&W with everyone else?" I asked.

"How about some us time? Just you and me?"

"Okay," I said. The idea made me slightly nervous. Apparently in this alternate-life, Duncan and I had had some pretty serious make-out sessions. So far I'd gotten away with just a kiss here and there.

"Let's go to my place," he said. "I've got some hot chocolate with your name on it." He knew my weakness for the sugary warm nectar of the gods.

And so for the second time ever, I drove to Duncan's house. It looked exactly the same. Even down to the bowl of peanut M&Ms on the counter.

"Where are your parents?" I asked, popping a green one in my mouth.

"I think they were meeting some friends for dinner after the game."

"Oh." Was all I could think to say as Duncan heated some water.

"Don't worry; they won't be home for a while." He winked, but then his face fell.

"What's wrong?" I asked.

"What's going on with you?" he countered.

"What do you mean?"

"Well, you've been acting strange for a few weeks."

"The dreams are gone. Is that what you mean?" I asked.

"No."

"Could you elaborate then?" I asked. I knew I was dodging, but how could I explain the truth?

"I don't mean to sound like a girl, but you've been avoiding me."

"Busy with school, I guess." I said.

"Seriously, Ems." He rounded the counter to where I was sitting on a stool. He leaned on the counter next to my arm so that we were almost at eye level.

"I'm not meaning to," I said, slightly flustered. And it was true.

He looked thoughtful for a few moments, then his face lit up. "Wait, who did you last dream of?"

"Um... Lucy?"

"Lucy, huh?" Duncan walked to the cupboard and got some mugs out, then scooped chocolate powder into both.

"Did I tell you about her?" My Lucy dreams started before the change. I wondered what exactly alternate-me said to Duncan about them.

"A little." He was being careful with his words too. "You said this would happen." He said quietly, almost like he didn't want me to hear.

"I told you—"

"She was engaged to a Harker, right?" he interrupted.

"Charles," I answered. "What did I say would happen?"

He poured the steaming water into both mugs and handed me the purple one with flowers to stir. "Did I ever tell you that I'm a Harker?" Duncan asked.

Yup. But that was alternate-you, so... Instead, I played along. "But your last name is Stewart!"

"Mom's maiden name is Harker."

I slowly brought the mug to my lips and scalded my tongue with the hot liquid. I still wore the ring he gave me the last time he told me he was a Harker and absently wondered what he'd told the other me about it and how long I'd had it.

"Maybe Charles or whoever is like my ancestor or something," he said thoughtfully.

"So if you're a Harker…" I thought aloud.

"I am."

"Then that means…" Something just occurred to me.

"What does that mean?" he asked when I didn't say more.

Carefully, I sipped from my mug again. The sweet chocolate was almost the perfect temperature. "I have to go," I said setting the mostly full mug on the counter.

"Wait. What?" Duncan practically dropped his, setting it down. Some of the liquid sloshed down the sides and onto the white quartz counter. "You have to go?"

"Yes." I had to leave, to think this through uninterrupted. "Homework," I shrugged, hopefully covering the lie.

"Em, this is what I've been trying to talk about. You seem distracted lately." He paused and reached for my hand. "And… different."

I pulled away. "I kinda am, Duncan," I said.

"Distracted or different?" He shook his head and raised his hands in the air in frustration.

"Both? I dunno." I shrugged and grabbed my coat and keys. "See ya," I said and walked out the door.

He followed without his coat. "I thought things were good between us."

"They are," I said, flipping through my keys. "We're fine."

"Are we?" Duncan held my hands, stopping me and forcing me to look up at him.

It had begun snowing again. Huge flakes caught in his honey-brown hair. *So close, but the wrong color*, I thought absently. One large flake hung onto his short lashes, drawing my attention to his gray colored eyes with flecks of green. *Also wrong.*

"Say what you need to say, Duncan." It came out more clipped than I wanted.

He drew in a big breath and let it out, nearly enough to steam my glasses. "I don't know what is going on, why you are different, or what you are going through."

"Sorry?"

"No. Tell me what's happened, Em. What's wrong? I want to help you. What is going on in that cute head of yours"—he kissed my forehead—"that you suddenly can't confide in me?"

I searched his face for a moment. Attractive, yes absolutely. But his wasn't the face I wanted to confide in.

Stupid time difference.

And stupid medication that won't let me see him again.

"I've gotta go," I said and slid into my car.

"Maybe we need a break." He looked across my hood as he said it, not willing to meet my eyes. It was obvious that he didn't mean it.

"Ok," I said and gently pulled my car door closed.

I banished the conversation from my thoughts as I drove away. Something he said before our little clash kept bouncing around in my mind. I needed to think it through:

Duncan was a Harker. His mother was a Harker. I didn't even meet him until I had my first *Harker* dream about Nora Harker. My Nora dream, where she suddenly spoke for the first time in her life—thanks to me. Which was possibly what saved her brother, Colin.

Colin, who was the progenitor of Lucy's Charles. And Andrew.

And possibly Duncan.

Suddenly it all made sense. The reason I'd never met Duncan until recently even though we'd apparently been going to the same school for years.

Charles, Andrew, Duncan. None of them existed until I saved Colin.

CHAPTER 23

...

SATURDAY

"It's just you and me, Emily. Can you tell me why you came?"

"Mom made me."

"Do you remember why your mother wanted you to come?"

"She said I was screaming."

"Yes, but then they couldn't wake you."

...

"Why do you think that happened?"

"I...I don't know. I don't remember."

"What were you doing before you started screaming?"

"Sleeping. I think."

...

...

...

"Were you screaming because of a nightmare—er, a bad memory-dream?"

"I don't remember."

"Then why do you think you were screaming?"

"I don't know!" The shouting made my head hurt more.

...

...

[paper shuffling]

…

…

"Have you been taking your pills, Emily?"

"Yes."

"Did you take one last night?"

"Yes." I reached a hand to my face. My cheeks were wet.

"Have you had any memory-dreams since you started taking the pills?"

"No."

…

…

…

[more paper shuffling]

…

…

"Emily, a lot of people are worried about you. Your parents are *very* worried about you. You gave them quite the scare this morning with your… episode."

The fog in my head was penetrated by a flicker of a memory. Sparking emotion. And more wetness on my cheeks. *It hurts.* But I don't know why. I don't remember why.

Gritting my teeth, I pushed down the sob that threatened to surface and allowed the fuzziness in my head to return.

The room was spinning. Back and forth. In swirls of color. Too bright. Faster and faster uncontrollably. I closed my eyes.

"Come back!" Shouting. "Emily, come back now!" Closer shouting. The room stilled. "Come back or I will have no choice but to commit you. *Now.*"

The emotional wave hit suddenly and hard. And it hurt even more because I didn't remember the cause. *It's too much. It's so much. I can't.* The devil on my shoulder screamed for me to disappear again. To disappear further back. So far back that I will never surface again, but the threat of a padded, locked room brought me back, and the fuzziness was gone in an instant.

I kept my eyes shut tight. Before opening them, I took several deep breaths.

In.

Out.

In.

Out.

In.

...

...

...

Open.

But the world was blurry again.

"Better?" Dr. Shew asked.

I squinted, but it still didn't help my vision. "I can't see?"

She handed me my familiar plastic frames. I put my glasses on and the world finally focused.

"I'm afraid that you are dealing with something much worse than night terrors," she said, then wrote something in my file. She never used to be rude like this, writing so many notes during a session. Her focus had shifted for some reason.

"That's what I've been saying for years," I said, under my breath.

"I think you are still having the memory-dreams," she said, either ignoring my comment or she hadn't heard it. "But the medication is causing you to forget them."

They hadn't stopped? "I'm still having the dreams?" My breathing became fast again as my mind raced through all of the terrible possibilities. What if I was murdered? Okay, maybe that was an acceptable dream to forget, but what if I had another dream like Carly's? What if Arianna and I weren't speaking again or *worse*—maybe she didn't exist at all because of something I did in a dream last night that I didn't remember.

"Despite that, I think you should continue to take the medication," she said.

I finally looked at her. "You look different," I blurted out.

She set down her notes and gave me a half-smile. "I didn't have time—"

"Did I change something again?" I began to hyperventilate. "What's different? What's different about you, doc? I can't think." I grabbed a fistful of my hair. "I can't remember the dreams, I can't remember if I changed something."

"Emily?" Her voice was firm. "You are starting to spiral again. Take deep breaths. In"—she breathed in—"and out"—she breathed out. "In and out."

I obeyed and mimicked her exaggerated breaths.

"Better?"

I nodded, relaxed the grip on my hair, and let my hands fall into my lap. "You aren't wearing any makeup," I said. "That's different. And you have dark circles underneath your eyes, and your hair is out of place. That's not like you, right?" I glanced at the clock on the wall. The time panicked me, but I continued, "It's almost six thirty, but it's a Saturday. Maybe you don't make yourself look so perfect on the weekends?"

"You didn't change anything, Emily," Dr. Shew said calmly.

How would she know? "So I'm right?" I said. "You were just lounging at home on a Saturday. You don't wear makeup on Saturday's sometimes, right?"

"When exactly would I have had time to put on makeup?" She wasn't accusing, just curious.

"What do you mean?"

"Your mother called me at five o'clock in the morning."

I glanced at the clock again and pointed at it, my mouth hanging open. "It's morning?"

She nodded.

"So I didn't block out the entire day?"

"You might have if your mother hadn't called me. Or..." she stopped herself.

"Or what?"

"Or you might have been hospitalized. But you sound more like yourself now," she said quickly. "Do you feel better?"

"I feel like I'm here now, so I guess that means I feel better."

"Good," she said. "I want to see you again next week. I think if you practice some techniques, with the help of your parents, we can avoid another episode. Or at least you can calm yourself down without another emergency appointment."

I nodded and stood up to leave.

"And again, continue taking your medication," she added as she stood.

"Wouldn't it be better if I remembered the dreams?"

"I don't mean to scare you, Emily, but I believe it was fortunate that you took the pill last night."

I narrowed my eyes at her. "How do you figure?" I asked. It was the first time I questioned her instead of agreeing and trusting implicitly.

She folded her arms over her chest before she spoke, the gesture made me trust her even less. "I think whatever it was, was so traumatic that it *would* have landed you in the hospital if had you remembered it."

Not likely, I thought. She had no idea what I'd endured. "Do you think I'll ever remember them?" I asked. "The ones I've forgotten, I mean?"

She reached out to gently grip my elbow. "You might," she said, "but I wouldn't worry too much about it."

"Ok," I said. Her tone implied that I was scared to remember them, but I wasn't afraid.

I wanted to remember.

To hell with following her instructions. The panic of not knowing where I'd been or what happened while I slept was so much worse than remembering the bad. I had to know what had happened. And if there was a good chance I was headed for the looney bin either way, what did it matter? I was never taking those pills again.

rose ritual

SATURDAY

om didn't say anything the whole ride home. She kept looking at me out of the corner of her eye, almost like she didn't want me to notice her doing it. Like I might snap at any minute. Who knows, maybe I would. I felt bad for putting her through all of this. My "episode" must've been scary for her and Dad.

I wanted to talk to her, but I didn't know how to articulate what I was going through. I couldn't even tell her I'd decided not to take the pills anymore. She wouldn't understand my reasoning. I knew she'd side with Dr. Shew.

And I didn't have the energy to argue. So I remained silent.

I was exhausted when we got home, but I didn't want to go back to sleep. The medication was certainly still in my system, and I didn't want to risk another memory-dream I didn't remember. I trudged up to my room and threw my white comforter over my pillow, lazily making my bed to lie on top of it. Hopefully I would stay awake if I wasn't cozy underneath the covers.

What happened last night? I wondered, putting my hands behind my head and staring at my purple walls. It was hard to imagine something worse than anything I'd gone through before. It felt worse not knowing and letting my imagination run wild.

With so many horrible experiences to pull from, my imagination was good.

It was only a little after seven, but I needed to talk to Grandma, so I picked up my phone still next to my bed charging, unplugged it, and called her.

"You're up early, Emily," Grandma answered on the first ring.

"I guess I didn't wake you?" I asked.

"I'm an early riser," she said. It sounded like she was eating something, then she swallowed. "But you're not. What's wrong?"

"Why do you assume something is wrong?" I asked.

"Because you're calling me before nine in the morning on a Saturday." I could hear the smile in her tone, but then she sighed. *She already knew.* "Actually, your mother called me while she drove you to the doctor."

"Oh."

"Are you feeling better?" she asked, hopeful.

"Not one hundred percent," I said, "but better than I was."

"What happened, sweetheart?" Her voice had dropped to a whisper.

"Mom said I woke up screaming," I said. "I don't remember anything that happened this morning until we were already in Dr. Shew's office." I hadn't admitted that part to even myself until now. "And even bits of that are still… fuzzy."

"What did the doctor say?" she asked. Her tone was weighty, full of gravity. And she hadn't referred to Dr. Shew as my "shrink" the way she always did. I could hear her serious concern.

"She thinks I'm still having the memory-dreams," I said, "but I'm not remembering them."

"So last night was a bad one, huh?"

"I can only assume."

"But you've been fine until now, right?"

"Yeah, I was probably having Lucy dreams until last night." I said it matter-of-factly, but the thought shot a pang into my chest. How many times had I been with Lucy without remembering it?

How many times had I talked to Andrew but forgot everything when I opened my eyes the next morning?

Then something dawned on me. *What if last night was October 3rd? The day Lucy died? And I didn't remember it?* The thought panicked me.

"Do you think I could try to remember what happened?" I asked. "Is there anything in Grandma Cole's journals that would help with that?"

She didn't say anything for several seconds. "Grandma Cole never took medication to forget them," she said slowly.

"I know—" My voice cracked, so I cleared my throat. "But did she forget them for any reason?" Even as I asked, I knew the possibility was unlikely if even existent.

Grandma didn't answer right away again. "If she did, how would she know?"

"True." I felt defeated. After all, I didn't know I was still having them until this morning. "Do you have any suggestions?" I asked quietly.

"You could try the Rose Ritual," she suggested.

"But I don't even know who to visit," I said. But my mind was already making plans. I could start with Lucy.

"Then I don't know what else to tell you," Grandma said. "What did Dr. Shew tell you to do?"

"She said I should keep taking my pills, can you believe it? Like not remembering my memory-dreams is somehow better."

"Are you going to follow her instructions?" she said, suddenly sounding more grandma than girlfriend.

"No." I considered lying to her, but the thought came too late.

"I really think you should do what the doctor says."

"You're probably right," I lied after all, but made my voice sound like I was actually intending to. "I'm sure Dr. Shew knows best."

"Where do you think you're going, young lady?" Dad asked. My hand wasn't even on the doorknob yet.

"I, uh... just talked to Grandma," I stammered, not because I'd actually been sneaking out or about to tell a lie, but because of Dad's reaction and tone. He sounded like I was three and about to run into traffic. "She suggested that I try the Rose Ritual... you know the one Dr. Shew taught me that helps after the bad ones?"

"I thought you didn't remember the night terror?"

I cringed, but tried not to react too obviously. Dad was usually more sensitive about his word choice—whether he believed the truth or not. My breakdown must've hit him hard. "I don't," I said, "but it wouldn't hurt to try, right?"

"Well, I don't want you to go alone," he said, opening the coat closet behind me to grab his.

My breathing became shallow again in my panic. If the Rose Ritual *did* work, I did not want my Dad there to see it. "Is it alright if I call Ari instead?"

"Call her right now," he said, not taking his coat off, but not disagreeing either.

I fumbled to grab my phone from my pocket. His eyes didn't leave my face as I searched for her name and pushed the call button.

It rang three times. Then four. My heart pound harder and harder. What if she didn't answer? But on the fifth ring, she picked up.

"Hey, Ari," I said, a little shakily. "Could you—would you come with me on an errand?"

"Sure!" she said as cheery as ever, despite the probability that I'd woken her up. "What time?"

If Dad hadn't been hovering, I might have told her a later time and made up another "errand" to go on when I was finished. "Meet me at the cemetery in twenty minutes?" I asked.

Dad raised an eyebrow.

"Cemetery?" Ari was confused. "What—?"

"Just meet me there?" I cut her off.

"Yeah, twenty minutes. Got it."

I hung up and took another step to leave.

Dad blocked me. "You said twenty minutes," he argued.

"Yeah, and it's going to take me about that long to walk there," I said, "unless you're okay with me taking the car."

He raised his eyebrow again, but didn't say a word as he allowed me to pass.

It would really only take me about ten minutes to walk, but once I was outside, it occurred to me that I needed time to walk to the floral shop too. If I was going to do the Rose Ritual, might as well do it right and get a rose.

I should've told Ari more like forty-five minutes, I thought as I tried to come up with a solution. I pulled my phone back out of my pocket to call her again when something sticking out of the mailbox caught my eye. The phone went back into my coat pocket as I rounded to face the mailbox and see what was there.

Wrapped in cellophane and tied with a white ribbon was a single, white rose. Carefully, I retrieved the flower and checked the back of the familiar *Brewster Floral* tag. It was blank. I looked around to see if there were any suspicious cars or people slinking nearby who might've put it there, but everything looked like normal—just my usual, non-suspicious street as always.

Who could have put it there? I wondered. I almost stuffed it back into the mailbox, but it was too much of a coincidence that it would be there, the details so perfect, right when I needed it. Like someone *knew* I needed it, and needed to do this alone. I took the rose and power walked to the cemetery, making it there in record time.

I found Lucy's grave first. For more reasons than one, I hoped I hadn't lived Lucy's death, but I needed to check. I folded my legs underneath me and read her dates again. I don't know why I expected to see something different, but it read the same that it always did.

Taking a deep breath, I cleared my head and closed my eyes. I remained that way for half a minute, much longer than any other flashbacks had ever taken. When I opened them again, I felt conflicted relief. Either I hadn't dreamt her death last night, or the ritual didn't work on forgotten dreams.

What now? I pulled my phone from my pocket to check the time. I only had about five minutes until Ari would be here, unless she was running late. I was almost certain that the flashbacks took virtually no real time, but there was still the complication of finding who it was in the first place.

I stood up, not sure whether to meander or give up. But not knowing what happened last night was driving me mad. I *had* to know. I *needed* to know. And there was a very real possibility that I'd dreamt someone new. Someone whose name I didn't know. That reality frustrated and saddened me all at once.

Not knowing what to do, I took small steps, walking around nearby headstones and reading their names and dates. Hoping one of them would trigger something.

Ari's familiar silver car slowed on the street and pulled over. She could have driven along the cemetery roads right to where I was, but I was grateful she'd decided to park on the street and walk. But that still meant I was running out of time. I watched her get out of the driver's seat, and when she moved I saw that she wasn't alone in the car. The brilliant red-haired person in the passenger seat could have been none other than her sister Carly.

I'd seen her alive and well after the dream where I'd saved her, but it was still so surreal seeing her again. And knowing that the hole in Ari's heart that hardened after her death and pushed me out of her life was whole again. Not fixed, but nonexistent.

As Ari slowly walked toward me, I thought about Carly. The fact that I'd lived her death twice gave me an idea. *What if I repeated someone else last night?* I wished I'd brought my tally journal I'd kept over the years to systematically locate each one.

I racked my brain instead. Deaths were easier to remember, so I could start with those. *Sandra died in that car accident,* I thought. For some reason she was the first to come to mind because she'd been driving the exact make, model, and color of vehicle Ari had. *But I can't remember what her last name was.*

Think. Think. Think.

Nora. Why didn't I think of her sooner? But the thought sent all kinds of waves of panic through me. Nora's death and everything surrounding it had affected some very real people in my life. Namely Charles. And Duncan. And Andrew. But I had to find out. Her grave was not far from where I stood, so I sprinted—not worrying if I alarmed Ari—and fell to my knees when I arrived.

I tried to slow my breathing, though it seemed near impossible, but closed my eyes anyway and cleared my head.

Everything flashed purple. Then blinding white.

not again

"Nora wake up, please wake up!" young Colin desperately pleads. "We have to move!" His sniffles are loud, and he chokes on his words. "Nora, c'mon, c'mon, *c'mon!*" A small hand tugs at my arm again and again. "C'mon, c'mon, c'mon!"

Wait. No, not again.

My head throbs between my brows, past my temples and around to a sharp pulsing at the back right side of my head.

Oh, it hurts. I forgot how much it hurt.

I struggle to open my eyes without success. My fingers are already woven through my—*her*—thick hair. I can feel the wet, sticky blood pooling against her scalp.

Ugh. I would shudder if I could.

The blood is warm, almost hot in the freezing temperature, and trickles through her fingers at a steady drip.

Drip, drip, drip...

No. No. No. Not this one. I can't do this one again.

Her eyes prick with tears in reaction to my thoughts. Before Lucy, I'd never noticed how much my interference affected those I dream-walked.

Drip...

Drip...
Drip...

"Nora, please." Colin's voice is softer now, despondent. But he doesn't stop talking. "Please, Nora. C'mon, c'mon, c'mon!"

With great effort, her eyes open, rimmed with fine white crystals. She blinks to unstick her ice-encrusted lashes. Her shallow breath is barely visible against the gray winter sky. Blocking half of it is Colin, of course. His face is pale and streaked with dirt, tears, and blood.

"You're awake," he says, breathing a sigh of relief.

That's different. He didn't say that before. Though my head pounds, I try to remember what I've done differently.

"C'mon, let's get you up," He says tugging at my sleeve, but the pain in my head sends sharp needles coursing through me and I resist, letting out an inaudible cry.

Inaudible.

Older Colin told Lucy—er, me—that Nora was mute. In the first memory walk, I spoke to Colin. The "miracle" is why he was saved. I haven't spoken yet. That's the difference.

Grandma Grace says it isn't right to change things. Will he still make it off the ice if I don't talk?

Nora struggles to lift her arm enough to touch his face.

Colin clutches her hand with blood-stained fingers and sobs harder. "Please, Nora!" His voice cracks. "Nora, the ice is breaking! We'll fall through!"

What is the purpose of reliving Nora's death again? Did I do wrong by changing things before? Should I do as Grandma Grace says?

The frozen river underneath us groans and cracks.

Or should I talk? Should I make a "miracle" again and save her brother? What will happen if I don't? Will he get off the ice anyway?

What will happen if he dies?

What will happen to Charles if Colin dies? To Andrew?

To Duncan?

Will they cease to exist?

Though I don't know his Harker line, something tells me that it might affect him too. What should I do?

"Nora! Colin!" a voice from the bank calls.

"Papa!" Colin calls back. "The ice is breaking!"

I try to plead with my eyes, willing him to get off the ice.

"It is okay, Nora." He says his voice suddenly firm. "I won't leave you."

No! I attempt to shake my head, but the pain is so intense. Nothing more than a weak moan escapes my lips.

"Not until I figure out a way to get you off too." Colin looks around, like a way to transport Nora will suddenly appear. He is running out of time.

Get off the ice! I want to scream. I want to beg like I did before, but something is holding me back. *My internal voice, one which sounds a lot like Grandma Grace, is holding me back.*

Finally decided, I remain quiet and hope I can convey to Colin how desperately he needs to leave her side.

Nora is trying hard, so at least it's something I know she'd do without me here.

"Maybe if I run to the shore, I can get something to drag you off the ice with." Colin talks to himself while the voices on the bank grow increasingly more frantic.

"Papa!" Colin calls. "Find something to drag her off with! She's hurt!"

"Colin! Sweetheart!" a female voice shouts. Their mother I'm sure. "Come off the ice!" Her tone of voice indicates that she must know Nora won't make it regardless.

The amount of blood loss must be obvious even from the shore.

"I love you, Nora Violet Harker." Colin says squeezing her hand. He's not going anywhere anytime soon.

Go to the bank, *now.* I want to order, but I black out for an indistinguishable amount of time.

...

Several loud wails of grief carry through the icy air from the bank. My heart lurches. Is Colin still nearby? Hopefully not because I remember what happens next:

The ice rips and spills river water upward, mixing with the blood.

Craackk.

Nora's head snaps upward at the sound. Time slows for the poor girl bleeding out on the ice who is unable to move or scream or cry as she watches the finally free branch tumble.

And I cry for her again.

Showers of ice and snow stab the parts of her skin that aren't already numb as the branch breaks the glass river and plunges underneath, pulling us in with it.

Fortunately she fades fast. The loss of blood and the icy water quickly take her away into unconsciousness.

Just like before. Except this time I don't know if she died alone.

***

"Emily!" Ari shouted in my face. Her nose was only inches from mine.

My limbs instantly thawed, I found myself lying on my back in the grass of the cemetery. I'd never been knocked so senseless before.

Ari turned her head, and I could see tears glistening on her cheeks. "Carly!" she called in the direction where she'd parked.

I pushed myself up with my elbows and instantly spotted Carly's flaming red hair, her curls wild in the breeze as she ran. Within seconds she was on the ground with us too.

"What happened?" Carly asked, a little breathless. I couldn't take my eyes off of her. Seeing her, here, alive was still so surreal.

"It's nothing," I said, rubbing my head in the same location as Nora's injury—totally the wrong gesture.

"That didn't look like nothing," Carly said. "Emily, what happened?"

My first instinct was to lie, but I could see Ari's phone already in her hand, threatening to dial the paramedics—or worse—my parents. I reached up to touch her phone. "Don't call anyone," I said softly.

"Then. What. Happened?" Ari asked, gritting her teeth. Probably to push back more tears.

I looked from one sister to the other, so different in appearance, but clearly sisters in their mannerisms and personalities. They were fiercely loyal to one another and bonded tightly due to their difficult circumstances at home. Again, I was reminded of a universe where Carly hadn't survived and what it had done to Arianna. For the first time, the difficulties of my life—my missing memories, sudden boyfriend, and newfound popularity—felt small and insignificant compared to Ari's loss of her sister.

And the thought filled me with even more guilt.

"I had a flashback," I said, lowering my eyes.

"A what?"

"A flashback," I repeated, then related what had happened that morning. My *episode.* And how Dr. Shew explained that I was still having the memory-dreams, I just wasn't remembering them because of the pills. "I wanted to remember what happened."

"And... it worked?" Ari asked.

I looked up at her, then at Carly who was open-mouthed as I spoke. "It worked," I said, turning back to Ari.

"Who was it?" Ari whispered.

"Nora. Again." The guilt swept over me as I said her name. "Except I didn't save Colin this time." I choked on the words, tears swimming. "I let it play out the way it was supposed to, I guess."

Ari threw her arms around me, and I let out a sob. I felt devastated. It was a pain unlike anything I'd ever felt before. My chest ached, pulsing sharply with each ragged breath. *Just like this morning.* The cause of my breakdown that morning was clear now. Even though I hadn't remembered it, this same pain had been there, just beneath the surface.

"Why didn't you save him?" Carly asked, her voice even. I could hear the underlying question. Why her but not this boy? Would I save her again if the choice was presented again, or let her die on the tracks?

I pulled away from Arianna so that I could look at her sister to answer, even though tears were streaming down my face. "Someone suggested that it wasn't right to change things," I said, the shame of it washing over me. "But they were wrong." I looked Carly square in the eye so she could feel my meaning. "In my heart, I *know* they were wrong. I will *never* regret changing the way I acted the second time I dreamt of you."

Carly swallowed hard and looked down to study her hands. There were tears in her eyes too.

I looked back at Ari. "I didn't save Colin. I don't even know if he died." My voice cracked.

"Is there a way to find out?" Ari asked, confused that I was looking to her for the answer.

I could think of two ways to find out. Colin's grave was in the cemetery, not far away. I could march right over and look at his dates. Or I could ask Arianna a simple question.

"Do I have... a boyfriend?" I couldn't bring myself to ask if Duncan existed. Merely saying his name was painful. I couldn't even bear to think the other one's name. The thought that they both might have been obliterated from existence because I couldn't save Colin—their possible common ancestor—made me want to crumble.

"Oh, sweetie." There was pity in her voice, and her eyebrows rose in concern.

I kept my voice firm. "Do I have a boyfriend? Please, just answer the question, Arianna." I lowered my voice to a whisper. "I need to know."

"No, Emily. No, you do not have a boyfriend."

My heart sunk into my stomach, but I brushed the tears away and stood shakily. "Could you take me home?" I asked.

"Of course," she said and nodded, also pushing herself to her feet. "Do... do you want to talk about it?"

I shook my head, not trusting my voice to stay even. I made myself a vow right then and there. I would never again let someone die if I could save them. And I was never taking that medication again.

reunion

I awake to familiar blond curls in my periphery on the pillow. I'm back with Lucy. The thought makes me giddy. It had been so long since I was last with her, and though I had tried to banish the memory from my head, being back here with her shoved it fresh into my head.

My last Lucy memory-dream was at the engagement ball when Andrew finally found out about me, *Emily*. I'd essentially run away immediately after a la Cinderella.

"Oh no. Not you again," Lucy moans.

My elation evaporates. *Wait. What does she mean? What have I done?* I must have been right about continuing to dream Lucy, but not remembering any of it.

"Enough," Lucy answers my thoughts.

You don't understand, I say to her, *something happened... It was an accident. Well, sort of. I didn't know the pills would—*

"Stop, Emily."

I open her mouth to speak, "But—"

"No!" she shouts. It's loud. Especially considering that I'm right in her head. I couldn't get any closer if I tried. "I cannot stop you from lurking in my mind, but you are *not* taking over my body today. No talking. Nothing."

Okay.

"How long should I expect you to stay?" Her tone is cold.

I have to think. This is new territory for me. I mean, it's rare enough that I even know who I am. No one else has ever been *aware* of my presence, let alone communicated with me.

No one has ever asked me that, I said. *I don't know.*

"General idea?"

Sorry, I really have no idea. Usually I'm only present for a few hours, sometimes longer, sometime shorter. I really don't know.

"Fine. Please, do not get in the way. It is a special day."

Is it—?

"No," she cuts me off. How does she do that? "You will not direct my thoughts about anything. My sister is coming home today, and I have an entire afternoon planned for just the two of us... and you, now, I suppose. But you will not tell her—or anyone else—that you are here."

I will not tell her I am here.

"Or that you even exist."

To do that I would have to tell her that I am here...

"Just promise, please."

I promise.

"We can leave the subject about the little girl who lives in my head for another day."

The little—?

"Or whatever you are! Today I do not care," she says. *They are* not *sending me to the sanatorium today,* Lucy thought.

Sanatorium. Nut house. Mental institution. Insane asylum.

And I thought I had a messed-up life.

Until very recently, it has never occurred to me just how my intrusion affects others. (I mean, other than that time when I changed one little detail and the entire universe flipped. Besides that.)

So, I stay out of her way as Betsy braids and weaves Lucy's hair elegantly, and dresses her in a deep-blue gown. It must be new, because I don't remember seeing it in Lucy's closet—er, wardrobe... or whatever they're called, now.

"You look lovely, miss," Betsy says.

"Thanks to you," Lucy replies.

Betsy curtsies. "We've all missed Miss Hannah. It's an exciting day, and you should be looking your best."

Lucy gives her a genuine smile, and we head to breakfast.

After what seems like only a few bites, I make sure to stay out of the way as Lucy checks in on Mrs. Holt in the kitchen, which is buzzing like a hive in a cloud of flour and heat.

"Everything's in order, miss," Mrs. Holt says, brushing a lock of brown hair away from her glistening forehead. "The luncheon is being prepared, and I made sure that your and Miss Hannah's favorite soufflés are on the menu for dessert."

I almost don't recognize the kitchen from when I last entered Mrs. Holt's realm. Dirty pots and pans encrusted with sauces and crumbs are piled on every available table. Dishes of food cover the workspaces. The fire blazes furiously, with a stack of wood nearby to keep it going. A savory meat I don't recognize roasts in the hearth over a spigot. The smell is mouthwatering. Papers with neat scrawl, recipes I assume, are scattered next to fruits and vegetables and tucked in between food dishes. Several also cover the floor. I want to read what they say, but Lucy keeps her attention on Mrs. Holt.

"Thank you, Mrs. Holt," Lucy says. "And I see that you have recruited help?"

"Had to, miss," Mrs. Holt says and then introduces a kitchen maid—now furiously making pastries—from a neighboring house.

"Miss," the young maid says with a small curtsy, barely looking up from kneading her dough. Her nose is specked with flour, and her forehead is smeared with it. Which is understandable because I count at least six types of desserts in various stages surrounding her.

"And William is running errands," Mrs. Holt says, gesturing

to a young boy who is maybe ten. He fidgets in the corner until Mrs. Holt rattles off a list of errands to him.

"Ma'am," he says to Lucy, nodding once, then takes a brown package from the edge of the table and rushes out the servant door. In his movement, one of the recipes kicks up from the floor and flutters several feet away. Nearer to the fire.

This looks like a fire hazard, I say, but Lucy shushes me, and we move on to the stables.

"Are the horses rested and the carriage cleaned from top to bottom for our outing?" Lucy asks Matthew, who is brushing a spotted mare. Again, I make sure to steer clear.

Matthew tries but fails to hide a smile. "Everything's ready for you and Miss Hannah," he says. "Horses are in top condition and will be harnessed and hitched up on time, Miss Lucy."

"Thank you, Matthew."

Lucy's busy morning helps me keep my mind off of things too. It's nice not to worry and let her take the lead. Sure, she demanded it, but for me it's restful.

It's probably how most people feel about sleep.

"Restful?" Lucy asks. Her tasks are finished, and she heads for her room to rest for a moment.

What? It feels... undeniably strange to have her picking thoughts out of my head. Especially the ones I didn't think she could hear.

"Ha! Yes, I can hear all of it. That must be quite *disconcerting* for you," she says, again reading my thoughts. "But seeing as I have absolutely no say in the matter, you'll get no sympathy from me. After all, you never asked my permission to be here," she says, tapping her temple ever so subtly.

But it's not on purpose, I say when we enter her chambers. *I don't have any control either.* I don't think I do.

"You mean, you didn't choose to come?" she asks and lounges on her chaise.

No, not exactly, I reply. *It is not the most pleasant thing for me to be in people's heads either. I mean, your life isn't bad. It has kind of been a relief to live so many of your days because of that fact. A lot of what I experience is very painful.*

"I am not the only one you visit?"

A quick procession of every person I've ever walked runs through my memories. With a longer pause at my recent ones: the horrific sound of crunching metal in Sandra's car accident; the dreaded panic to get Carly's foot free from the rails; Nora's dazed, pain-racked mind on the frozen ice.

The last one floods me with guilt once again.

No, you're not, I say, wondering if she too witnessed my memories.

"I cannot imagine what that must be like," she whispers.

Part of me is used to it, I say. *And I've learned how to cope when I'm awake.* For the most part.

"Please do not think I am being unfeeling for asking, but you mentioned when you are awake? Are you a person? A real person?"

"Ha!" I inadvertently laugh out loud. *Sorry. And yes, I am a person. When I'm not with you or someone else, I'm awake, living my own teenage life.*

"Teenage?"

Right. Probably not a word they used in 1901. *I'm sixteen. And I'm... from the future.*

"When? I mean what year are you from?"

I can feel her excitement stems from some event she wishes to know the outcome of, but before I can answer, a silver bell rings.

"Oh! They are here!" Lucy sits up. "Could we continue this conversation later?" she asks kindly, checking her reflection in her mirror and pinching her cheeks a few times.

Of course.

Lucy makes her way down the grand staircase and out the front door to meet her family. Wringing her now-gloved fingers, and tapping a foot anxiously, we don't wait long before a covered carriage pulls up.

The horses, clearly about spent, puff air through their lips as they come to a stop. Matthew almost immediately unhitches them to take them to the stables.

Drake, standing stiff and proper, raises a hand to unlatch the carriage door and almost immediately Uncle Harry bounds out to embrace Lucy.

His coat is scratchy wool, but Lucy breathes in the much-missed musky scent of her guardian.

"I am so happy you are home safe!" Lucy says when they pull back.

Uncle Harry removes his black bowler hat, revealing graying hair that matches his short beard. "I am sorry our trip was so extended, Lucy. But Grandmother sends her regards."

"I am sorry I was not there to say goodbye to Grandfather," Lucy says, tears pricking her eyes.

"He understood why you could not come, darling." Uncle's eyes well up too. "He wanted me to tell you how much he loves you and hopes that you are feeling well again soon."

"I am feeling much better now."

You were sick? I ask. How much time has passed? I try to keep the last thought to myself.

Shush, she says silently. *Let me greet my family.*

"I am so glad to hear that," a motherly, female voice says behind Uncle Harry.

"Aunt Penelope!" Lucy breaks from her uncle to embrace her aunt.

"Are you really feeling better, darling?" she asks.

Lucy nods. "I am." She smiles. "The cough is mostly gone, and the doctor says my lungs have finally cleared."

Lungs have cleared? I say. *Did you have pneumonia or something?*

Quiet please, Emily.

"Oh, that is good news," Aunt Penelope says. Then her expression turns to a stern look. "And you have been resting? As much as possible?"

Lucy nods.

"You haven't been overexerting yourself?"

"Just resting," Lucy says.

"Lucy!"

Lucy's heart soars at the sound of her sister's voice.

"Lucy, I've missed you so much!" A curly, blond-haired girl leaps into Lucy's arms.

"I have missed you too, Hannah." Lucy says, hugging her back tightly. The embrace is crushing, and I wonder just how long it's been since the sisters have seen one another. I will have to ask later. After a moment, Lucy pushes back to look at the younger version of her. With her long blond hair, blue eyes, and fair complexion, I suspect I am looking at the exact image of Lucy at age eleven.

I feel what can only be described as an internal nod from Lucy.

"I have instructed Mrs. Holt to make a delicious supper for all of us," Lucy says, addressing the group. "All of your favorites."

"That sounds wonderful, Lucy," Aunt says. "Thank you."

"But for luncheon, I am stealing my sister." Lucy winks at Hannah. "Mrs. Holt has prepared something for Aunt and Uncle, but we are taking a carriage ride and having a picnic."

"In this biting cold?" Aunt Penelope's voice is laced with concern. "Is that wise with your condition?"

"Do not worry, Aunt," Lucy says. "I have made arrangements for us to eat indoors."

"Where are we going?" Hannah asks the moment we part from their guardians. Mrs. Holt needs a few more minutes to finish preparing the lunch, so the two—well, three—of us walk toward the garden.

"It is a secret," Lucy says, linking arms with her sister. "But how was your trip?"

"Oh!" Hannah gasps. "I have something for you." She releases her grip and heads back toward the stables. "Hopefully Matthew has not taken my trunk up yet. I will fetch it now!"

"Hannah!" Lucy calls, laughing. "Can it wait?"

"No!" Hannah yells without looking back.

Lucy laughs to herself.

What was that about? I ask.

"I don't know," Lucy says, keeping her voice low.

We are silent for several moments. I find myself sinking into Lucy's happiness.

"Do you have a sister?" Lucy asks, maybe feeling my contentment.

I am an only child, I say. *But I have a best friend who is like a sister.*

"Have you ever been separated from her for a long time?"

My mind flashes through all of the months when Ari hated me for dreaming her sister's suicide. *Yes*, I say.

"Is it not so wonderful when they return?" Lucy asks, then coughs twice.

Are you okay? I ask, remembering that she is recovering from some sickness.

"Fine—" she says but coughs again three times before she can get another word out. "I am fine."

Are you sure? What did you have?

"Pneumonia. But I'm fine, really," she says. "The doctor says my lungs are clear."

Pneumonia? My heart lurches. That can be fatal. *Wait, what is today—?*

But she reacts before I can finish my question, and I don't interrupt because I smell it too.

Lucy's neck snaps to look at the house, and her eyes rake the house. Bright, licking flames pour from the lower windows near the kitchen as thick, black smoke escapes in rolling waves, staining the blue sky.

mortality

"Matthew!" Lucy shouts, racing to the stables. "Get the fire brigade! Hurry!" she shouts. "The fire brigade!" Over and over she calls for help, stopping several times to catch her labored breathing. She sets into a coughing fit, and has to stop to recover.

Eventually Matthew pops into view, hearing her cries. His expression is confused until he follows her gaze to the black smoke spewing from the windows. He immediately rushes to the stables, and quicker than I thought possible, races away on a brown steed, kicking up dust in his path away from the house.

"Hannah!" Lucy yells, continuing toward the stables. We're almost there. But then she doubles over in another coughing fit. Panting for air and holding the stitch in her side, Lucy walks as quickly as she can—a pace that is anything but brisk. *Hannah*! she shouts in our head, unwilling to risk another hindering fit. The few moments it takes to walk, each step like lifting a lead weight, feels like hours as we make our way to the stables in search of Hannah.

Fortunately she did not head toward the house, Lucy thinks. At the same moment I say, *Your aunt and uncle are inside!*

Lucy's moment of relief turns to panic. *The servants too,* she says to herself as we enter the stables. Her eyes take a moment to adjust to the lower light, but it is not dark enough to hide the fact that only one person is inside, and it is not Hannah.

"Where is my sister?" Lucy says to the boy. "Do you know where she is?"

"Naw, miss," he says, "Miss Hannah was here, but she say she be needing somethin' in her trunks. They was taken inside already."

Oh no. She's not my sister, but my heart falls into my stomach. Joining Lucy's.

"Get far away from the house and out of the stables, Jacob." Lucy says, eerily calm. "The house is on fire!"

She rushes out the door and toward the nearest entrance to the house before the boy can react.

Wait, we're going into the fire?

"My sister! My family!"

No, no, no. No! You are not *going in there!* Lucy ignores me, throwing the door open, and pauses for only a second before barreling inside. The fire hasn't reached this part of the house yet.

The servants' entrance, Lucy explains in thought, clearly preserving her breath for movement instead of talk. *We can take the back stairs up to Hannah's room. Hopefully that is where she went next.*

This is a very bad idea. You've got to go back, Lucy! I plead.

Lucy doesn't respond, but it is clear that nothing I say would sway her.

So I push on the brakes. *Lucy, stop!* I force my will on her and turn her feet to stone, refusing to move another inch.

"What are you doing?" she shrieks. "My sister! I have to save my sister!" Her will is strong, and she manages to take another step before I can stop her again.

You could die in here, I say. *And with your health... there's no way you can make it.*

She thinks for a minute, blocking her thoughts from me

before responding again. "I will die standing right here if you do not let me move. Then both my sister and I will be dead."

I don't have an immediate response to that. Lucy takes advantage of my hesitation and rips back control of her legs and feet. When we reach the stairs, she wants to take them two at a time, but the coughing that ensues after only two steps is enough to make her—us—retch all over the narrow wooden floor.

We can't keep going, I say. There is no sign of smoke yet, but the house is heating like a furnace. You *can't keep going,* I amend.

We're going, she insists.

Then at least put something over your mouth, I say, thinking about all of the movies where the character puts a wet bandana over their mouth and nose in a smoke-filled room. Because we will eventually find a smoke-filled room if we don't get out soon.

But that will suffocate me!

No, the smoke *will suffocate you.* I say calmly. *Find something thin and get it wet if you can. It will filter the air a little.* I think.

Lucy is annoyed at the detour, but she darts back down and into a small bedroom. It probably belongs to a servant. The room only houses a twin-sized bed, a trunk at the foot, and a small nightstand holding a bowl of liquid on it.

Rummaging through the trunk, she finds a threadbare rag. It was once probably white, but is now gray. It looks like a handkerchief.

Why does it need to be wet? she asks, eyeing the water in the bowl. A servant's sink essentially. *The water doesn't look clean...*

Lucy, hurry! It's the only thing that will help keep your throat from burning.

Lucy hesitates, trying to talk herself into it.

Do it. Now, I say. *Or else, let's go back,* I suggest but figure its wishful thinking that a little bit of dirty water would cause Lucy to give up.

She dips the rag into the water and wrings it out on the floor, then hesitantly places it against her mouth.

Your nose too, I say.

It smells, she says—and she's right—but obeys and soon we're back on the stairs.

After tiptoeing past her mess from before, we reach the top. But Lucy's breath is labored. She sucks in air like she's drinking it through a straw and tries without success to prevent coughing. There's nothing left in her stomach, so she dry heaves when the hacking turns forceful.

You should get out, I say, but know my words fall on deaf ears.

I have to warn them, she answers. Lucy takes a few breaths when the coughing stops, then continues to move down the hallway.

When Hannah's door is in sight, Lucy quickens her pace and reaches for the handle.

Feel the door first! I shout. *You don't want to unleash an inferno if it's burning inside.*

She feels the wood with the back of her hand like I instruct. It's not warm to the touch, so she opens it and rushes inside.

"Hannah!" Cough, cough. "Hannah!"

Our eyes sweep the room, but it is unoccupied.

"Hannah," Lucy says quietly. Dejected.

Maybe she got out, I say. The effect of the heat is making her disoriented. Sleepy. Lucy's heavy feet try to move out the door.

Our throat begins to burn. *Put the cloth back over your mouth and nose.* She is having trouble listening to simple instructions. Gray smoke begins to seep into the room.

We need to get out, I say.

Not without Hannah.

Then crouch down. You don't want your head up in the smoke, I say, trying not to let my panic seep into my tone. *Get on your knees.*

She practically collapses to the floor.

Crawl over to the window and see if you can get it open.

"I... can't." Lucy's head is fuzzy. It is amazing that mine is not. Another coughing fit spasms her body. But she conjures up some strength and slithers to the window, collapsing underneath it.

Can you open it? Or break it? Even as I ask, I know she doesn't have the strength to do it. And then it hits me:

This is it. If I ask, Lucy will tell me it's October third. The day she dies.

I think we have more pressing matters at the moment, she says when I ask the question about the date.

It's important.

Very well. It's… October third, I believe. Why?

Her headstone is burned into my memory. It is conjured immediately. I try to force it back with all of the strength that I have so that she won't see it, but the details push through:

Lucy Marie Rhett

Born: January 12, 1884

Died: October 3, 1901

October third. Today. This is it.

No, this is not it. I have to save her. I will save her.

Can you pull yourself up to the window? I ask her, directing her thoughts away if she did hear me. *See if your family made it out?*

I can't, she says to me. She's losing consciousness. *Why is today important?*

Let me take over, I say, ignoring her question.

The weight of her control falls on me. And like with Nora, I have some power to keep going. With oxygen-deprived limbs from her labored breath, I struggle to use Lucy's arms to pull us off the floor and up to the window sill.

Fumbling for the tiny latch, I am able to turn it and shove the window with enough force that it swings open, smashing against the exterior wall. Pushing Lucy's head out the window, I help her take in huge gulps of sweet air. Through the haze, there are figures visible on the lawn. Tiny figures, but I know Lucy will recognize them.

Aunt Penny, she says weakly. *And Uncle Harry.*

Is Hannah there? I ask.

A half dozen people gather on the lawn, one looks like Hannah's size, but her clothes are wrong.

No, she says. *I think the servants are safe, but Hannah... we have to find her.*

Let's find her then, I say. But I am only stringing Lucy along at this point. I fully intend to get us out, with or without Hannah.

The going is even slower now as we crawl along the floor, attempting to keep the handkerchief over her mouth. The now-visible smoke is thick. It's almost impossible to see anything, but we make it out of the room with only one coughing fit. The ceilings are higher in the hall, but the fire is visible from below and is racing up the stairs.

Damn, the window! I curse myself for opening it. The fire is certainly drawn to it. I've sealed her doom that much quicker.

With one last push, I scurry Lucy's small body the opposite way of the flames on her hands and knees. The air becomes thicker, and now my consciousness is becoming fuzzy. Maybe it's for the best, I think as her hands begin to scald against the hot floor. Painful, blistering sores appear on her palms and I feel them just as vividly as if they were my own hands. Which is why I scream with her in pain.

"Lucy?" The voice coming behind me is familiar, but it's faint and I can't place it. I pause to turn.

A dark form crawls toward us, skirts trailing behind. It isn't until she's only a few feet away that I recognize the dark curls and petite face dusted with ash.

"Tessa?"

"Emily?" Tessa asks.

How does she... "Grandma Grace?" My panic begins to rise even further. Lucy's lungs can't handle the talking, and I double over in another painful coughing fit.

"My sister," Lucy emerges again and manages to get out. "We have to save my sister."

"Where is your sister?" Grandma asks Lucy.

"I do not know," Lucy says with sudden renewed energy, and takes physical control too continuing forward. "I was about to check my room."

"I'll help," Grandma says crawling forward and passing us. She's wrapped cloth around Tessa's hands to prevent them from burning and is ripping some of her skirts to also wrap Lucy's hands.

"No, Grandma, Lucy is going to die," I say. "We have to save *her*. Hannah doesn't need—"

No! Lucy gags me as I try to form the words with her mouth.

Lucy, you don't understand, I say. *I've seen your grave.* I pause. Telling her about her fate wasn't the plan, but... desperation. *You die today! I cannot let that happen.* But my plea is weak. She won't listen and we are moving again.

With unknown momentum, we reach the next room—Lucy's room. It is rapidly filling with black smoke, and we see a familiar form lying on the ground. Her peach dress is barely visible, but Lucy recognizes the tiny shoes that were once hers.

Hannah! Lucy says, but then she's gone.

Grandma/Tessa rushes into the room and checks on Hannah's lifeless form.

"Is she okay? Can we get her out?" I ask. *We've come this far. Might as well try to save them all.*

"I can't tell," Grandma says, "I'm not a doctor." But she lifts Hannah by grasping underneath her arms and begins to drag her toward the exit.

I move forward to help by lifting Hannah's feet.

"Why did you come?" I ask, but then lose my grip with a sudden wave of weakness in Lucy's legs and arms and crumple to the floor.

Grandma doesn't seem to be bothered by the added weight, or by the fact that I'm incapacitated for the moment. She continues to drag Hannah at the same pace. "Is Hannah supposed to die today too?" she asks, dodging my question.

"I don't know. I haven't seen her grave." I try to move, but my strength hasn't returned.

She gently lays Hannah on the wood in the hallway to look at me. "But Lucy is."

"I'm not going to let Lucy die in here—"

A loud crash sounds somewhere below, drowning my words. I pray nothing is blocking our way out.

"Emily, you shouldn't be changing things," she says, not at all minding that there are more hot embers flying and burning holes in our clothing.

I hit each one that lands on me to extinguish it, hoping that none of them feed enough to spread through Lucy's skirts.

"Grandma, I *have to.*" I say. The air is so dry that tears don't form. My eyes only burn instead. "I didn't save Colin..." The memory of not helping fills my chest with overwhelming remorse.

"Then perhaps Colin wasn't *meant* to be saved."

"So Charles and Duncan and... *Andrew*—they shouldn't even exist?" I want to scream, but my voice is scratchy and burning so it comes out hoarse and faint. "An entire family tree erased because Colin wasn't supposed to live?"

"Life's not fair," Grandma says, shrugging Tessa's shoulders. It's getting harder to see her in the thickening smoke.

"I'm not making the mistake again," I say. "I'm not letting Lucy die." I push myself up to crawl once more, but Grandma blocks me.

I scowl at her.

"Why are you here?" I dig down to put as much force into my words as I can. "Tessa shouldn't be here."

Grandma remains silent. I can't see her expression clearly, but it seems that she is at a loss for words.

So I continue, "You'd kill Tessa, possibly something that *isn't* supposed to happen, just to make sure that Lucy dies? Just to stop *me* from changing anything?"

With more gusto than before, Grandma picks up Hannah like a baby with one arm cradling her head and neck and the other beneath her knees, then stares at me with a serious look. "I want you to listen to me, sweetheart," she says. "I am getting Tessa and Hannah out of here. If they die, hopefully it's because they were supposed to. But *you*—" she chokes on her words, but swallows loudly and keeps her penetrating gaze, "Emily, my darling, *you* won't die from this fire. But you and I both know that Lucy isn't supposed to survive today. So stay with her, be with her until the end. It's your calling." She pauses a miniscule moment. "I'll talk to you in the morning," she says, then turns and goes, faster than I thought possible. Leaving me—us—in the smoke and ash.

I wait until I can no longer see Tessa's dark form before exerting my own strength to escape. Our exit is a blur, but somehow I rush down the stairs, past the flames and smoke and sparks.

A few minutes later we collapse on a side lawn at a safe distance. I can feel unconsciousness pulling at us both. It feels like it's already taken Lucy.

"Lucy!" Her uncle is instantly by our side, cradling her head. "Lucy, you are alive." He scoops us into his arms and rushes toward a hospital or doctor, I'm certain.

"And Hannah?" I ask with a drunken smile, as he walks. I'm fighting with all I have to keep her eyes open. There isn't much left. "Did Tessa get Hannah out?"

Uncle Harry's eyes grow wide and he stops in his tracks. "Hannah was inside?"

But the dread isn't enough to keep me awake. "I saw Tessa Harker carrying Hannah out," I whisper.

My eyes close to the blackness before I hear his answer.

grief

Fortunately I woke up as soon as the screaming began and was able to stop it quickly. Still, it was loud. I braced myself for one or both of my parents to come barging in at any second. Maybe it was time to start saving up my allowance to soundproof my room. Secretly, of course. If I was determined to keep having the dreams—and I *was*—the least I could do was spare my parents from stomach ulcers.

Especially after a memory-dream like last night's—traumatic, painful. But not deadly. Really, the screaming was just a residual response to the pain of being burned. Because I had saved Lucy.

I saved Lucy.

I smiled as I readied for school. The relief of saving her was almost all-encompassing and nearly cancelled out the guilt I felt over Colin. *Nearly. Not absolutely.*

But this felt good. Once I explained to Grandma how good this felt, and how terrible losing Colin had felt, I'd be able to convince her that I had made the right decision. I should be saving people, not just letting them die. She'd come around to my way of thinking. And hopefully she'd quit thwarting my efforts. Either way, I'd needed to come up with some ground rules about her piggy-backing my memory-dreams.

It was only as I walked down the stairs that I remembered the voiceless concern hiding in the back of my consciousness. *Hannah.* I'd saved Lucy, but I still had no idea if Hannah or Tessa had made it out. Immediately I made plans to visit the cemetery before school to search for both of their graves and find out.

My stomach twisted. I hoped that both Tessa and Hannah had survived. If not, maybe Grandma would have to find someone new to be.

Mom was on the phone when I walked into the kitchen. Dad was sitting at the counter, also talking on his cell. Neither of them seemed to notice my presence, and it looked like breakfast wasn't on their minds, but that was okay. I'd planned to turn down anything that wasn't portable anyway so I could get to the cemetery before school. I tiptoed to the cupboard to grab a bagel and smeared it with strawberry cream cheese, before heading for the door.

"Emily?" Mom's voice was choked when she called my name.

Something was wrong. Her tone was all wrong. I froze where I stood.

She met me in the entryway, her face puffy and red from crying.

"What's wrong, Mom?" Anxiety rose from my stomach to my throat.

She pressed her lips together, attempting a smile, but tears welled instead. She swallowed. "It's Grandma Grace." She covered her hand with her mouth to hold back the sob.

When she removed her hand to say the rest I dropped my backpack and bagel onto the floor.

I REFUSED DAD'S OFFER TO WATCH A MOVIE WITH HIM that morning. I refused the pancakes Mom eventually cooked for breakfast. She made a double-batch since my aunt and her kids had invaded the house. The only thing I didn't refuse was the option to skip school and bury myself in my room for the day. Seeing as the house was being increasingly overrun with relatives, my parents conceded without much of a fight.

They said it was a heart attack.

"B-but she's young and healthy!" I had argued.

They said that heart-attacks can even happen to the young. Plus Grandma was in her late sixties. It wasn't uncommon.

I would have argued more, except I suspected an even more horrible truth. I still needed to find out for sure, but if my memory-dreams affected me enough to make me wake up screaming and occasionally cause adrenaline to rush and my heart to race, maybe... If Tessa had died in that fire, her death very well could have given Grandma a heart attack.

After all, it had been Grandma Grace's first *death dream*. And it had been someone she had walked multiple times, someone she knew. I'd nearly lost my mind after Nora's death, and I'd only walked with her twice.

For the first time in my life, I snuck out of the house. I wasn't about to climb out the window and scale the drainpipe. I just waited until downstairs was at its peak of chaos and commotion and I was certain that the ones who might stop me were congregated in TV room so they wouldn't see me escape.

Even though I had been alone in my room the entirety of the day, I hadn't realized how claustrophobic the energy in the house was until I distanced myself half a block down the street. Sucking in a ragged breath, I finally let myself break down, silently crying as I walked. With the hood of my coat up and my hands stuffed into my pockets, any passerby would assume the red patches on my face were due to the cold. And when the snow began to flurry around me, I knew my face and tears were even more obscured.

The snow also meant that I had the cemetery to myself. Dad had closed the office for the afternoon, and I could have swiped his keys to get into the office, but that would have meant further risk of being stopped. So I searched the old-fashioned way.

First, I went to the location of Lucy's grave but didn't even glance to see if it had changed. That wasn't why I was there. Then, spiraling out, I systematically checked the surrounding headstones for the names I looked for. First, I found Hannah only ten feet away. Skimming the information quickly, my eyes rested on the death date: October 3, 1901.

No.

But not allowing the despair to fill me just yet, I continued to search. Thirty minutes I searched, scanning each stone for the familiar name of Harker. Spiraling further out, then zigzagging through. I began to worry Tessa wasn't buried in Meadow Grove and felt a spark of hope that she'd survived and moved elsewhere before she died, but then I remembered that Tessa was from Savannah and they might have shipped the body anyway.

My fingertips, toes, and my nose were beginning to go numb, so I made the decision to stop looking. But I didn't want to face the household full of people either so I absently searched the cemetery with less vigor for a while longer.

I nearly tripped over the curb when I passed through the cremated section and a sinking feeling prompted me to search there.

If she died in a fire, and the body was too badly burned, would they...

Sure enough, toward the back row laid a white stone with bold letters reading *HARKER*. I neared it to study the fainter letters of the first name: *Tessa*. I sunk to my knees, willing the flashback to wash over me. But nothing came. *Died October 3, 1901.* I closed my eyes, concentrating on the memory of the fire, the way Lucy's hands and throat burned. I wanted to be with Grandma. I wanted to be with Tessa.

But Lucy was with neither of them when they didn't make it out of the house. So I couldn't be with either of them as they both died.

The flashbacks didn't work that way.

I knelt in the frozen grass until the cold seeped through my jeans and numbed my knees too. When I was too cold to say any longer, I rose to my feet stiffly and trudged back to my warm, but crowded house.

No one noticed me enter. And no one noticed me slink back to my bedroom. I shook off my coat, slipped out of my boots, and climbed back into my bed to wallow. I wanted to cry some more, or perhaps fall asleep, but neither came. Instead, I stared at my full bulletin board and daydreamed about possible memories that might be attached to the dried flowers and ticket stubs to distract my thoughts. I was once again a little uncomfortable in my changed universe and angry that I couldn't speak to the one person who had some memory of my original one.

My plan to distract myself had backfired.

But I erased the feelings, reminding myself that it was better that Carly lived.

And an idea occurred to me.

For the second time that day, I did something I'd never done in my life. Sneaking to the bathroom, I took some nighttime cold medicine though I didn't have a cold. Then cozied back into bed and concentrated on Lucy and the fire until the drugs took me back.

CHAPTER 29

Second Chance

"Matthew!" Lucy shouts, racing to the stables. "Get the fire brigade! Hurry!" she shouts. "The fire brigade!" Over and over, stopping several times to catch her labored breathing that sometimes sets her in a coughing fit.

I'm back. It worked.

Knowing what's coming should fill me with dread. Instead I am bursting with determination.

"What worked?" Lucy asks. "Never mind. We have to hurry. We have to get Hannah out of the stables and away from the house."

Matthew appears, and he is soon riding off.

"Hannah!" Lucy yells, walking swiftly toward the stables.

She isn't in there, I say.

Of course she is, why wouldn't she—

Trust me. Inwardly, I sigh. Again going against what I'd planned not to tell her. *I am redoing your memory.*

"Hannah!" Lucy yells again, then doubles over in a coughing fit. Holding the stitch in her side. *What do you mean redoing?* she asks me, walking slower than before.

I mean, I've been here with you before, I say. *We went to the stables and a boy told us that Hannah went inside the house.*

"No... you are wrong," she says aloud, like it will make it truer.

We enter the stables. Lucy's eyes take a moment to adjust to the lower light. Again, there is only one person inside.

"Where is my sister?" Lucy asks Jacob. "Do you know where she is?"

In the house, I repeat.

"Naw, miss," Jacob says, brushing a stray-stringy strand of blond hair away from his eyes. "Miss Hannah was here, but she say she be needing somethin' in her trunks, but they was taken inside already."

Lucy's stomach falls, and she freezes with the realization that I was right.

I want to say I told her so, but not about this. That would be too cruel. *Now you tell him to get out.* I prod when she can only stare.

"Get away from the house, out of the stables, Jacob," Lucy says with strange calmness. "The house is on fire."

We rush out of the door and toward the nearest entrance. Lucy throws the door open and pauses for only a second before going inside. "I expected you to try to and stop me from rushing into a burning building," she says to me, smirking.

I did try, I say. *Last time. But you didn't listen.*

Lucy doesn't respond. We reach the stairs, but another coughing fit ensues after only two steps. And she vomits. "Where to next?" she asks when she recovers her breath. "If you know what happens, did we find Hannah?"

I pause before answering. *We found her, but we couldn't save her. Or Tessa.* I almost don't mention Andrew's sister, but since she is the biggest reason I initiated this replay, I thought Lucy should know.

"Tessa?" She is surprised as expected. "What is Tessa doing in the house? I did not even know she was in town."

I don't know, I say, *but let's keep moving so we can save them both.*

"Great. Where do we go?" Lucy pants. The house feels hotter than it did before. I can feel beads of sweat gathering on her forehead and scalp.

The servant's bedroom. I say. *Get the handkerchief out of the trunk and get it wet with the water on the night stand. It will filter the smoke a little and hopefully slow the burn to your throat.*

"*Slow* the burn?" She slowly walks back down the stairs and into the bedroom. "So my throat will burn?" She's hesitant this time, not a rushing heroine like before.

Do you want to save your sister or not? I ask.

"Yes." Lucy fumbles through the trunk for the rag and dips it, then wrings it like instructed.

This is how we save them. I give both of us a pep talk.

"But we burn my throat."

Quickly, Lucy, I prod. *You were faster last time.*

"And how do you know it will work this time?"

This time I know where she is. Luckily Tessa/Grandma found us the first time, so we won't need to search for her.

Lucy doesn't say more but quickens her step. With the rag properly on her nose and mouth, she mounts the staircase, and retches again at the top in another coughing fit.

Hannah is in your room, I say. *Don't waste time going to hers.*

There's no visible smoke yet, but I know it is coming soon. Lucy's limbs are like lead again, and the air heats even more. This time I realize it's her illness that is slowing her down. Not the fire.

"My aunt and uncle?"

Are safe. They got outside. Along with the servants.

Lucy nods as we arrive at her door. Her head is getting fuzzy. Pushing the door open, Hannah is crouched on the ground, conscious this time.

"Hannah!" Lucy breathes, taking the last few steps swifter than I thought she had strength.

"Lucy!" Hannah says. "Here, this is for you." She presses a sealed note into Lucy's hand. "He said it was important."

"Hannah, the house is on fire! We have to get out of here!"

"I know," Hannah says with a trembling lip. "I'm scared, Lucy," she says, tears rolling down her cheeks. "I was trying to find you."

"Let's get out," Lucy says, with renewed energy. She gently grabs her sister's tiny wrist and pulls her out of the room.

Where is Tessa? I wonder, not meaning to let Lucy hear.

"Where should she be?" Lucy asks but another, more forceful coughing fit racks her small frame.

"Lucy!" Hannah's voice is filled with fear.

Black smoke is beginning to fill the hall. Slower this time since we didn't open a window to fuel it this time, but the heat is nearly unbearable.

Get on your knees, I say. *Under the smoke. It will give you more time.*

Lucy collapses to the floor. Fortunately the layers of dress and petticoats protect her knees from cracking on the hard floor. *I continue to scan the area for Tessa's silhouette to emerge through the smoke.*

"Get up, Lucy!" Hannah cries. "We need to get moving!"

"No, Hannah," Lucy says.

Another hollow coughing fit. Wasting so much precious time. She gasps between each hack, desperate for air. Her body jerks violently. A loud *pop* is immediately accompanied by a sharp, stabbing pain in her side causing Lucy to double over.

She's broken a rib.

"Get on the floor," Lucy says through gritted teeth. "Under the smoke." It hurts so much to breathe; she gasps quick, shallow gulps of air.

Without another word, Hannah drops too, and the two sisters crawl at a too-slow rate toward the back stairs. The floor is scalding hot. Hannah cries out with each movement as her palms redden and blister.

I want to suggest they rip off some fabric from their dresses to protect their raw hands as Tessa/Grandma had done before, but I don't know how much time that will take. Especially in Lucy's dramatically weakened state.

Where are they? A deeply saddened feeling creeps through me as I begin to doubt I'll be able to save Grandma this time.

It'll be a miracle if Lucy can get out.

The familiar guilt of not saving Colin snowballs, adding to it the guilt of living the fire a second time—on purpose—and not saving Lucy.

"Go ahead of me, Hannah," Lucy says, biting against her own pain. She heard my thoughts, but came to the only conclusion she could think of in her disoriented thoughts. To save her sister.

"Not without you," Hannah's voice breaks.

Part of me expects Hannah's words to trigger another Nora flashback, they are so similar to young Colin's. It is not lost on me —the similarities and stark differences between this and Nora's death. Ice and fire. Brother and sister. Nora and Lucy: both brave, both injured, one terribly sick, but both trying to save their younger sibling. But I cannot allow myself even a moment of distraction from being here for Lucy.

I've helped Nora. Twice. And though coming back is my own doing, my own fault, I will stay with Lucy. Twice.

"Go get help," Lucy says. "No one knows we are in here." *Except Tessa/Grandma if she ever gets here,* I think but then realize that Lucy is possibly lying to get Hannah out. When Hannah still hesitates, Lucy says. "I cannot make it on my own. Go down the servant stairs. Hopefully the fire has not reached there yet."

Hannah takes a moment to embrace her sister. Clutching so tightly that Lucy has to muster all of her power to keep from coughing again and crying out in pain.

"I will get help," Hannah whispers, then dashes to the stairs.

I do not make it out, Lucy says. It isn't a question.

My guilt expounds since I have been here once and saved her. I should never have come back. Still, she wasn't supposed to survive the first time.

No, I say, cowardly not saying more. *I've seen your grave. You die today.*

It hurts so much. I'm not sure if she meant for me to hear that, but I know what she means. Her chest, her lungs, burn and ache with pain. Her stabbing, broken rib. Her throat burns. Her blistered hands. Even her head throbs loudly despite the haze of her mind.

And after so many dreams, after so many deaths, this will mark death number fifty-eight—unless I count the repeats—then the numbers get confusing. Grandma Grace mentioned that I am some sort of guardian angel, meant to be with people in their moments of happiness and sorrow. But I didn't really feel what she meant until now.

I am here for *her.* For Lucy. She is in pain. She is scared and alone and at death's doorstep, and I am here to be with her. To be here for her. To bear her pain with her.

Even if it is my fault and I can't save her this time.

Let me take over, I say. *It will make it easier.*

But why? she asks in her head. No longer able to speak.

Because that's why I'm here. I'm here to help you. Let me take over.

I don't have to ask again. Instantly I feel the weight of her control and pain overwhelm me. But again, I somehow have the strength and endurance to keep conscious even as I feel her drift away.

Attempting to keep moving toward the stairs, I hiss at the pain in her palms as I touch them to the floorboard. *There is no use.* I sit still, waiting for the end to come, however it might be.

Something pokes at her wrist. With so much pain everywhere, I am surprised to even notice the corner of the small note tucked in Lucy's sleeve, digging into her skin. The letter Hannah so desperately needed to give to Lucy.

Without a single ounce of hesitation, I rip open the letter.

the end

Dearest Emily,

It's addressed to me? But who? Lucy's sick lungs throw me into another coughing fit. I clutch my side at the sharp pain as each cough trashes Lucy's chest, making me cry out in agony. Her body won't hold out much longer. With the smoke getting thicker with each second, the letter will be impossible to read within moments. It's a miracle I can read it at all in the smoke. *Read faster, Em!* I scold myself.

YES, I MEAN YOU, EMILY CHANDLER. I KNOW WHO you are. I know what you are. But I thank you. I thank you for being with my sister in her last moments. I thank you for taking over her lips. Her lips which never spoke a word in her entire life until that fateful day she ordered me off of the ice.

Something strange happened. I have two memories of the day my sister died in the frozen river. I know which one really happened—the one when my sister did not speak. When I stayed with her for too long. When I almost fell in

myself and drowned. I know you were there with her for both.

WAIT. I SCAN TO THE BOTTOM OF THE LETTER. IT WAS written by Colin Harker. He was saved. And that means—

"Lucy!" A familiar voice. *His* voice is faint through the smoke, but I can hear it as though he is inches from my ears.

"Andrew!" I call out weakly, bracing my arm across my chest tightly as more coughing takes control and aggravates my broken rib.

Get out! I want to yell. But her body is getting weaker by the second, and the words won't come.

"Lucy!" He calls again. He is closer, maybe near the top of the stairs.

"Get out," I say. "Save yourself." My voice sounds like barely a whisper, and my eyes begin to droop. But then I see something crawling through the haze. It's dark. Merely a shadow at first, but as he draws nearer I can see the soot smeared across his forehead and near his eyes, and the dirty rag covering his nose and mouth.

Andrew.

"Let's get you out of here," he whispers when he reaches me.

I shake my head. "Grandma—Tessa is in here" I say. "Go find her first." Then I turn my head so I don't cough in his face.

He uncovers his face. "Emily?"

I nod. "Lucy is gone. Unconscious."

Suddenly my face is pressed against a soot-filled, scratchy wool coat as he embraces me. It catches me so off guard that I cry out from the pain in my side. Immediately he lets go.

"Her sickness," I explain. "She broke a rib from this horrible cough."

The gold flecks in his eyes blaze even with so much haze between us. His dark hair falls into his eyes, longer than when I last saw him. And graying? No, it's just the soot—he kisses me quickly and hard. He is frantic and hurried, but so am I, because it is surely our last.

I feel guilty, but a big part of me is grateful that Lucy is unconscious. "I've missed you," I say quietly.

He pulls back. "Missed me?"

"Long story," I say, not wanting to get into the whole—I was here, but on medication so I don't remember any of it—conversation. "Now please go save your sister." *And my grandma.*

He doesn't move to obey and though I know that we are in a dire situation, that he needs to get out *now*, I just can't bring myself to hurry what will be our last moment together. Ever. So I don't release my grip on him and instead spend a few precious seconds studying his face.

"I'm getting you out first." His voice is firm, decided, and without another word he scoops my knees and begins to crawl-carry me toward the servant stairs.

"Please save her," I whimper in his arms. "Please get Tessa out, I can't—"

A loud crash immediately followed by the fireworks of hundreds of dangerous flying sparks, interrupts my pleas and the servant's stairs collapses in front of us. The shaking of the floorboards causes Andrew to drop me to the floor, hard. We both cover our faces with our arms to block the heat wave that comes next.

Getting Tessa and Grandma out seems impossible now. "You need to leave," I say, changing my plea, though I'm not certain if he can hear my weak voice.

"No, I'm getting you out. I won't leave you here to die."

"I am not dying," I remind him. "But you might if you don't hurry." I try not to dwell on the fact that Tessa, Grandma, and Lucy will all perish. "Check the main stairs, perhaps those are clear."

"If she dies, I'll never see you again." Andrew stands with me in his arms, turning in the direction I suggested. "I am saving you both."

"Lucy is supposed to die today, Andrew," I say. "You can't save her."

"Watch me."

Everything goes black.

SOMEONE BREATHES IN AND OUT SLOWLY NEAR MY bedside when I finally wake up.

Inhale.

Exhale.

Inhale.

It's probably Dad. Mom's breathing isn't so noisy. But I don't dare open my eyes to see if he is watching me or if Mom is nearby watching me too. I am terrified to find out where I am. I don't dare even think about my most-likely guess. Lucy's death seems to have thrown me into a catatonic state even worse than Nora's.

The unfamiliar roughness of the sheets almost confirms it.

When I take a deep breath of sweet-clean oxygen, he shifts next to me. He knows I am awake. Might as well face the inevitable. Opening my eyes, I note that I am in a hospital ward, though a white curtain blocks out most of the room.

But it's strange. I hear no beeping of a heart monitor, or even the indistinguishable sound of someone talking over a PA system outside the room.

Where—?

"Lucy?" he says hesitantly at my bedside.

Andrew.

My raw throat confirms it: I'm still Lucy.

Slowly, I turn to look at him. He's clean. Wearing a loose-fitting white shirt that is free of soot and stain. He absently twists the silver ring on his finger.

My elation at seeing him is immediately overshadowed by the fact that I am Lucy. And must act as such.

"Where is Charles?" I ask, but it sounds more like a croak.

Andrew's face falls a minuscule amount. I doubt anyone but me would have noticed. "I sent him to supper," he says stiffly. "He has been at your bedside day and night since the fire. I am sorry he is not here now, but he had to eat."

"Wait." My head reels. "*Day and night?* She didn't die? You got her out?"

"You said *she*..." Andrew mutters to himself. Then his eyes glint with hope. "Emily?"

I search my—Lucy's—head for her. She is unconscious but alive. I can hear her subconscious buzzing at the back of my head. "It's me," I say.

A low hiss escapes my parched lips. The embrace is painful —again.

"Sorry." He pulls back, but doesn't go far, still hovering inches from my face.

"Water?" I ask, hoping he will give me some space. Who knows how long Lucy's betrothed will be, and seeing his cousin so close...

"Of course." Quickly, he fills a glass and brings it to my lips.

I drink long and deep. Lucy's throat still burns, but the cool water soothes it instantly. But her thirst is hard to quench, being so dehydrated.

After draining two and a half glasses of water, I finally feeling satiated enough to stop. I'm anxious to ask the question, but I have to know. "Tessa? Did you save her?"

He lowers his head. "I couldn't save her." Suddenly the oxygen is sucked from the room, almost like I'm back in the house with the smoke stealing it all away. "I told you," I gasp, "Lucy was supposed to die. You should have..." I will him to look at me. He looks at me through welling tears. "You should have saved your sister." *You should have saved Grandma Grace.*

"She met Hannah on the servant stairs before they collapsed," he continued.

"Wait. Did Hannah...?"

"Hannah is fine," Andrew assures with a kind, crooked smile.

"Your bedside has been quite crowded. Margaret has been here too. But Hannah rarely lets go of your hand. Your uncle forced her to take supper and get some sleep in an actual bed."

"At least she made it out this time," I say mostly to myself. "So if Hannah made it out, what happened to Tessa?"

Andrew shrugs and looks like he's trying not to breakdown. "The only thing we can figure, is that when she heard that I ran inside, she went back in after me. And they couldn't stop her."

Of course. Andrew wasn't supposed to die in that fire either. So the sisterly love, mixed with Grandma making sure only Lucy died, was enough motivation for them to run back in after Andrew. The thought makes me angry, but then I realize that Grandma was probably doing it for me.

Keeping Andrew alive.

"We think she was on the servants stairs again when it collapsed. Her body—" His voice hitches, and he looks down to regain control. "Her body was found in the rubble of the stairs."

"You should've left me," I say even though it's pointless to continue my protest. "I've seen her gravestone. Lucy Marie Rhett. Born January twelfth, eighteen eighty four. Died October third, nineteen-oh-one... She wasn't supposed to survive the fire."

"Not Harker?" He looks truly confused, his grief forgotten for a brief moment.

"She isn't married yet." I shake Lucy's stringy golden locks. I absently note that for once she isn't *lovely as always*.

Andrew ducks his head, hiding the flush in his cheeks. "Right. If she had died on the third..." He half says to himself. "Well, the wedding hasn't happened yet."

"Right," I repeat.

I study his features for several moments. Dark circles hang underneath his chestnut, gold-flecked eyes. His dark hair is disheveled and in desperate need of a trim. He didn't say, but I suspect he's been holding vigil near Lucy just as Charles has. I just hope he hasn't been too obvious.

"Does Charles know you are in love with Lucy?" I ask.

"I am not in love with Lucy. I love—"

"Charles doesn't know about me," I cut him off. "And I need to remind you that I am *not* her. That fire was never going to kill *me*."

"But Lucy dying would be the same thing as you dying... to me."

I shake my head in frustration. "Andrew, I was born more than one hundred years in the *future.*"

"I know. But how else would I ever speak to you again?"

Believe me, I know the feeling. I want to say, but I don't because it shouldn't matter.

"Have you ever relived a memory?" I ask, changing the subject.

"What? No." He looks confused, surprised even. "Have you?"

"I've relived *three* memories."

"Why?" he asks. "What was the purpose?"

"I don't know, but in the first one I was so devastated, so *scared* to experience—" My heart pounds, and my eyes prick. I shut them tight, praying that the flashes don't come. Even though she was saved. Even though Carly is okay, I can't even experience a small flashback. Not now.

"It was a death," he said in a low tone. It wasn't a question.

I nod. Then open my eyes again and realize that my fingers are clutching Andrew's tightly. I shake my hand to release his. *What if Lucy wakes? What if Charles comes back?* "A suicide actually," I croak.

His expression is knowing. He has walked a few of those; I can see it in his eyes.

"My best friend's sister," I say.

"Someone you *knew*?" Andrew's tone is shocked.

"She's buried in the cemetery near where I live." I shrug. "Well, *was*," I amend. "I saved her."

"So you saved your dear friend's sister, and yet here you are telling me that I cannot save Lucy?" Andrew leans back in his chair and crosses his arms over his chest, putting as much space between us as he can without actually leaving the room. "That is very hypocritical, Emily." He is truly angry. Or hurt.

"No, you don't understand," I lean forward, ignoring the sharp pain in my side. "The first time I had a redo, I saved Carly. And my whole world changed."

"Changed? How?"

"I woke up with a boyfriend I didn't know I had. I woke up with my best friend back. I woke up and Carly was alive and well."

"Boyfriend? What's a boyfriend?"

"Suitor, or something," I say, explaining. "I guess that's what you would call him."

Andrew shakes his head, not in disagreement, but like he is trying to clear his thoughts. "What is so bad about all of that?" he asks. "What did your life look like before that?"

"No boyfriend, but I was okay with that," I say the last part softer. "No best friend. No friends at all really." I pause and breathe deep. "And Carly was dead."

"Can you tell me why those changes were so bad? So wrong?" he asks softly.

"They weren't bad," I say after a pause, "but they were wrong. I'm sorry, I don't know how to explain it." Andrew shakes his head, clearly bewildered. "But when I found myself repeating again, reliving another death, I knew I had to do things differently. At least I thought I should."

Andrew's eyes never leave my—Lucy's—face as I speak. His expression shows deep concentration, like he is trying to figure something out. So am I. I am tempted to hide in my thoughts too and sort things out, but I continue. Lucy could be back any second. Or Charles. And even though Lucy is saved, it's never certain when I will have this opportunity to talk so freely again.

I take a deep breath. "There was no saving the second girl. I showed up too late for that. But in my first memory-walk, I had saved her brother in a miraculous way that caused quite a stir." I remember Colin's awe—older Colin, Andrew's *grandfather*—when he spoke to me about the miracle of Nora speaking and ordering him off the ice. My fingers itch for the letter. I never finished reading it. But other than thick bandages, my hand is empty.

"You decided not to save the brother." Andrew's head is hung down, refusing to meet my eyes.

"Yes."

"And do you realize what that would have done?" He still won't meet my eyes.

I am almost afraid to speak. *Does he know?* "Yes," I say softly, I'm not sure he even hears me.

His head snaps up, the gold flecks in eyes aflame as they bore into mine. I don't have to look to see his fists clenched at his knees; his entire posture is taut, ready to bolt from the room at any second. "You *knew* that by not saving my grandfather, I would never be born."

"How do you—?"

"You knew!" he almost shouts. I'm sure he would have if he wasn't worried about alerting a battalion of concerned nurses.

"You have no idea the amount of guilt I've felt for making that wrong decision," I say, unable to meet his eyes.

"Just because you found a way to be in control, just because you *can*, doesn't mean you should."

"I agree, but why have control?" I shout back, but the resulting coughing fit stops me from continuing right away. Andrew gently helps another glass of water to my lips, although if it's for Lucy or me, I don't know.

"You decided to let Lucy die too." He says when I've settled again.

"That's not the point."

"Then what was the point? To find my sister..." his voice cracks and he swallows loudly, "She wasn't supposed to be in there, but I couldn't have found her anyway." He straightens, the emotion wiped from his face. "I do not regret saving Lucy."

"And that's what I realized, Andrew. That's what I've been

trying to tell you." I sigh deeply, swallowing my own hard lump. "Lucy was never going to make it."

He raises an eyebrow. "Clearly," he says, waving a hand at Lucy's still-living body.

I smile, but quickly sober again. "I deeply regret not trying to save your grandfather, I don't know how..." I trail off, choking on my regret. "I don't know how he made it. But I am so *grateful* that you saved Lucy."

Andrew is astonished. "I thought..." he says, then closes his mouth, apparently speechless.

"The fire was my third redo." I almost blurt out that I think I managed to redo the fire on purpose, but then he'd ask why, so I keep that part a secret.

"You lived through that twice?" His voice is shaky with emotion.

"Yes, and I managed to save Lucy on my own the first time," I say quickly to keep my emotions under control. "I don't know exactly what made the second time impossible, maybe it was her broken rib that prevented me from getting us out... I don't know." Inevitably, my voice hitches at the end. I take a deep breath and continue. "I guess what I'm trying to say is thank you for saving Lucy. I think that's why we sometimes have control. To use it to save them if we can."

"That was a long-winded," he teases.

I shrug and smile. "I thought you should know about the redos too."

We are both silent for several moments.

"Why did you stay?" he finally asks.

"What?"

"With Lucy? If you were convinced she wasn't going to make it—you know, before I came?"

"Why stay?" I repeat his words.

"You once asked me how to get out of the ones too difficult to bear. Death by fire is one of the worse ways to go in my experience."

Lucy's hands burn under the clean dressing. Like they are being reminded what they went through. "It's high on the list," I agree.

"So why stay?" he repeats again.

"Lucy?" Charles's voice is not far. He's come back.

"Because she needed me." I say quickly. "Grandma Grace once told me that we are like guardian angels, or something. That's why we walk, to be with people in their best and worst times." I blink several times in attempt to stop the tears after saying her name.

"You are awake!" Charles says, pulling back the curtain.

I smile for him. *Wake up, Lucy!* I think to her, but realize she already is. I wonder how much she heard.

"I am," Lucy says to Charles.

Andrew slowly stands and looks intent on slinking out quietly to give the couple some privacy. I plan to do the same. But he stops. "Will you tell her it was me?" he asks Lucy.

"What was you?" Lucy asks, knowing he means me.

"With Colin," he says causing a confused look on Charles face. "The second time. It was me."

a beloved wife, a wonderful mother, and friend

I'd been leaning against the brick wall, pretending to be engrossed in my phone texting or flipping through Instagram, for at least fifteen minutes now. Of course I was doing neither. I was trying to look the part of tuned-out teenager so that my relatives would stop bugging me to talk about my feelings.

Grandma's death hit me hard. I was probably the granddaughter who spent the most time with her, and everyone knew it. Mom was nearby talking to three of her cousins, dressed in their Sunday best with nearly identical skirts, probably from the same department store sale. I was almost certain that I was the subject.

The funeral ended almost a half hour ago, and we were supposed to head to Grandma's grave, but Mom still needed to assure everyone who stopped her on our way out, asking in hushed tones if I was *okay*. Because I *looked* fine, but Grandma's death on top of my recent *episode* meant something was clearly wrong with me. They all seemed to know about my recent mental breakdown.

I should have headed to the cemetery with Dad when he did to avoid the stares, but there was something about being here that made me not want to leave. Plus, I would have attracted stares at the gravesite too. Something about being inside the church walls made me feel like I had some sort of sanctuary from... I don't know. Even from several feet away, I knew Mom was discussing every detail to anyone who asked. So it wasn't sanctuary from that.

It was too bad Ari couldn't come. If she were here, at least I'd have someone to talk to. But her family decided to sneak away to their no-cell-service cabin for a few days. Their mom had been getting better, nicer, more like a mother to both girls since Carly's time in the psych ward. And since Carly was joining them, it didn't seem right to ask Ari to skip that family time for Grandma's funeral.

I shook my head to clear my thoughts and was almost surprised to see my ponytail of straight, dark hair swing into my peripheral vision, like I expected it to be a different color.

Keep it together, Emily. I chided myself. My "mental breakdown" had really done a number on my psyche. I had another appointment with Dr. Shew tomorrow; maybe she'd have some insight.

The swarm of cousins dispersed, and Mom slowly approached me—like she'd spook me if she walked too quickly. "Ready?" she asked.

"Yeah." I slipped my phone into my coat pocket.

"How are you feeling today, honey?" she asked as we moved toward the exit. "Still tired?"

"I feel okay," I said. "Fine really."

"Well, you are not skipping your appointment tomorrow," Mom said in her best motherly voice. "It's important that you talk to Dr. Shew about... what you're going through. Let's prevent another *episode*."

"Aye, aye, Mom," I said, nudging her playfully.

Instead of pushing open the double-glass doors, Mom pulled me into a hug and let out a little yelp, like she might start crying. I let her hold me for several moments. "It's times like this —" She choked on her words, she was crying. "It's times like this that I feel like I have my little girl back. And at a funeral, of all places."

"Mom, I haven't gone anywhere."

"I know. I know." She pulled back and reached in her pocket for the used tissue. Up close, her eyes were filled with tears and rimmed red. She'd been crying a lot the past few days, understandably. "But you used to be so happy and without a care in the world. And I feel like sometimes I get a glimpse of that, but it never lasts."

"I cried at the service too," I reminded her.

"No, I know. It's just... different."

I shrugged, confused. It was hard to tell her what was going on in my head, especially when even I didn't know what was going on. "Let's go," I said, even though my body was reluctant to leave the building—like it was whenever I was inside the church building.

She nodded and pushed open the doors.

I almost collapsed on the concrete steps the moment I stepped outside into the crisp winter air as everything came flooding back. But I only stumbled and made a comment about my clumsiness to hide the reality. That part was always the worst. And suddenly the conversation I had just had with Mom seemed like a lifetime away.

Of course I knew why I had such a hard time being that carefree girl. I almost died in a fire. Twice. And Grandma *did* die because of it.

The memory of lying in that hospital bed came rushing back. Andrew saved Colin. Even if I shared Grandma's philosophy that we shouldn't change events, I couldn't really blame Andrew for saving his grandfather since his very existence would have been snuffed out if Colin had died as a child.

But I didn't share Grandma's opinion.

I was glad Andrew had saved Colin. I was glad I saved Carly. And I was glad he saved Lucy. Nothing would change my mind about that.

"Could you drop me off at the cemetery entrance when we get there?" I asked Mom when we pulled out of the parking lot. My voice gave away the rush of memories and pain, I hoped Mom didn't notice.

"I know I just asked you, but are you feeling okay, hon?"

"I'm okay," I lied. "I just want to walk for a minute before getting to Grandma's grave. I have a headache from crying, and I think it'll help."

I could hear her thinking of a reason to say no. But she and dad wouldn't be far so she agreed. She seemed even more okay with it when we both recognized the familiar strawberry-blonde hair pulled into a ponytail just entering the cemetery.

I'd only stepped one foot out of the car when I was met with a crushing embrace. I almost winced in pain, but my ribs were thankfully intact.

"How are you holding up?" Ari whispered in my ear.

"I thought you went to the cabin," I practically squeaked, due to my sudden lack of air.

"Sorry," she muttered, pulling away. "I didn't go."

Mom drove past us, and we began walking.

"But, wasn't Carly finally going? Didn't you want to see her after—" I didn't finish my sentence. She didn't remember a world without her sister.

"I can see Carly whenever," she said. "Not when my best friend loses her favorite grandma!" She put both hands on her head, exasperated. "Trust me," she lowered her hands to her lap. "They understood why I didn't want to go."

"I'm okay," I said. "Really, Ari, you didn't need to cancel your trip."

"We're going again in a couple of weeks." She shrugged. "Are you really okay?"

"About Grams? Not at all," I said. "But I've been thinking about her all day. Could we talk about something else?"

"Sure. What's... new?" she asked.

"Well, I've done a lot of dream-walking," I lowered my voice.

"Walking?" She cocked head in confusion.

Oh no, did something change again? Does she not know about the dreams?

"What's that?" she continued when I didn't elaborate. "Did you dream someone who walked a lot?"

Whew! She did know. "No." I laughed nervously. "It's a term I picked up from Andrew, you know, because he has the dreams too. He calls it dream-walking."

She nudged me. "And why are you picking up terms from Andrew?"

I flushed.

"If you're having the dreams again, then that means you've stopped taking your meds." Her tone was accusatory. And loud.

"Shush!" I hissed.

"S-sorry," Ari tried to whisper, but it wasn't much quieter than before.

"I'm not taking them anymore."

"But, why?"

"Because when I take them I still have the dreams, I just don't remember them. It's what caused my *episode*."

"Did your doctor tell you to stop taking them?" she asked.

"No, she told me to keep taking them."

"You're going against doctor's orders?"

I nodded, then tried, but failed to hide a smile. "Lucy didn't die. I saved her."

"What are you talking about?" Her face was blank.

My stomach lurched. "I thought I mentioned her."

"Why so jittery, Ems?" She pulled me next to her in a side hug. "I know about Lucy. I just didn't know she was supposed to die."

"Oh. Right." I held a hand up to my chest to calm my suddenly racing heart. Who knew that having my life change once would make me so anxious? "Yes, Lucy was supposed to die, but Andrew saved her." I tried to sound nonchalant, but the smile that crept up my lips betrayed me.

"Ah!" Ari winked at me. "Now I know why you don't want to

take your meds. One word: *Andrew*." She practically sang his name.

"It's not like that!" My cheeks flamed. "He's not the reason, really! It's too disconcerting to wake up in a panic but now know what happened. Plus, I feel like I should be helping people in the dreams if I can. But I guess Andrew..." Okay, maybe he was a bonus.

"Right. It's fine, I see how it is." Ari gave me a knowing smile. "One boyfriend while you're awake"—she held up a hand palm-up—"and one boyfriend while you're asleep." Then she held up her other hand.

"Boyfriend?" In all of the madness I had not thought about Duncan once. "You said I didn't have one."

"I heard about your fight," she said sheepishly. "Duncan called me right after and sounded pretty upset. I just figured it was probably over for you two."

I didn't have a response "You should probably talk to him," she added.

"I think you're right."

I MISSED THE GRAVESIDE SERVICE FOR GRANDMA. MOM and I arrived a little late anyway, but my slow walking with Ari made me miss the rest of it. I didn't mind though. I had been at the funeral, and I'd seen a graveside dedication before. Plus, part of me felt like I wasn't really saying goodbye like everyone else. I had walked Carly, I could very possibly walk Grandma.

I stayed in the cemetery long after the other mourners had left. Mom and Dad had some business in the office anyway, so I meandered among the graves. And my feet once again found Lucy's plot.

I panicked for a brief moment because her headstone wasn't where it was supposed to be, but I found it close by. And in large all caps lettering, across the top read *HARKER*.

"Lucy Marie Rhett," I read aloud. "Born. January 12, 1884. Died July 31, 1958." *She made it to her wedding.* I sighed in relief even though I had lived her rescue. And next to her lay her beloved Charles. I noted their death dates were only a few months apart.

"In loving memory," a voice continued behind me.

I whirled around to see Duncan. His hands were shoved in his pockets, due to cold or something else, I couldn't be sure.

"A beloved wife," Duncan continued, studiously not looking at me. "A wonderful mother. And friend."

"Duncan," I said.

"I always find you right here," he said. "With Lucy and Charles."

"I, uh..."

"I know you and Lucy are close," he said, answering my unasked question.

"How much do you know?" I asked, braving the next question. "I just don't remember exactly what I've told you—"

"Enough." He cut me off, but his voice sounded far away. He seemed troubled about something else.

I wondered how much he knew about Andrew. Ari did say that they had talked on the phone after our fight. Would she have mentioned Andrew to him?

"There was a fire," I blurted out without thinking. "I mean when I walked Lucy."

"I assume she made it out okay?" He gestured to her grave. "Unless you jumped ahead a few decades."

"No," I shook my head. "I mean, yes, she made it out okay." I paused. Warring with myself about whether to tell him more. "I lived it twice."

"Twice? That sounds horrible."

"It was," I said "I felt every second of it both times. I was burned, my throat was scorched. Twice."

He didn't respond.

"She was sick too," I added, not quite sure why I was telling him all of this. "She broke a rib coughing. That's a whole different kind of pain; you can't take a deep breath because it hurts so much."

"I can't even imagine," he said. His eyes closed tight. Suddenly I noticed a familiar object was on the grass beside him.

"Why do you have that?" I asked, pointing.

He picked it up. "I heard about your grandma," he said, handing it to me, "I'm sorry for your loss."

"Thank you." I took the yellow birdhouse that was such a permanent fixture outside Grandma's house. "You know the same could be said about her."

"Hmm?"

"My grandma," I said, looking wistfully at Lucy's marker again. "A beloved wife. A wonderful mother—and grandmother—and friend."

Duncan shoved his hands in his pockets again and nodded. "You were close."

"Yes." I looked back at the bird house. "You took this?"

Duncan shrugged and smiled guiltily. "I knew you loved it. Figured I'd grab it before one of your relatives decided they wanted it."

"Thanks," I said. I didn't know if any of them did want it, but it was thoughtful of him.

"Did you ever figure out what the numbers meant?"

I pointed at the *VI* painted on the side, and he nodded. It was a little strange that he'd called it a number when it was unclear if it was supposed to be a roman numeral or letters. "No, we never did," I said.

"Maybe someday." I could have imagined it, but it looked like there was a glint of something in his eye when he said it. I shrugged it off.

A pregnant pause enveloped us "About the other night—" he said.

"I want to break up," I whispered, cutting him off.

"I am sorry about the other night," he repeated. But he looked resigned. There was something in his face, in his features that reminded me so much of...

"Can we stay friends?" I asked quickly. Even though I couldn't in good conscience be involved with him and have such conflicting feelings toward... someone else. But I desperately needed him in my life. "Please?"

"Friends." His tone was full of resentment.

"Please," I said. "I just need some time. Grandma stuff, plus my recent mental breakdown." They were poor excuses and not the actual reason. "But maybe, in the future..." It was cruel to give false hope, but I couldn't lose him.

Even though I just met him.

Duncan nodded once, then walked away.

there's my girl

In through the nose.
Out through the nose.
In through the nose.
Out through the nose.

Concentrate. If I don't think about it, the putrid rag shoved halfway down my throat won't make what little is left in my stomach come out. The rag is so much worse covered in bile.

In through the nose.
Out through the nose.

The sticky tape stretched across my face pulls at the skin and tiny hairs near my hairline. It hurts.

And it keeps me awake.

But so does sitting on the wobbly wooden chair with my ankles strapped tightly to the legs. They were smart pulling my pant legs up this time, since I shimmied out of the bonds and kicked one of them yesterday. Or last week? My sense of time is so screwed up.

Being locked in a dusty, dingy basement with rusty pipes, no windows, and only a naked light bulb hanging from a cord has really messed with my circadian rhythm.

But I suppose the drugs did that too.

Click. The door unlocks, whines as it swings open. Heavy footsteps enter the room.

My heart jumps in my throat, then pounds in my head as adrenaline rushes through my body. Part of me is surprised I have any of the hormone left.

I close my eyes tight. Pretending to be asleep. Or high. Maybe they'll leave me alone this time.

I jerk back at the pressure at my wrists, ready to swing or claw at whoever is untying the ropes. My eyes betray me and fly open, always too curious to see which one it is.

But I don't recognize him.

Ash-blond hair. Young. Maybe a year or two older than me.

"Whoa," he says, startled by my sudden motion. "Easy there." His smile is kind. But a kind smile can always be faked.

He raises his hand and in one swift, painful instant, the duct tape is gone. I almost gag as he extracts the rag, but I don't miss the opportunity to sink my teeth into his last finger before it pulls away from me.

I expect a yowl and smack in the jaw, but instead he merely hisses, shakes his hand, and squints his eyes.

He's trying to be quiet.

"What was that for?" His eyes are still shut tight, and he holds his injury tenderly.

I don't answer. I never do.

A moment passes, and he opens his eyes to look at me. "What did they do to her?" He asks almost absently, but still directed at me.

I cock my head to the side. An old habit when something does not compute.

"I'm trying to help you. Remember?" He motions to my wrists, his eyebrows asking if it's safe to continue untying. I don't tell him it's not. "I know this isn't the typical change, and I can see that this one is a hard one for you." He resumes, though carefully, unknotting the cords.

"Am I—?" I croak. Weeks with a rag in your mouth will do

that to your voice. I clear my throat, hack up some gunk, then spit it on the stained linoleum next to me.

The guy tries not to show his disgust.

"Am I supposed to know you?" I ask.

"Seriously?" He looks annoyed. "You died in a fire in another life." A strange thing to say with an irritated tone. Seeing no realization on my face, he goes on, "You saved your friend's sister from killing herself?"

But then everything flashes purple. Then blinding white.

And I know myself.

Then I start to cry. The weight of emotions this poor girl is holding back spills out. Fortunately for my sake—and hers—she's blocked out a lot of what has happened to her since she was taken.

"Sorry," he mutters as he makes quick work of getting the rest of the bindings loose. "Let's get you out of here before someone realizes you are missing."

I nod. Playing along with whatever the mysterious rescuer has in store.

"Can you stand?" he asks.

Immediately I push off of the chair, but my knees instantly buckle in weakness. The blond boy catches me under the arms before I crash to the floor. Then half-drags, half-supports me to the back of the room.

"I thought you were rescuing me," I joke.

"I am." He is concentrating on the puke-green wallpaper.

"Well, the door is over there," I point with a shaky hand.

"And there is a hidden one here."

He feels around, then finds a button painted the same color as the wall and pushes it, revealing a small door next to it. It slides open to reveal a dark tunnel. Rushing through, he slides the door back, and we are enveloped in darkness.

We race in silence, as quickly as my weakened legs will allow.

Left, then right. I memorize the turns in case this rescue isn't really a rescue, but then another sliding door leads to a dimly lit cylindrical concrete room with ladder.

And blinding sunlight bleeding through the cracks.

I can't help but smile.

"I'll check first," the blond boy says, breaking the silence. "Make sure no one is guarding above."

I nod and lean against the cold concrete to support myself.

He scurries up the metal rungs and seems to take a deep breath before pushing up the round cover. Several breath-holding seconds pass before I notice his shoulders relax and he looks down at me.

"We're clear," he says. "Do you think you can climb?"

With all of the will I can muster, I take three wobbly steps toward the bottom rung. There's no way she is staying down here, so with *my* strength, I launch myself up and out. The suddenly bright light assaults my senses, but I feel the boy hook an arm underneath my legs and carry me several yards before gently putting me down in the cover of some green. When my eyes have adjusted I note we are among some trees on the side of a road.

I try to search her head for a name as a classic white Chevy Impala drives by. Maybe I can figure out a date by the cars. An old —no new—station wagon speeds in the other direction. Then a black Mustang. *Sixties?* I wonder. *Or seventies.*

"She wasn't saved, you know."

"Who wasn't saved?" I ask.

"You—*er*—Mary." He shrugs sheepishly. "Mary wasn't saved before."

I point to myself. "I... am Mary?"

He nods, then grins. "Seriously, Em, you really need to start wearing your ring all of the time." He looks back at the road.

Did I hear him right? Does he know my name? Or is Em short for Mary? "I thought you said my name was Mary?" I test him.

"Yeah, Mary Piper." He seems distracted watching the cars and doesn't look at me as he talks. He seems to be waiting for something.

"You just called me *Em*."

"Sorry, *Emily,*" he corrects himself with a grin. "This one really disoriented you, didn't she?"

"So you know who I am?"

Finally he looks at me. "Is she, I mean Mary, present?"

I listen. She's checked out. Probably from emotional trauma and exhaustion. I shake my head no.

He smiles again. "Then yes, *Emily Chandler,* I know who you are." He chuckles softly. "How often have we done this?"

I don't answer, because I still have no clue what he is talking about. A small part of my head wants to believe he is who I want him to be, but it's impossible. You go *backwards* in time when you memory-walk, not *forward.* Unless he's about a hundred years old, there shouldn't be any Chevy Impalas.

"So, why are you saving this poor girl, other than because it's a noble thing to do?" I play along.

He looks back to the road. "Because she was engaged to marry Matthew Harker before she was abducted.

My heart pounds again, but for a different reason. "Andrew?" I whisper.

"The one and only." He laughs then leans toward me and kisses me softly. "There's my girl."

End of Book One

Get three FREE short stories when you join Joanna's email list at joannareeder.com

thank you for reading

Thank you for reading *In Her Dreams*!

If you enjoyed immersing yourself in Emily's world and meeting Lucy, Andrew, and Duncan, please leave an honest review! Reviews are essential to indie authors like me.

acknowledgments

First of all to my readers for reading this book! Thank you!

But seriously it never would have come to fruition without the support of my family. From my sweet husband who may not understand my need to tell stories but supports me anyway, and my crazy kids who are completely content to watch Netflix or nap for a couple hours a day so mommy can write. Also my parents, siblings, and extended family who have been my beta readers, emergency brainstorm session heroes, and for supporting me and encouraging me all of these years.

I also couldn't have done it without my amazing writer's group (Go Team Fellowship!) and critique partners, Jesse Booth and Aaron Herd who have helped me brainstorm, develop my stories to make them stronger, kept me motivated, and boosted my confidence along the way (you are my rock, Team Istari!).

Lastly, a huge thank you to my editor Katrina Beckstrand (editsbykb.com), who completely understood and visualized my vision for the *In Her Dreams* trilogy and helped polish them to make them all lovely and shiny.

about the author

Joanna Reeder is a USA Today Bestselling author who takes readers time traveling through dreams, shifting into fantastical creatures, and tossed into Faerie. Her fantasy stories always have a dash of romance, leave readers turning pages long into the night, and eager to recommend them to their daughters and grandmas and coworkers!

When Joanna isn't writing, she enjoys bike rides and kayaking with her hubby and kids, vacations at the beach (with a book to read, of course!) and learning new songs on her blue electric guitar.

She's a believer in the paranormal (seriously, she has stories) and her motto is, "A Dr. Pepper a day keeps insanity away!"

If you love fantasy romance too, you can sign up for Joanna's weekly newsletter at joannareeder.com. You can also chat with her on Instagram @joanna_reeder.